DISCIPLES

Austin Wright was born in New York in 1922. He was a novelist, an academic and, for many years, Professor of English at the University of Cincinnati. He lived with his wife and daughters in Cincinnati, and died in 2003 at the age of eighty.

DISCIPLES

Austin Wright

ATLANTIC BOOKS
London

First published in the United States in 1997 by Baskerville Publishers Ltd.

Originally published in Great Britain in 1994 by Touchstone,
an imprint of Simon & Schuster Ltd.

Reissued in Great Britain in hardback and export
and airside trade paperback in 2010 by Atlantic Books,
an imprint of Atlantic Books Ltd.

This paperback edition published in Great Britain in 2017 by Atlantic Books.

1 3 5 7 9 10 8 6 4 2

A CIP catalogue record for this book is available from
the British Library.

Paperback ISBN: 978 1 78649 215 9
E-book ISBN: 978 1 78649 216 6

Printed and bound by CPI Group (UK) Ltd, Croydon, CR0 4YY

Atlantic Books
An imprint of Atlantic Books Ltd
Ormond House
26–27 Boswell Street
London WC1N 3JZ

www.atlantic-books.co.uk

To Sally

PART ONE

1

Harry Field

Only a couple of hours before the baby was kidnapped, the grandfather reached a reconciliation with death. It happened at some deep level of his mind while he was thinking about other things. He was a retired professor of the history of science and was writing a speech for the ladies of the Afternoon Club about fakes, charlatans, and pseudo-sciences. It was one of his favorite topics. The speech was to be delivered on Saturday.

His name was Harry Field. He was alone in the house with the baby, who slept while he worked. His work went slowly because of the distractions on his mind. There was a letter he had received recently from an old friend named Lena Fowler whom he had not heard from in fifty years. Three weeks had passed and he had not answered it. He looked out the window thinking back and forth between his speech and the letter. He did not notice that he was also thinking about death.

It was a pretty afternoon in early March, the sun shining on his dusty window. It glared on the arm of the leather chair and reflected on the screen obscuring the words. This morning Harry almost fainted after breakfast. It scared him, the blotted vision and pressure at the back of his skull. He hoped it wasn't precursor to a stroke. This too distracted him while he worked on the speech. He was obsessed with death. He had been thinking about it all his life and though he was often able to postpone the question temporarily he had never been able to reconcile himself. He was seventy years old and might last another twenty or twenty-five years. Or he might not. Either way did not make much difference to the horror, which was unimaginable, of the coming nonexistence of his consciousness, his mind, his eyes and ears, memories, thoughts, self.

The unexpected news of his reconciliation with death came up from his inside mind in the midst of these distractions. It came with a strong warm feeling and words: See, it's all right. It amazed him and he wondered how he had reached that conclusion. It must have been by some unconscious process or sequence of ideas which arrived at the point full of ergo and voilà: here you are, Harry, it's your answer after all these years. He looked forward to the evening when he could retrace what the reasoning actually was.

Then the baby was kidnapped and everything went into chaos. While he worked that afternoon she slept in the room across the hall. The responsibility for her made him uncomfortable, and he was waiting to be relieved. His wife Barbara was in San Diego. She flew there three weeks ago to help her extremely old and recently bereaved mother get used to living as a widow. His daughter Judy, the baby's mother, was at work. The baby sitter Connie Rice would come at three-thirty. The baby's name was Hazel and they called her Hazy. Concerned because she had been sleeping so long, he tiptoed across the hall to take a peek. He saw her padded rear end sticking up and he closed the door softly not to wake her.

If she cried he would pick her up. Then he would rest her thick padded bottom in the crook of his elbow and hold her against his shoulder not changing her diaper unless absolutely necessary.

4

Usually she could last unchanged until Connie Rice came back. He would take her downstairs and put her by the toy box next to the fireplace while he sat in the armchair and watched. There was the stuffed penguin and the mailbox and the inflatable alligator. If she was crabby he would carry her around thinking how old he was, over seventy, and how young she was, sixteen months, and how heavy she was and how fragile his back. He would talk language to her saying here we go around the living room and see the hall closet and those are overcoats and that's the piano and now the dining room and this my friend is the kitchen and what do you think of that rack of spices? Don't like it? In that case take a look at the china closet and the plates which are decorative and that's an Indian relic and that picture a sample of modern art and wouldn't you rather get down and walk around on your own feet? Are you hungry, what should I feed you, a piece of bread, a cracker, orange juice?

Sometimes his talk was good enough to make the baby relax against his old cheek and he would feel the little hard knob covered in silky hair full of trust while he soaked in sentimentality. He would think my daughter Judy to whom you belong and my wife Barbara to whom Judy belongs and all of us getting older on this cool sunny March day inside out to the yellow winter-killed lawn and the bare trees with peeling bark and the early spring birds at the feeder, titmice, house finches, chickadees, all precarious waiting for the better days to come. And Connie the baby sitter should be here by three-thirty.

The kidnapper was a man named Oliver Quinn. He was the baby's father. He took the baby right out of Harry's hands, which Harry allowed since he did not realize the extent of Oliver's estrangement from Judy. This Oliver came and rang the door chimes around two-thirty. Harry interrupted his writing, went downstairs with mild alarm and opened the door. It took him a moment to connect, this big man with the round fat face and glasses, scarf with tassel, plump purple jacket, smiling like a salesman. Hi Professor, Isn't this a great spring day?

Judy's at work, Harry said.

I forgot. She works. How's she doing?

She's fine.

And my child? Does she walk yet?

She toddles around.

Great. Does she talk?

Judy thinks so, I can't tell.

Where is she now?

She's asleep.

But I hear her, Oliver said. Can I see her?

I'll have to get her up.

So old Harry, who didn't much like this Oliver Quinn, let him sit in the living room while he tended to the baby. The baby quieted when Grandpa came into her room. The room was humid. He picked her up, heavy in his arms, in a little shirt and fat rubber pants full of diaper. She settled comfortably against his shoulder, hot and moist. He put her on the changing table, cleaned her up and dried her and put another diaper on while she watched sleepily. He put on her purple playsuit, and brought her down.

She looked at Oliver, no recognition. Hi kid. He came to take her and she tightened her arms around Harry's neck. Sorry kid, too fast. Harry put her on the floor where she sat, looking around.

Cute kid.

She got up and toddled to the toy box. She pulled things out and threw them. She carried a rag doll to Oliver without looking at him. He reached for it and she pulled it back and threw it at the piano.

How's Judy's social life?

Harry's dislike of Oliver Quinn had to do with how he had dropped out of Judy's life when she got pregnant and came back when the baby was born and then left again. He didn't like the things Judy said about him.

I heard she had a boyfriend. He said it pleasantly with point.

I can't speak for her, Harry said.

Sure. I won't interfere. Friend of mine saw her the other night at Clippers. She's got progressive ideas.

What do you mean?

Nothing.

Harry was annoyed. If he's talking about David Leo let him say it. Expose himself for the bigot he is.

The baby thrust the stuffed octopus at Oliver Quinn.

Look at this, an octopus. Thank you, lady.

He handed the octopus back to the child, took it back, handed it back, not paying attention.

Nice day, he said to the child. Like to go to the playground? He looked at Harry. How about it? he said. Let me take her off your hands a while.

Harry tightened, not prepared for this. That's all right, he said, I can handle her. He wished Connie Rice were here.

I'll bet you're busy, Oliver said. I saw your article about science and religion. Judy showed it to me. Right interesting. I bet you're writing all the time.

I'm busy, Harry admitted.

Keeping busy in retirement. What are you writing now?

Miscellaneous.

Right enough. So let me take Hazy to the playground, you write your miscellaneous.

That isn't necessary, Harry said. I can take care of her.

No, Professor, you don't understand. I want to take her to the playground. She's my daughter. Sand box, slide, tunnel. Like that, kiddo?

The man's looking at him as if his fears were unreasonable irritated Harry but embarrassed him too.

Judy won't mind, Oliver said. I'm the father. I wouldn't let anything happen to her.

I know you wouldn't, Harry said. He was thinking how mean and suspicious he looked. The child climbed up on Oliver's knee, putting a butterfly net over his face. The rich chuckling laugh of the child, while Oliver made faces and played her game.

So Harry gave in. Okay, he said, but please bring her back in an hour.

Sure thing, Professor.

The red jacket with white fur and a hood. While Hazy sat on Oliver's lap, Harry put the jacket on her. He watched them out the door, Oliver carrying. Her face looked out from the hood over Oliver's shoulder while she waved bye with two fingers down the steps. An old brown Toyota with a dented left fender. Somebody in the passenger seat. Already he wished he hadn't done it, and there was still time to stop them if he ran out, but he told himself it was too late, and it was. He saw Oliver strapping the baby into a child seat in the back. The child seat reassured him, the sense of responsibility it implied.

It took a while for Harry to realize that he had delivered his daughter's baby to a kidnapper. Connie Rice came at three-thirty. She was the baby sitter and housekeeper while his wife was in California. He heard her walking around downstairs. After a while she came up.

Her voice sang up the stairs, Where's my lovey dove, still asleep this gorgeous afternoon?

Surprise in the baby's room. Not here? Where did you go?

From the study Harry called. Her father took her to the playground.

What father?

What father? Oliver Quinn, Harry said.

Connie Rice stood in the study door thinking it over. Did he really? This Connie Rice was a healthy young woman with long sandy hair and a sandy outdoor face full of bones. Not only was she helping out in Barbara's absence, she and Joe her husband were editing a Festschrift in Harry's honor. He saw the thoughts working inside her face behind the bones. Well, she said, after a while. I'd better do something useful around the house.

He went back to work. The house was no longer silent. He heard the vacuum cleaner and smelled cooking. The presence of someone else in the house gave him only a specious relief, it did not help the anxiety, neurotic as it was. Then he got absorbed in his work and forgot the anxiety until he realized with a jolt that a lot of time had passed. What?

Five o'clock. The idea took shape, a shock. He hurried downstairs and saw Connie in the living room reading *Time*.

She said it: Weren't they supposed to be back by now? Then suddenly she sat up. Which playground did they go to?

I don't know.

I'll go look, she said. She got her coat. This suggested emergency, so she softened it saying, They must have got carried away by the beautiful day. Adding, I'd better find them before Judy comes home. He watched her down the steps her unbuttoned coat flaring, her car turning around quickly, zipping away.

No chance of working now, he brought the afternoon paper in, looked at it, couldn't read. Carried away by the beautiful day. He walked back and forth in the living room. Hazy's toys were back in the toy box. Connie had replaced them while she waited.

The aroma from the kitchen promised good things ahead once the future was cleared.

But Connie didn't come back. Twenty minutes passed, then more. He tried to imagine Connie at the playground with Oliver and the baby relieved to have found you enjoying the beautiful but now chilling early March afternoon, with a chat to get to know you while forgetting the worried old grandfather at home. It was time for Judy to come home. If she passed the playground on the way, she would have seen her child there with Oliver and Connie.

He saw Judy's car coming up the street. He thought, she'll have Hazy with her. She pulled into the garage but came out alone. He watched her in her office suit up the walk unaware.

I'll have to tell her her child isn't here, he thought.

She came in the back while he was in front watching for Connie's car. He went to the kitchen. She dropped her coat on a kitchen chair.

Smells good, what is it? she said.

Lasagna.

How's my baby?

She went to the playground, he said, as calm as he could manage. We're waiting for her to come back.

That's nice, she said. It's such a nice day.

He realized she thought Hazy had gone to the playground with Connie. They're late getting back, he said. Connie went to look for her.

Connie?

He told her quietly: Oliver took her.

Oliver?

He came by. He took her to the playground.

Oliver? You let Oliver take my baby?

10

Calmly as possible he said, He wanted to see her for a little while.

What?

His daughter Judy looked at him. He had never seen such a look on her face. She paused, then uttered a sound. Not really a scream, not loud, a little shriek but it was like lightning.

What did you do with my baby?

She put her hands to her face and took them off and stared at them. Daddy, Daddy how could you? She turned around and paced with gasps and moans. My baby, my baby.

Connie Rice came back. I drove to all the playgrounds, she said. I drove all around looking at the streets.

Judy sat on the sofa, her shoulders hunched, face twisted.

I'll never see her again, Judy said.

No no Judy, Connie said. She's all right.

She's dead.

She looked despairingly at Harry. You gave my baby away. He had never been accused by his children before. It shocked him and filled him with fright like the unknown.

She sat up straight. Call the police, she said. She looked at Harry. You call them, she said, you're the one who let her go.

He saw the rightness of that and went to the phone. He heard Connie say softly to Judy, Don't be hard on him, Judy, he didn't realize.

He should have realized, she said. A moment later, I'm sorry, Daddy.

He called the police putting the word kidnapping into his own voice at last, thereby confirming it an event. Once that happened everything else was displaced. He remembered the reconciliation with death that he had reached earlier in the day. He never did get a chance to track the forgotten reasoning that led to that conclusion. It seemed remote now. Everything did.

The speech he had been writing, the campaign against the charlatans and fakers and pseudo-sciences he loved to demolish, as well as Lena the old girl friend and the letter he wanted to write. All were irrelevant and perverse in the light of the unnatural disappearance of his daughter's child.

2

Nick Foster

When we finished packing we got into the car and fastened our seat belts. It was changed from cloudy to sunny. I looked at the house when Oliver pulled the car into the street. It disappeared so did the street.

And now Nicky where do you think we are going Oliver said.

To Miller Church I said.

First a necessary stop or two he said. He pulled into a gas station. Why do you think we are stopping here.

To get gas I said.

Why do we need gas.

To make the car go I said.

Righto man. That's the old understanding at work.

He made me pump the gas. He gave me money which I gave to the guy with the machine. We went on.

Now Nicky another stop. Do you know this neighborhood he said.

No I said.

This is a residential district. Resi-dential. This is where the university people live. Do you know what the university people do.

They go to the university I said.

Correct. Do you know any university people.

You are a university person I said.

Right and wrong he said. I was but I am not. Once upon a time but I have ceased to be.

The street had a circle at the end. It had big houses and didn't go anywhere. He parked the car. I waited while he went into the house. He stayed a long time. Kids came by from school looked at me. Birds on the grass mud wet ground. Bare trees with branches shiny in the sun. Crows flying above the trees saying caw caw talking to each other in a crowd going somewhere caw cawing as they go. If I was them I'd caw too.

After a while Oliver came out of the house carrying a package in a red and white Santa Claus suit. It wasn't a package it was a baby. Look what I got he said. Company for our trip.

He strapped the baby into the seat in back. Now you see why I got the child seat he said. Because the law which says you can't take an infant in a car except a car seat so says the law.

So says the law I said.

It's important to obey the law he said.

The baby looked at us not saying anything.

Meet my daughter.

Pleased to meet you I said.

The baby stared at me eyes brown. Oliver started the car. You didn't know I had a daughter he said her name is Hazel. Ask her if she recognizes her name.

I turned to the back seat and said is your name Hazel. I told Oliver no answer.

That's because you're being too direct. It takes knowhow to handle a baby. You need to know how. Watch this. He pulled into a parking lot next to a row of stores. Wait here and don't let my daughter go away he said. I waited in the car with the baby who looked out the window at the passing scene. This was people going in and out of the store with shopping bags. After a while Oliver came back with a package wrapped in pink plastic that took both arms to carry. He put it in the back seat next to the baby.

Now what do you think is in the package he said.

Baby stuff I said.

What kind of baby stuff.

I don't know.

Figure out. When you see a baby what do you think of.

Crying I said.

What else do you think of.

Mothers I said. Milk and juice.

Well shit take a look at that baby in the back seat what shape would you say she is.

Round I said.

What part is roundest most padded stuffed and swollen up.

Her behind I said.

Righto and what makes her behind so padded and swollen up.

Diapers I said.

You're speaking truth man. So what's in the pink package.

Diapers.

Good man. Do you know why a baby needs diapers.

Everybody knows that I said embarrassed.

That's knowhow. You weren't expecting a baby on this trip were you he said.

I should have expected it I said.

Why should you have expected it.

Because I should have known whatever you do that's what you would do.

Very smart answer. You're a genius Nicky.

We went on. We were out of the city now. The country was flat. Fields flatting out to the sky. It must be lonely to live in a shed in one of those fields next to the brook between the pastures and that one tree by itself.

Her name is Hazel but do you know what they should have named that kid he said.

What I said.

They should have named her George. I always wanted a kid named George it's a patriotic name.

That's a boy's name I said.

That's no reason he said. Girls can be George if they want to be. There's a writer named George and a movie named Georgie Gal and a song named George On My Mind. It's best to name a girl George or Sam or Paul because it makes people notice. It's like spice on Indian food it says this ain't no ordinary girl. Nick would be almost as good he said.

That's my name I said. To show I understand I said it's the same as naming a boy Mary or Dorothy. That would make people notice.

He said you're not kidding they've been good men in the history of the world named Evelyn and Maria and Leslie though I can't think of a good man named Dorothy off hand.

He said what do you think Judy the mother is doing now.

Cooking dinner.

What else do you think she is doing.

Going to the bathroom.

Maybe that. Do you think she's wondering where her baby is.

She's wondering where her baby is.

I told her father we're taking her to the playground. Do you see any playgrounds along the road where we could stop.

Across the fields I saw wires and a road above the fields and trees around a farmhouse and a barn and silo. I didn't see any playground.

Too bad he said. Do you think Judy'll worry because we can't find a playground.

She'll worry.

Will she cry.

She'll cry.

Do you think we should turn back.

I thought about it. The sky was getting mellow. I don't usually see sky where I live. Fields either. I wonder what it would be like to be a farm animal.

Do you he said.

I don't know.

The baby started to cry.

Well fuck it there is no question of turning back he said. We didn't start this trip with the intention of turning back. Because where are we going.

To the Miller Church.

Righto man. Three days it will take us. What do you think of that.

The baby was twisting and screaming in her seat.

Tell her to shut up Oliver said.

I turned around. Shut up I said.

The baby was sobbing all over itself. She won't shut up I said.

Jesus what will we do with the baby for three days.

I thought about it. We could get someone to take care of her I said.

What. Who. Who exactly did you have in mind Nicky.

There was a farmhouse across a field. Someone in a house I said.

What house. The house was gone. Do you see anyone.

17

We could leave her by the roadside and someone rescue her.

This is my daughter you're talking about. Hell man why do you think I got the child seat and the diapers because I told you I'm taking her to Miller. Dummy.

I didn't say anything.

Why am I taking her to Miller. It's because who Miller is he said. Do you remember that at least.

It's because who Miller is.

Who is Miller then.

Miller is God's right hand man.

More than that man more than that.

Miller is God's son.

Shit you're being stupid again. You've got to remember.

It wasn't that I remembered it was that I was scared to say. Miller is God I said.

Miller is what.

Miller is God.

God who.

Miller is God Himself.

You're getting there. And what did God do to you.

He made me what I am today.

Say it again.

He made me what I am today.

I thought about that. I thought of something to say to Oliver that I had never said before. I didn't know what would happen but I said it. I said you treat me like I was a idiot.

You is a idiot he said.

No I isn't.

How do you know. What evidence have you got.

Good evidence I said.

Well well look at you. Good evidence you say.

The doctor psycho in school. He told me I wasn't an idiot.

He told you did he. What did you do ask. Did you go up to him and say please tell me am I an idiot or is it only that I feel like one.

He didn't tell me he told the class.

He told the class you're an idiot.

He told the class no one in school was an idiot. He said if you were an idiot you wouldn't be in school.

You think that got you off the hook.

I thought about it I said. I thought nobody in school is an idiot. I'm in school. I'm not an idiot.

Good thinking he said. Well if you're so smart don't forget this either. We're going to see Miller. We're taking my daughter to see Miller. I'm taking you too because who Miller is. Tell me who he is.

Miller is God Himself.

And what else.

He made me what I am today.

Right. Tell that damned brat to shut up and go to hell will you.

Shut up and go to hell I said to the brat.

3

Judy Field

Oliver Quinn has my child, I can't work. I wake in the morning without my baby, and it's still true, it has been true now for fourteen hours, then sixteen, now eighteen. I have to do something, it does no good to claw the Oliver face in my mind. I think of the police with their tools, tracking equipment, networks, and I will give them no peace. Keep calling so they don't forget, set them on fire with a mother's flames.

Last night we considered a private detective. After calling the police, Connie and I went looking ourselves, tracking Oliver in his haunts. We went to Wexel, his last known address, a little white house crammed between others with an apartment on each floor. A light in his window, I knocked on the door. The occupants, women, students at the university, had never heard of Oliver Quinn. The McPhairs upstairs were glad to see me but knew nothing since he moved out a year ago. They advised me to get a lawyer, because he doesn't have any rights if he doesn't contribute child support. That's not exactly the problem just now. Next we went to where Luke and Veronica used to live but the house was dark. We went to the Tabasco Bar and asked Mike, who said Oliver was in last Friday. Three days ago, not close enough. After that we had no more ideas and we came home.

This morning I got dressed in my office clothes and went to the police myself in spite of having called them last night. I drove down the hill to District Five. I want to report a kidnapping, I said, which started the news up all over again. I interviewed a fat policeman in a laundry white shirt with a large yellow mustache of the bushy type. He had authority like a television comedian or children's show host. His fatherliness was not a display, just an emission, wince and cluck like still not accustomed to evil in the world after all these years on the police force, like where have you been, man? I told him I called in this information last night. Oh, he said, and went looking for files. He looked at folders a long time while I wondered. Yes, he said, we have the report.

What can you do? I said.

Ask more questions, that's what you can do. Or the same ones over again. Age and name of baby. Name and last known address of Oliver Quinn the alleged abductor. Job, I don't know. Quit graduate school after one semester. Worked in a restaurant. Name of the restaurant. Car, license number, how should I know? Why did he kidnap the child? His twisted mind. Was there a dispute about custody or visitation? Did he visit the child frequently? Why didn't he?

Well ma'am, the good policeman said. You hear anything, let us know, you hear?

So I came back home to my father at his computer, writing. I had lunch with him. With nothing else to think about but wait, I went to work in the afternoon. I drove to the office, parked, walked in the office door. I saw Henrietta at her desk, and blurted it: My baby has been kidnapped.

What?

People jumped up from their desks. I burst into tears like the sea was following me everywhere. Henrietta and everybody, comforting arms, hugs, questions, I told everything again while everybody cried. I got control and hung up my coat and sat at my desk.

Go home, Cynthia said. We'll cover for you.

I came to get away from home, I said.

I did a little work, a report for Mr. Getz. Computer focus, tapping keys, clickety click. Mr. Getz came and said go home, do it tomorrow. I burst into tears again. I don't want to go home, I said.

In the middle of the afternoon another policeman showed up. Like a scout master straight up and down covered with electronics, a human robot with controls. No news, more questions. I went into the coffee lounge with him and shut the door. He wrote my answers in a notebook. Actually they were the same questions as those of the fatherly policeman in the morning. I asked if they had made any progress and he said they couldn't do anything without this information. They already had this information, I said. Well we did find one thing, he said. Mr. Quinn has moved out of his apartment. Is that so? I said.

Then that evening Oliver called. Himself on the telephone in the midst of kidnapping my baby. Connie and David Leo were at the table and my father answered the phone. Oliver? he said. Oliver? I grabbed the phone out of my father's hand. We talked, his damned voice pretending to be calm and cool. He was in a motel, he said, and Hazy's fine, you don't need to worry, it's for her good. He's rescuing her for her religious well-being. Do you want to talk to her? Then he put her on the phone or said he did, though she didn't speak and all I really heard was silence full of her face holding the phone to her ear listening to me. Oh my child. I spoke to that face, crying, trying not to, saying This is Mommy, darling, can you hear me, baby, hoping she was really there and not just Oliver grinning at me. At the same time I was trying to think what Oliver meant by religious well-being and I remembered something but not enough, and then he was gone.

The name crashed over me too late. Stump Island, I said. He's taking her to Stump Island.

What's that?

I remembered Oliver's last return, talking about a man who called himself God. No joke. The guru who claimed to be God Himself, which crazy Oliver wanted me to take seriously. Because he was going to live with him and wanted Hazy and me to go too. It was the final proof that Oliver was mad and cleared my conscience as far as he was concerned. Stump Island, that was the place.

Now we know something, Dave Leo said. Let's go after them.

Dave Leo is a serious young man, a junior professor in the English Department. He admires my father and wants to be my boyfriend though I am white. He has a smooth brown face, African-American, with large eyes, a careful voice, a thoughtful and competent manner, a sad look. His presence these last two nights has been comforting. When we chatter about what to do, Dave Leo makes a steeple of the pointed fingers of his hands and mulls it over. I know he has an opinion about Oliver Quinn but he is tactful and keeps it to himself.

Where is Stump Island? he asked. Maine, I said. If that's the right name. We got the atlas, where Dave Leo and my father looked it up. No listing in the atlas index. How sure are you, they asked, that it's Stump Island and not Bump Island or Stone Island or Broken Leg Island? Not very sure. We need a larger scale map, Father said. He went to the computer and brought up a listing of place names. Stump Island, state of Maine, Penobscot County. He called Professor Henrich in Geography. I'll get back to you, Henrich said.

I called the police to tell them about this call. A man named Jenks. I gave him the same information I had already given three times before. Now I added the guru and Stump Island. Thanks for the information, Jenks said.

Professor Henrich called back. Stump Island is a small island in the Penobscot area. It's privately owned. Mail goes through Black Harbor, itself not big.

Let's call them ourselves, Dave Leo said now.

Call who?

Somebody. The Maine police.

I don't know about these small New England towns, Father said. I don't know. Well go ahead. Let's see if you can find police in Black Harbor at this time of the night.

This was Dave's project. He called Directory Information for Maine. Somehow the operator located Black Harbor. So who do you want to talk to in Black Harbor at nine-thirty on Friday night? There's McMahon's Garage, the operator said. Post office is closed. Board of Selectmen no answering machine. I told you these small New England towns, Father said.

The operator was interested. How about the State Police? she said. The office in Augusta. Why are you calling us, the State Police in Maine wanted to know. It took a lot of explanation, Dave doing it now. Because we think they're heading to Stump Island. Where's that? the Maine policeman said. It's near Black Harbor, Dave said. Where's that? In Maine, Dave said. Well, son, the man said, this is across state lines, shouldn't you call your FBI?

FBI, Father said. Of course. Call them, I said. So Father looked it up and called the 800 number in the telephone book. Another interview, more questions. Meanwhile Dave was thinking.

The FBI will send a man around tomorrow morning, Father said. Fine, Dave said. And I think I'll take a little trip to Stump Island.

What are you talking about? It's hundreds of miles.

I'll take my car, I'll drive. I mean it. I'm serious.

What about your classes?

I can cover them.

If you go, I should go too, I said.

You? he said. I saw the quickly dashed flare of hope, the glance at my father, the thought of traveling across the country with me. What more could a would-be lover want? But he didn't dare, not quite, not yet.

Just me, he said. You're needed here. It's something I can check out while you deal with the FBI.

He wanted to be a hero. All right. Father said it would be more sensible for Dave to fly and rent a car in Bangor. I'll pay, he said. You might even get to Black Harbor before they do.

If that's where they're going, Connie said, to keep our hopes down.

I went to bed. This was the second night I went to bed without my baby, and it was worse than the first. Worse because I had let myself be distracted during the day. I had spewed language, nouns, verbs, adjectives, syntax and grammar, all that human jabber all day long.

There was a pale light from the street lamp on the wall like every night. Lacy tree branches through the upper pane against the sky. Sound of night traffic on the highway in the industrial valley. No siren at this moment, though there would be another soon for there were always sirens. The baby crib at the foot of the bed, that's what was empty. Its emptiness opened into the underworld. I had not thought about the empty crib all day. Now it was back, still empty.

For twenty-six years of my life there was no baby, and I never missed her. I was accustomed to sleeping alone in my room with no sounds except my own sounds and what was outside the window. Then the baby came. Though I sometimes missed my privacy, I welcomed the change. This new little life which came out of me would cry and I would hold her on my breast and she would stop and belong to me. I put her delicately in the crib and as I lay in bed I would hear her snuffling and turning, and if she whimpered I would pick her up again and she would stop. Henceforth there would always be tension in my life, alert to the dangers of relaxation. My sleep was never as deep as it used to be because my ears were still listening, and I was permanently watchful for every possible mishap that could threaten this bud growing in my room so close to me.

But now I was alone in my room again as if my old life had never been interrupted. No snuffling from the crib, as if the last year and a half had not existed. She's not dead, I said to myself. Now. Think about now. I put my baby into now, which meant finding her in a motel somewhere between here and Stump Island. Crazy Oliver taking care of her, if he could. She cries looking for something familiar in a world mostly still chaos in which the one clear certainty, Mommy, is absent, replaced by some crude thing she doesn't know what it is. I spoke aloud in my private room. Hold on, baby, I said, we'll find you. I promise.

4

Oliver Quinn

Everything depends on preparation. That's why I bought the car seat. If you want to do something, you must think the future step by step. Likewise the time spent training Nick. How many times I had to explain because it takes him a while. Next was set a date, which was hard because of the unpredictable element. There's always an unpredictable element, you could fall dead of a heart attack while eating your cereal on the morning of a day of no importance. The fine weather solved that. With foresight I stopped for diapers, it being common knowledge that babies require them.

Drive three days, two stopovers in motels before our destination. Two rooms, one for the baby, the other for me and Nick. I planned to eat in restaurants and counted on the waitresses to tell us what babies eat, many of them being mothers themselves.

I did not anticipate the crying. It got worse through the afternoon. Across the barbaric country of farms, it was hard for a person like me to bear. The message was full of rage and insult and nothing I could do but ignore.

We needed supplies. All societies have babies, therefore baby supplies like others should be available in areas of commerce.

We exited by a cluster of buildings with illuminated signs up high. The sky was fading. If you have a poetic temperament you'll notice the twilight approaching across the terrible flat Republican land of middle Ohio, the deepening color behind the silhouette of a farm house and silo turning pink and gold. In this setting the commercial signs by the exits riot like devils of orange and green against the departing sun. That's what we saw, while inside the car the noise produced by the child who couldn't describe her needs reached storm dimensions.

Next to the gas stations, we found one of the great discount stores, a big red sign across its front, K-MART. We left the baby in the car and went in. Baby food, stacks of small glass jars, a baby face on each. I got an assortment for balance, yellow, green, shades of brown. Nick took the babyfood out to the car while I looked for baby clothes. A woman asked if I needed help. I said I wanted baby clothes. She asked what kind. All kinds, I said. I got a little of everything, guessing the sizes. The woman laughed like I was joking. She said if my wife didn't like it I could bring them back, but I didn't have a wife. I also got toys, selecting on the basis of what I would like if I were a baby. A bulldozer, a machine gun, a rattle. I got the rattle because this baby is still young and might prefer young toys. Enough variety in the toys would shut her up.

Back at the car I found Nick shuffling the sidewalk holding the baby. He told about three women around the car when he brought the baby food. They weren't very nice. They asked what kind of father would leave his child alone in a parking lot and they mentioned the police. He tried to say it ain't no baby of his, but when he opened the door the crying activated his instinct, which saved him. It caused him to pick the baby up, and she shut up like he was her savior, because of exhaustion probably. This took the rhetorical steam out of the ladies. The strangest thing when I tried to take the child to put back in the car, he swung away not letting me, and when he turned back he started to cry. A grown man, don't ask me. I humored him, let him put the baby back himself, so that we could go on our way.

Back to the Interstate in the dark. We ate in McDonald's. The baby was stinky but not too bad, just don't get too close. She sat in a high chair, with a jar of baby spinach. I gave her a spoon which she banged and threw on the floor. Nick wanted to feed her so I let him, and she got spinach on her face and the tray but we did the best we could. Nick got her a glass of Coca-Cola with a straw, but she lacked the conception of the straw. An idiot woman at a nearby table kept making cute-type noises intended to evoke a display of cuteness in the baby. After a while the baby cried again. It made Nick edgy, or else some softening of his mind from walking the baby in the parking lot turned him into a mother. He picked her up without permission and walked her around, and she stopped. As for instinct, it's well known that as mankind developed intellect, so his instincts died away. In comparison with migratory birds, for example, we are stupid when it comes to instinct. We have only a few, an instinct to eat, flee from danger, sex. We make up for it by brain. It follows that Nick, who's not so bright, would have more instinct than I. Note also his instinct is feminine, maternal, across the lines of sex, which I attribute to his primitive development, it taking a higher development to bring out sexual differentiation in animals.

We put the baby back in the car and drove on, looking for a motel like Red Roof or Cheap Couples. The baby was quiet like she thought the stuff she had spit out was dinner and she had actually been fed, and it would have been fine driving in the peaceful dark with the other cars humming along only that Nick Foster who seems to think his newly roused maternal instinct means something kept murmuring baby all the time, I love babies oh do I love babies.

I told him to shut up. We found a Day's Inn and stopped. Two rooms, one for me and Nick, the other for the baby, with the baby on the second floor and us on the first. We put the baby to bed. I let Nick carry her because of his instinct. The question was whether to change her diaper since she was getting pretty foul. I tried Nick. I said, let's test your smarts. What should we do about the baby's diaper?

We should change the baby's diaper.

I asked why.

Because the baby will be happier, he said.

That's anthropomorphic, I said. The question is not the baby's happiness but the baby's health. It's healthier to change the baby's diaper. Have you ever changed a diaper?

No. I spread a newspaper on the bed. The baby was a mess. It took a lot of toilet paper, more than for an ordinary person, because the baby was smeared all over its behind. When we were done I'll admit I would not have been satisfied with the cleanup if it had been me, but we did the best we could.

We put on the new diaper and the pajamas I bought at the store. Nick dumped the dead diaper and toilet paper in the toilet. I don't know what's to prevent it plugging up. The stuff didn't go down when I flushed, so I left it for the maid to figure out. We left the baby in the middle of its bed, locked the door for its protection, then back to our own room on the ground floor.

We watched television before sleep. I don't know if the baby cried, because we couldn't hear her where we were. She was crying when we left, but not loud, and I figured she either fell asleep or didn't. In the morning I thought she had been kidnapped but we found her on the floor by the window. She was asleep. She seemed chastened. That's the word I'd use, chastened or less arrogant than before.

I explained to Nick. What you've got to understand, I told him, is the incompetence of this child's mother. She's a mother not by nature but by accident, making the best of a bad situation. Ann Landers will tell you love based on the best of a bad thing is not to be trusted. That's the first count against her. Second is the environment in which she's raising this child. Not only does she work nine to five, leaving the care of the baby to others, a new man has entered her life. Apparently she has not noticed his black face, which implies colorblindness not merely physical but moral. Worse still if she has noticed, she being the daughter of a professor who thinks he is wiser and more intelligent than anybody else. I know better. Never forget the moment of creation of this child. In the dark of a motel in sound of the pounding surf of Cape Hatteras. How she lusted then, laughing, giggling, no sense of significance at all, it was embarrassing. Yet so vindictive later. Now this alliance with a man not merely black but trying to rise above who by nature he is. It's my daughter she wants to raise like a black man's child, soaking her in black culture like cornbread and molasses, not to speak of moral relativity nor the revolution ahead when children rise up against their fathers. That's why. She has no right to scorn me and look down on me. She has no right to deny me my part in the baby, my claim. To ignore me, pay no attention to my warnings. To care so much about that baby to the exclusion of everything else.

I am taking her to Miller. I told her on the telephone the second night. She thinks I'm crazy. She doesn't understand, nobody does. I tried to tell her once, she didn't hear, she wasn't interested. Don't say she don't deserve what she gets.

*

They called me preacher's kid, which was my father's fault. He stood up front in his gothic church talking to the ladies. Snobbish sermons interpreting the Bible. He kept God's distance, telling the ladies what God meant, like his job was to protect God from people instead of bringing people to God. If I wanted to speak to God, I had to go through channels, through my father. Pray my prayers in his words like the people praying in church.

As a kid I was too sensitive. I got over it by making other people cry. Jump out from the bushes at the swaggering kids going home with their school bags, beat them up. My father wanted to make me a copy of himself only inferior. I was to be a man of God like him, by his permission. He would introduce me to God but keep an eye on us to make sure we didn't get too chummy. I refused. Silently, for everything was unspoken between us, my father and me. His rules were unspoken, like the curfew when I was a teenager, likewise his punishment when I violated it. His punishment was silence for me to figure out like remorse. Since he wouldn't punish me in a conventional way I violated every rule I could identify. I violated the curfew. I refused to do well in school until I realized my bad grades pleased him. After that I studied to learn how ignorant he was.

I read about what it was like in a world without God. It hadn't occurred to me there might be such a world. I learned about Raskolnikov from *Cliff's Notes*. He believed a strong man can do anything he likes, and to prove it he murdered an old pawnbroker and her daughter. I wondered if I could do that. From *Twombly's Study Guide on Sartre and Existentialism* I learned that in a world without God you have an obligation to do what you can get away with because otherwise your life's a waste.

My mother had been dead a good many years. My father expected me to eat dinner with him, cooked by his housekeeper,

Melissa Drew. Sometimes I did, sometimes I didn't. I practiced friendliness like how are you this morning Pop, what kind of a day did you have. I practiced doing what I could get away with. Speeding in the car without getting caught. I was an excellent shoplifter. Women's sweaters, cameras, stuffed animals. I put them in the living room. What's this? my father would say. What do you want with a woman's sweater? You already have a camera.

I wasn't satisfied, something was missing. I moved out, left town, came to Cincinnati, a room of my own. Didn't tell my father so there were no letters. Later I heard that my father had died alone in the house. They found him when he didn't show up for church. He left me some money but not enough.

I had another reason for leaving town, Priscilla Mantel. We had a fine thing going. She was a clerk in a record store, never mind what I was doing. She liked sex, and we made a lot of it on weekends. She liked to take risks. We would lock ourselves in her apartment and take off our clothes on Friday night and not put them on again until Monday. Sometimes she would stand naked in her window that looked down from the third floor to the busy neighborhood street where the kids jumping rope could look up and see her and she would wave to them. Sometimes we went to a hotel and pretended we were man and wife and sometimes we went out to the park at night and found a place behind bushes off a path while watching the people strolling who didn't know what they were missing if they would only look. We had a great time until she got pregnant. That spoiled everything. She had no right to get pregnant. She expected me to take an interest. She was wrong. Her pregnancy took all the fun away. I dropped her, that made her mad, and the next thing I knew she tried to sock me for child support. I had to leave town. Shook her off finally, she never knew where I went. Never again, I warned myself.

I met Nick Foster at the United Dairy Farms where I was working the night shift. He was pumping gas next door. He would take a break to sit in a booth and drink a milkshake and I talked to him. Nick Foster had inferiority feelings and sometimes when he found it hard to talk he cried. I thought he'd be good to practice on. I made him realize he was not bright. He already knew but I made it clearer, after which he became my faithful and doggy follower. He was living with Billie Hambrell. She encouraged his dependency, so I made him get rid of her and live with me. She made a fuss. I helped him write her a letter which he signed. That was the last we heard from Billie Hambrell. Nick cried but he became my loyal friend. He learned to do what I asked, which made me feel better about myself.

Judy Field was not so nice. I met her at an AA meeting, thinking she was better than the rest of us. Because her father was a professor who wrote books. She acted smart so I went after her. I talked about Raskolnikov and the existential act and she said I was an intellectual in disguise. I told her my father was a minister, and she said I was in rebellion, how exciting. Her father believed in science not God and she thought we should get together. I had no interest in her father. She thought I was a good guy and I offered to take her home, but she was tied up. The next week we went to McDonald's and drove around the country and ended up at her apartment. She was good but not the best (not as good as Priscilla) because she was too self-conscious but it was better than nothing and I wasn't ready to quit yet. Only the next time she made me drop by her parents' house and meet her father and forced me into a discussion with him about religious beliefs. This was a mess because she told him I had been reading Raskolnikov and Sartre and the professor smiled like he knew all about me and he talked about science and the big bang and consciousness as if that's what I wanted to know. He told me science and religion can be reconciled, just don't expect God to intervene in every little personal thing, and I thought what the hell. He irritated me. He said every thought I ever had somebody else had thought before. He thought I was grateful for his wisdom since he was a scientist and only a scientist could know the truth about God. I made up for it with Judy at my place. She pushed under me while the juice rose and I thought of the professor looking at us and not knowing what to do.

I warned her not to get pregnant, if she got pregnant I wouldn't be responsible. I thought she understood that, she never said she didn't. At Cape Hatteras where we screwed inside all weekend ignoring the surfers sporting outside on the flying fringes of the sea, by the end of the weekend there was nothing left, and I thought that was the end of it. But a few weeks later she called to say she was pregnant, doing exactly what I had warned her against. I couldn't believe it. It made me laugh for the professor who couldn't control his daughter but mainly I was disgusted. She did it on purpose, just like Priscilla Mantel. How treacherous they all are, luring you with siren songs of naked flippery, and then sock it to you with results. To happen to me twice was more than I could bear. I needed to do something, to punish her some way but what could I do? I stopped seeing her. I bought an answering machine and did not return her calls. I figured the best way was to cut her like a cold turkey and hoped that would satisfy me. At the AA meeting I looked away. It worked. She moved back into the parents' house which served them right too. She had it coming for thinking she could screw me without consequences, for by God, there are consequences, which is something they all need to learn. You do things and you face the results. Nothing is free.

I went to work as a cook at Basil's Russian Parlor. Fancy restaurant near the university. When Estelle Gaines told me Judy was due, I got another idea. You never know in advance what feelings you're going to have. I thought, it's not often you can greet a baby fresh out of the abyss. It occurred to me that pregnancy is the natural outcome of sex, and maybe the proper response for me would be to take over the fatherly role. Instead of leaving it all to the woman, take charge as the man is supposed to do. Judy wouldn't like it, but that's her problem. So when a few days later Estelle called and told me Judy was in the hospital I went over and found the room and went in. I'm the father, I said, so they let me in.

Small room with people around the bed, Harry Field and Mrs. Field and a couple of Judy's irritating friends named Joe and Connie Rice and a nurse. The nurse said: You the father? Come on in. I heard Judy moan, Who? then saw her on her back with a mountain on top of her. Face ugly without makeup, corpse-colored, she winced when she saw me like a dog had bitten her. Saying, What are you doing here?

Come to see my baby born.

Go to hell, she said. In front of her father and mother and friends and nurse, to the father of her child.

I came to see my wife, and my baby born.

Wife?

There there, the nurse said, this is a time for joy, not family problems.

I stayed. The monitor showed the baby's heartbeat, the nurse went in and out, the doctor in green with not much talk while the mother grunted and yelled. When the baby was about to come they kicked out the parents but let me stay because I was the father.

Afterwards they let me sit alone with Judy in her room. The baby wasn't much, too small to be human, wrinkled and ugly, hard to look at on Judy's breast. Judy grumbling she would never forgive me. I said this was my baby and I wanted to play a normal role in her life. She asked where I had been the last nine months and I said it was none of her business. I had been minding my life and now I wanted to reenter hers in the role nature created for me. The baby, which looked more like an aardvark than a child, or maybe a gargoyle in the zoo, started to cry. The cry was inside a tunnel or a paper cup, enclosed and tiny. I remembered making this child, I remembered it coming out of my cock. With Judy whose capacity to be a mother was unproven and in doubt. The poor little thing. The cry inside the cup was so tiny and helpless the child could die from not being touched in a half hour or overnight with an incompetent mother. It seemed like I had been neglected all my life. Like walking in a cocoon of anesthesia, a blindfold mask. My father dying by himself and Judy hateful and resenting my absence and me acceding to being put down by going down before they began. How this was my baby but I'd never be allowed as father, and the baby would be raised like an absentee donor.

She said I could visit a little. Short visits to the baby in her home. She wouldn't let me take the baby out. Her distrust was insulting. We walked with the baby in the stroller discussing how to raise a child. Arguments. I wanted a hand in her raising and education, I wanted her to recognize and respect her father. I wanted veto rights over other men Judy might bring into the baby's life, as the true father I deserved some control.

She was vindictive and spiteful, I was surprised how much so. All because I had not stayed with her during those nine months while she was getting fat and ugly. Damned if I would put my-self in that servile position for someone who no longer attracted me. I told her that. I pointed out what a favor I was doing her by sticking around now, and that made her mad and she told me to get out. She'd rather score points, kick me out, break with me, raise the child as a single mother. Which only proved what I knew all along, she never cared about love or sex in the first place, it was all a trick to get herself a child. Well, if she wants a child that much I say that's her problem. Only don't expect me to sit by quietly and do nothing.

That's when I got the idea of taking the baby. The child was a couple of weeks old then and the mother was turning me out of my life. I thought, If she won't let me be father, then don't let her be mother. I thought if I could take it and give it to somebody else who really needs a child. Some couple wanting to adopt, maybe even make a little money on the deal. If that wasn't feasible, I could put it in a basket on the door of the Catholic church. You could say I was saving the child's soul. It was too hard though, I wasn't ready for drastic action yet.

About this time Miller entered my life. A guy Jake Loomer showed up at AA, where I went one evening after an argument with Judy. He gave a speech about a guru who turned his life around. He also wanted guys to play basketball with him in the gym the next night. I signed up for the basketball. Eight guys pretty well matched. Afterwards on the bench Loomer talked to a couple of us. He was just visiting on his way home from around the country, going back to where he came from, the Miller Church. Would you like to know about it? An orange leaflet.

THE MILLER CHURCH
Stump Island, Maine
Get to know God in person

He said, What's your problem? and I said I didn't have any problems, and he said that's your problem, I should come out to Stump Island and see for myself. You should meet Miller, he said, the greatest man in the world, see what he can do for you.

I said what can he do, and he said he can change you and make you new, he can innovate you and make you opposite to what you was. I told Loomer I was sick of God. I told him about my father who was God's only friend and God could fuck himself because I believed in Raskolnikov and Sartre. So Loomer got excited in a hush and said, You're serious, and he said, Then Miller is the man for you. Are you willing to talk to me about why Miller is the man for you?

I said Okay and we got rid of the other guys and went to Alex's Tavern where we could talk in quiet over a beer with no AA colleagues butting in. Loomer talked. First I gotta tell you something you may not understand. You see that "Get to know God in person" on the flyer? That's because the people in Miller Church will tell you Miller is not just some prophet or preacher, he's God Himself. That don't mean you got to believe it, so don't worry about it. All you got to do is think.

I was disappointed if this meant Loomer was crazy after all, only he kept talking and I changed my mind. Miller is God because he can make you new, he said. He can take you into his fold and if you live and practice in his fold you'll be different like he made you a different man with his own hands without even trying. Do you want to be a different man?

I never thought about being different before, it never occurred to me. I didn't know if it would be worth while. Loomer kept on. He said, Forget about Miller and think about God. You don't like God because your father has a monopoly on him, did it occur to you you misconstrued the nature of God, you and him? Think. Who is this God actually? This God who displays himself to you every day in every act of nature in the world around you. The dead birds, the shootings, highway accidents, obituary pages. Lived all your life and never realized what a murderer God is? Mass murderer, war criminal, terrorist. Never thought of that? You want to kill somebody and you think God disapproves? Wise up, half of God's work is killing. It's not God who punishes murderers, it's people. Nature is half birth and growth, half murder and death. You think God is less murderous than nature?

I said what has this to do with Miller, is he a murderer? Miller's your kind of God, Loomer tells me. He says he's God, does anybody strike him dead? No. What does that mean? Miller knows he is God, what do you know? Nothing. Miller knows the world is full of murder and hate, which any God who don't know that can't qualify. Your father stood between you and God. Well here's your chance to stick it to your father and be the kind of person you always wanted to be and were never allowed. Miller is God, that'll tell em, the Presbyterians and Baptists, along with the Catholics and Greek Orthodox, not to speak of the Jews and the Muslims and the Buddhists. Show them. Jesus man, he says, you don't have to believe him to believe in him. What's belief anyway except something you decide on without an argument? Why shouldn't God be Miller if you want him to be?

Think of it like this, Loomer said. We call Miller God, which means anything you want it to mean. For some Miller is a window into the Godhead. If you think where God was before Miller was born and where he'll go when Miller dies, you'll see God moves around, reincarnation, if you know that word. Avatar, that's another good word. It means different things to different people and we can still agree because the words are the same no matter what they mean. As long as we agree on the words it don't matter what they mean. Miller is God. That's the words, it don't matter what they mean.

He said, You live in the Miller Church you disappear from the world. Nobody know where you gone, nobody follow, it's a sovereign country independent of the U S of A, you do what you like. Haven, sanctuary, you know them words? Leave your troubles, back home don't know where you're at, good as being dead.

So I left a message on my machine that I had gone to New Orleans and I went to Stump Island with Loomer. Pine and fir on the Maine coast, a horrible place. Left Nick behind. Also Judy and that baby while I was swearing to myself I'll be back. Just because I was going to try out Miller, I wasn't giving up is what I mean. While Loomer said, if some smartass like your girl's professor asks, tell him God is direct knowledge, like your knowledge of Oliver Quinn.

I went to Stump Island and met him. Pleased to meetcha, Miller said, shaking my hand like an ordinary man. Welcome to the fold. The idea of giving Judy's baby to the Miller Community occurred to me as soon as I got there, I saw it in an instant. I didn't tell Loomer. In the evenings I had tutorials with him in the shed by the water. Talking about the new Oliver, who that would be. I could hear the waves slapping the rocks while we talked. He told me about the Raskolnikov Society, a secret enclave within the Miller Community. The Raskolnikov Society was a group of believers organized to execute God's secret wishes. I must not mention the Raskolnikov Society to anybody. I asked what I had to do to join, and he said figure it out.

I knew what he meant, something bold and radical that Raskolnikov would do. I wondered if the idea in my head would do. The more I looked around the place the better that idea seemed. At a Sunday meeting a woman named Maria stood up and spoke. She was the lady who gave me sheets and bedding when I arrived. Miller Community needs children, she said. That's because the future will outlive us. Exactly, I thought. I'll be doing a service for everybody while Judy learns the lesson she needs to learn. So I asked Maria if I brought her a baby would she take care of it? I didn't tell Loomer or Miller.

I went back to get her. I had to wait because the Community was moving to a different location. Leaving Stump Island, thank God. I found Nick Foster again and indoctrinated him. I saw Judy and told her about Miller. I wanted to give her a chance, so she couldn't blame me for taking things into my own hands. I suggested we all go together to live with Miller on Stump Island. I gave her good reasons, the extended family that would help her raise the child, the isolation from the world, the all-around love. She said I was nuts. I wasn't surprised, which was why I mentioned Stump Island rather than Wicker Falls, so she couldn't track us down when we had gone. Then when I saw the black man she was planning to raise the child with, I decided it was time. I alerted Nick. We acted quickly and now we are taking a child to God who will change us all.

5

David Leo

That's me in the middle between window and aisle, seat too narrow and no view unless I lean forward in front of the guy on my left. Somewhere, Pennsylvania, New York. I don't like to fly. The guy on my left has a laptop computer, the woman on my right reads a paperback. Nothing for me except the crumpled peanut bag the stewardess left and a plastic cup with no place to put it. Lean back and look at the roof. The luggage bins, the movable walls between sections, the sunny but viewless cylinder of discomfort into which I am crammed. Davey Leo the hero, pursuing a kidnapping, who do I think I am?

Now in Boston I wait for the unloading to reach my row, stand hunched not to bump the luggage bin, then out the tunnel to the concourse, looking for the plane to Bangor. Past lobbies and concourses with flags and high roofs to another wait in a sterile space by a plate glass view of planes on the apron, taxi strips and runways. Beyond the airport I see wooden houses on a ridge, domestic lives just out of public sight. I walk across the tarmac in the wind to a smaller plane, propellers and a view into the pilot's cockpit, then more taxiing and noise and bottled ears as we run down the airport until the ground drops, and we follow the coastline like an oversized relief map on our way to Maine.

At Bangor, a smaller airport, find the rental agency. I don't like to approach strangers, everywhere I go I am shy. No one knows I am a hero on a mission. I wait while the amiable woman looks up the computer. She's my friend, I rely on her. It takes time. Sign documents. The key. The lot is on the side, third slot, marked 24. Before I go I'll need a map. I find a shop and a Rand McNally atlas. I go outside to find the car in 24, this cool fresh day at a latitude more northerly than where I started, needing my jacket. Bag over my shoulder and the Maine wind blows. The chunky clouds scud in the bright sky, the weather makes my loneliness shiver.

How to operate this car I have never seen, modern, smells like new, locating the ignition, gear shift, brake, parking brake, lights and windshield wiper that I won't need yet. I study the map, which does not show Black Harbor. Remembering where it was on Professor Field's map last night in the living room, I can see where it should be on this map among names like Bucksport, Brookville, Deer Isle, and I plot a route on a card for the dashboard, US 2 into Bangor, State 15 to Bucksport, Orland, and beyond. Now I can start. The car hums like new through the lot to the highway, into the city looking for signs, across the bridge to the road down the river through villages. More comfortable as we go, I enjoy the driving short term.

Short because though there's nothing here but the road and traffic laws, the hum and muscular dynamics of driving, the more I go the closer I come, and then what will I do? Be a hero, that's what.

If I can find it I'll arrive in Black Harbor in the middle of the afternoon. What should I do first? Go to the post office to locate Stump Island? Find a place to stay so as not to be stuck in the rural wilderness with no place to sleep? Find a place to eat so as not to be afflicted with hunger or cramps and nausea while engaging in heroism?

Through Bucksport. Orland. I stop on the shoulder for another look at the map. Cut left before Castine. How smooth the car goes, how gently it takes the bumpy roads, past the ragged fields, the woods, farm houses and shacks, with silver glimpses of the afternoon bay, its shining inlets and coves reaching almost to the road. There's a flat aspect to the land but the road is full of ups and downs, straightaway stretches and curves, and the yellow fields tilt and slope. Suddenly there's a sign, BLACK HARBOR. Jesus, here I am.

Through a lane of shade trees the road ends in a T with another road and no sign which way to go. Large houses shuttered and closed, summer residences probably. Looking for a town center I turn right. The road comes to the top of a hill with yellow fields sloping off and a good view of the bay country. Miles and miles of water and islands, necks and inlets, with everywhere the same dark evergreen, the silver water in the late afternoon and blue hills or mountains on the horizons. No sign of a village.

So I go back where the road descends by more big houses. It turns at another intersection, the left going up again and the right down steeply to the water now visible. Go that way.

A few hundred yards to a little harbor. Facing the harbor is a black island covered with pine. On this side at the end of the road is a yellow wooden building, three stories, with a wooden platform, a sign indicating a general store, and a gasoline pump. Dirt parking and a path down to a dock with a row of slips where dinghies and fishing boats are tied up.

Is this Black Harbor?

Beyond the yellow building to the right is a stucco building with brown trim and a sign, HARBOR INN. That's what we need, let's stop here, I say. I have developed a habit of talking to myself in the car.

In my customary shyness I drive up to the Inn and park in the dirt lot. No other cars. Hoping it's not closed for the season, I go to the door, with a white lace curtain in the window, find it unlocked, open it and go in. Nice inside, varnished floor, house-like furnishings, lamps, a staircase with a mahogany banister. Little desk with a cozy lamp, a guest register, no people. A cooking smell, movement in back, a dining room. I wonder how they feel about black people coming in without knocking in a place where black people are scarce. The brass bell on the desk is shaped like an eighteenth century lady with a wig. Ring for service? The bell is loud like a noise in your sleep.

Shyness is protective, I wait in it through the steps in the hall of the young woman with long blonde hair and a denim shirt who approaches, watching her carefully for surprise or alarm when she sees the color of my face. Not this time, only the cool question, Can I help you?

Is this Black Harbor?

It is indeed. Amused.

Have you a room available?

Good. I sign the register; register my credit card, bring my bag in. Lug it upstairs to the front room facing the harbor, a complete view, what they call wonderful. Lace in the windows, mahogany bedstead, bedspread with bumps and knots.

This is nice, or would be except for my errand. No hero. Wash up, then look around. Think carefully where to start, what to ask, what my first inquiry should be.

I take my time before going out and start with only modest ambitions. The general store next door, with a sign on the front porch by the gas pump, BLACK HARBOR POST OFFICE. Just what I'm supposed to want. It's inside so I'd better go in. Soda fountain on the left, sickles and scythes in front, power mowers behind them, racks with pots and pans. A fat man sits in a lawn chair next to the garden hoses. Post office? He points to the back, a postal window with a room behind it, post boxes on the wall. Is it open? The man nods. A woman sits behind the window, but I'm not ready, I have to decide my approach.

I think I'd better eat first and get a better layout of the town. I go back to the car, up the hill to the road, out the other direction. Just around the bend under trees, there's a shack selling gas and eats and souvenirs. Hamburgers. Cole slaw, fries, I sit on a stool at the counter. Woman in a yellow apron, blank eyes.

I contemplate the stark insanity of this heroism I signed up for. Here in a village where I know no one, looking to intercept a kidnapping supported by a cult church, possibly mad, definitely out of the mainstream, with the possibility that anyone I speak to might be a member or sympathizer to thwart me. Beat me up too? It's bad enough calling, attention to myself by being black. I don't trust the woman in the yellow apron.

However, I'll have to trust somebody or never get anywhere. After determining there's nothing more in this town beyond the hamburger store I return to the harbor. There's a channel out to the bay on either side of the island. A fishing boat comes through the channel on the right. A couple of men on the dock watch. I could ask if there's boat service to Stump Island.

Later. I return to the post office. If you can't trust the post office, whom can you trust? But now it's closed. The fat man still in the lawn chair looks curiously but doesn't speak. He knows if I have questions I'll ask, no point knocking himself out trying to guess.

Back to the Inn. The young woman with blonde hair is at the desk, ask her. Excuse me, can you tell me anything about a place called Stump Island?

She wrinkles her face. Don't think so, she says.

Do you know anything about the Miller Church?

What church?

Miller Church? It's supposed to be on Stump Island.

Can't say I do, she says. There's two churches close. Catholic up the road half mile to the right. Congregational a quarter mile up to your left.

Thanks anyway.

Back at the wharf there's only one man now, out near the end looking over the water. Can't see what he looks like. I could ask him about a boat to Stump Island, but that's not safe if he's from there himself. I need a constable or sheriff, someone representing the law. Too late for anything today, I'll plan my attack and begin tomorrow. Meanwhile keep my eyes open in case Oliver Quinn and the child should happen to arrive.

No television in the Inn room, nor reading matter. What can I do with nothing on a boring evening, is boredom the price of being a hero? Once again I go to the general store, buy some magazines, cheap reading for a night. Full of hamburger, I skip dinner, get some potato chips later out of the machine.

Bedtime in the Harbor Inn. A floodlight on a telephone pole lights my room as I pretend to sleep. Once I'm settled in the uncomfortable bed and it's stopped squeaking and my brain passages have calmed down, a coastwise quiet moves in, magnifying the water sounds at the harbor, plop and gurgle. As the silence deepens I hear the ping of a bell buoy, marking something. The squeak might be a boat at the dock rubbing the pilings. Meanwhile the inside of my head is full of the day, flight attendants spieling, bags toted through corridors, new cars in strange countryside, plots schemes and betrayals, and especially rehearsals for tomorrow limited in scope considering that I have only the vaguest notion what the situation is.

In the morning, Good morning, sunny curtains in the Inn's breakfast room and again the young woman with long hair. Eggs or pancakes? I forgot to mention the Episcopal Church, she says.

After breakfast, following plans made in the night, I go back to the general store to ask the postmistress if there's a constable or sheriff in this town. But I failed to realize the post office won't open until ten-thirty so she can sort the mail. People wait. Hello they say to me, containing their curiosity. My shyness is either innate or the product of environmental causes, in either case making me helplessly polite. But since I'm not expecting mail it's silly to wait, especially when you think how simple my question is. Try the fat man after all. In the lawn chair where he always sits, probably all night. Excuse me sir, is there a constable or a sheriff in this town?

Constable you want?

If there is one.

Law?

If possible.

Well now. You a stranger here?

I think he knows that, but maybe it's another form of politeness. I suppose Martin Bilodeau's the man for you, he says. Martin Bilodeau for questions of law and the public peace.

Where can I find him?

Bilodeau Map Store, up the main road right. You'll see him.

Thank you sir. Now we're getting somewhere, unless things are corrupt like the movies and Bilodeau the constable or sheriff is in collusion. I shouldn't assume such things.

Bilodeau Map Store turns out to be the souvenir gas and food shop where I had my hamburger from the woman of the yellow apron, I not having noticed the sign last night. This morning a different woman wears the yellow apron. I ask for Martin Bilodeau.

He comes through the curtains, plump and rosy with silver glasses looking like a car salesman who drinks too much. Hi there, what can I do for you? Red plaid flannel.

You the constable?

Well, if that's what you want to call me.

I'm wondering what you can tell me about the Miller Church on Stump Island.

Oh my, let's go out onto the porch. Maybe you should tell me why you want to know.

Sitting on the porch, what can I do but take the chances I have to take? I want to know, I say, because someone has kidnapped my friend's baby. I'd like to get her back.

Martin Bilodeau leans back in his chair, eyes noticeably widened at the word kidnapped, just as they widened when he first caught sight of me through the curtains into the room.

So why are you asking about the Miller Church?

Because that's where we think the kidnapper is taking her.

He thinks a while before speaking.

Am I the one you want to see, he says, or should it be the state police?

That's what maybe you can tell me.

Well for that maybe you'd better tell me what happened.

To me his down east speech sounds exaggerated, deliberately juiced for outsiders, but what do I know? I tell him about Judy, Oliver Quinn, and Hazy. Why Judy thought he was taking the baby to Stump Island.

You came all the way here in hopes of finding them?

I thought it worth a try.

Just you or is the mother with you?

Just me.

And if you find them, what do you propose to do?

I don't know. I thought maybe you could help. Or someone like you.

Tell me my friend, what's your interest? I mean, why are you knocking yourself out?

Friendship, I say, to help out.

A romantic interest maybe, hey?

Is that a leer? Does it mean he has something against a romantic interest between people like me and people like Judy? On the other hand, he probably supposes Judy is a person like me and even possibly it's my own baby we're talking about, with reasons he hasn't yet figured as to why I should conceal it.

Not yet, I say foolishly.

You don't say? Well, here it is, the unfortunate thing I do believe Stump Island is currently uninhabited. It was inhabited but they moved. You might take comfort that my impression accords with yours thinking it was a commune of wackos. Old men with beards and wild-eyed youth and housewife types. Kept to themselves, though, didn't bother nobody.

They moved away?

Let's go down the wharf, talk to somebody. They get a closer view than I do.

Down in my car, measuring as we go my disappointment against the relief of heroism postponed, though where does that leave us looking for the child?

Where it leaves us is where we started. Trying to foil an intelligent person who has no intention of being foiled. Trying to undercut the advantage he took at the start. How can we do that except by luck, how else intervene before he lets us? By that line of thinking my heroism is just a show.

The man on the wharf is Jack Carmody, his granite face with specks of mica. His eyes have looked at the sea for sixty years.

Bilodeau says, This man is looking for a kidnapped child on Stump Island.

Jack says, Ain't nobody on Stump Island the last three months. Folks moved off before Christmas.

Bilodeau says, Guy swiped this guy's friend's little baby under her nose. Taking her to the playground, ran off with her.

Jesus, what do you know about that?

Everybody stands around thinking. What I'm thinking is get the state police, find where the Miller people went. What Carmody is thinking pops up in a moment: I maybe saw them yesterday.

Man and woman holdin a baby, he says, passed them in a motorboat headin out there.

Maybe your man got a woman to help him, Bilodeau says. You game to take us out?

Any time. Want to go now?

Bilodeau asks me, You want to go out and see?

Comfort from numbers, the shyness of my heart fast now with danger and excitement. Sure, I say.

Sooner the better, right?

A stinking lobster boat with ropes tangled in the bottom and lobster pots piled. Rusty hooks, buoy markers, nets. I climb off the dock, sit in the cockpit. Carmody starts the engine, backs out into the harbor. Takes the channel to the right.

A little motorboat comes into view beyond the island, heading for the harbor. It rides low with top-heavy people sticking up out of the water. Carmody steers in that direction and the shapes clarify. Outboard motor, two wrapped figures, one bent, the other erect, the bow high, stern almost underwater. Carmody heads directly at them.

Bilodeau asks it: That's them?

Them.

You sure of that?

Yep.

That's McCaskill.

So 'tis.

The boat passes close, the passage swift, man with a woman holding a wrapped up baby who wave as they go by.

Didn't get that good a look yesterday, Carmody says.

Bilodeau explains to me. McCaskill on Fig Island. Don't expect them out this time of year.

Want to go back? Carmody says.

Hell. Let's take a look, we come this far.

He turns up the engine fast heading out. The bay is full of islands, some near, some far out. A couple of islands are just rocks, others stretch for miles, I can't tell where one begins or ends with a uniform treeline of black evergreens above the rocks. The bay gleams in the cold sun, the boat makes a trough on either side and a froth of green and white rises and falls behind.

Going to see the island they left. Why, I wonder. The only reason I can think of is curiosity, of which constables and lobster boat owners have as much as failed heroes. Meanwhile Oliver and his victim escape, the air fare and rental wasted, sorry, Harry.

There 'tis, Carmody says.

An island ahead, not big, covered with trees like the others, no habitation visible. A dock emerges among the rocks, we go in, tie up, go ashore.

A broad path into the woods. I feel nervous, my shyness, or if the cult left a rear guard for ambush. In the woods a gate blocks the path. Barbed wire on either side. The gate is padlocked, Bilodeau climbs over, we follow, no problem there. The path continues.

There's a clearing with dead winter grass. Two structures opposite, one an old wooden house, the other a shed under a curved roof of corrugated sheet metal. We tromp across to the house. The grass disappears, trodden to dirt. Bilodeau tries the door, locked. Looks in the window. Cleared out good, he says. The door to the shed is open. Looks like a meeting room, dark without windows, a little light from gaps in the roof. Broken folding chairs against the wall. We walk around, outhouses, a trash bin, old bedding, old tanks for propane gas, dead tools and kerosene lamps. Yep, Carmody says, cleared out good.

How many was they, you reckon? Bilodeau says.

Twenty, twenty-five? Could that many live in that house?

Don't know. They go much back and forth?

Some for supplies, Carmody says. They only had an outboard.

Who owns the property, Pickins?

Likely. He owns most the islands round about here.

Wonder what he knows.

He's in Florida, takin in the warm and tropical mangoes.

Flamingos and alligators. Guess that's what he's doing.

To me Bilodeau says, Guess you got a wild goose on your hands son.

Wild goose?

Chasin the wild goose. You know the expression.

Maybe somebody knows where they went, I say. Post office should know, shouldn't they?

Post office, sure, if they want their mail to catch up with them, post office should know.

Back to the boat then, back through the islands, back to the harbor. Nothing is more important than time and distance, because the cold on return is freezing me to death, I not having anticipated what the Maine coast would be like this time of year. I stamp my feet and swing my arms, jaw chattering, nose running, eyes blinded in ice. Welcome death. After a long time Carmody digs in the bottom for a yellow rubber slicker. It's clammy and loose like a tent, a little help but not a lot, barely enabling me to endure torture while the distance closes between me and shore.

It does close though, proving once again that everything in the future will come to pass. Thank you Bilodeau and Carmody for your help even if it didn't get us anywhere and back to the post office, the plump postmistress writing in a notebook at her desk.

I ask her for the new address of the people who used to live on Stump Island.

What people? she says. They was several names out there.

How about the Miller Church?

Miller Church? Don't remember that. She thumbs through her file, I could do it faster. No Miller Church, she says, where'd you get that name? I've got a Miller. No first name. I remember that, mail addressed Miller, no front name. You want his new address? How about Wicker Falls, New Hampshire?

Wicker Falls. I'll take that, thank you.

According to my Rand McNally, back in the Inn, Wicker Falls is in the New Hampshire wilderness beyond Endicott, north of Gorham. It's on the map, but couldn't be much bigger than Black Harbor. I put my bag in the car and check out. There's a pay phone outside the general store, a bad connection, the professor's voice up and down in the static.

I spell it for him, W-I-C-K-E-R. No I don't know if it's the right Miller, think I'll go there anyway, I say. I'll let you know.

So here we are again, heading out on a long day's drive, still trying to be a hero, west now across the interior of Maine while afternoon folds in and darkens down. Miles of flat country, though not as flat as Ohio, fields and woods, barns and houses and wilderness to US 2 and on, fast between the towns and slow through them, on through back country, my mood stretched thin across the state. The heavy pounding road, my rental car less smooth and elegant than it was. Quick supper at a café along the road. I postpone the question of heroism ahead by the question of where to sleep, which depends on what time I'll get to Wicker Falls and whether I can find a place at that hour. That wilderness. Calculating and recalculating distance and time while clouds roll in over central Maine getting dark and the March afternoon gives way to the March evening and full night, estimating arrival at midnight or later.

Look forward. We're heading for the rugged mountain region of northern New Hampshire, above Mount Washington and the resorts, on the other side from where the tourists go. Out of season, not many tourist amenities on this road, and there'll be fewer where we're going. What would I gain by driving late and finding no place to sleep?

So I'll stop at the first decent motel I see along the way. I'll have half a day's driving or less tomorrow, which will give me enough time for reconnaissance. Then maybe, I tell myself, I won't have to do anything heroic until the next day.

6

Harry Field

Harry Field prided himself on being tough-minded and professional. He knew how easy it was to be fooled by wishful rationalizations. He took the tough-minded scientific view of death (death is death) so as not to be deceived.

His uncle died when he was a kid. Harry imagined his ghost floating into his room and looking him over. Likewise his grandfather. His grandfather's spirit watched everything he did and peeked into his thoughts. Well, his grandfather said, now I know more about you than I did when I was alive. Harry couldn't believe it though. He used to worry, what will happen to me when I die? Nobody knows, his father said. That's because no living person has had the experience of being dead. No witnesses, no evidence. His father was agnostic. It's beyond human comprehension, he said.

The dignified and certainly grown-up minister in his mother's church talked of heaven as a real place. His grandmother was there looking down on him. At some point in his still early youth it occurred to Harry to be shocked. Can this man, an adult with children of his own, who makes a profession of counseling people, really believe that? Even in his teens young Harry was amazed by the human credulity all around.

He went into science to be tough-minded. Not for the science as such but for the principle, whereby he became a historian of science and began his lifelong attack on wishful thinking. Determined to expose it wherever he could. He became a specialist in the misuses of science, in frauds and charlatans.

He tried to find a scientifically tough-minded idea of death that would escape the terror such tough-mindedness implied. This caused an inner struggle behind his serene outer face. All life dies. So natural a thing should not be terrible, why therefore did it seem so? For years he soothed himself by arguments. For example, time is an illusion. Therefore change is an illusion, and likewise mortality and death. The trouble with this argument was that he had no reason to suppose time was not what it seems to be. Such arguments were as wishful as the heavens and ghosts he attacked. But suppose we are God's eyes and science is God's knowledge of himself? That was soothing. Yet it too was wishful, for though you may be one of God's eyes, when you die that eye will go out, and that's the end of you. Back to the void. He could never get away from the void for long.

That's why, when he heard on the day of the kidnapping that his inner mind had reconciled with death, he knew it was major news. He longed to recover the reasoning that led to this reconciliation but he was still too distracted by the noise and danger of present events.

He was alone in the house at his computer looking out the window. The day was gray. The spring was suspended. The afternoon hung in a state of indigestion, waiting for worse. He had not moved for an hour, transfixed by a spell. Organize your thoughts, Harry. Using his rather old brain, trained in simplification, Harry reduced the things on his mind to four. Each thing paralyzed the others. The lost reconciliation with death that he would like to remember. The speech to the ladies of the Afternoon Club which he should be writing. The letter from Lena which ought to be answered. The kidnapping of his granddaughter, which should be fought with all the forces of the world. Do something, he said. Use the time, it won't wait forever.

He was also thinking about the undiagnosed cancer in his gut. An intermittent but recurring pain, not severe but not ordinary either, sickly and rotten. His annual colonoscopy next month ought to catch it. Dr. Andalusion was not worried, so Harry was afraid to say what he thought, his deep knowledge that it was too late.

The speech for the ladies. Fakes, charlatans and pseudo-sciences. The speech was stuck, he couldn't add anything today. He found Wicker Falls on the map, but his imagination stopped. Neither Wicker Falls nor Stump Island had anything to do with Judy's baby and Davey's trip was a mere distraction. Everything was a distraction from everything else. The interview with the FBI man was no help. His name was Jack Ford. He shook Harry's hand and told him to wait. All you can do is wait. Harry knew this. Things happen after a while, the future always comes. Until then, it could be anything. The news he waits for waits. While David studied Wicker Falls, Harry waited to hear that Oliver Quinn had given the baby to a baby farm in California.

He thought if I answer Lena's letter, maybe that will get me moving again. Dear Lena, how wonderful to hear from you, can't write now because of a family crisis. Don't say that. Be calm as if only the most radical events could knock his well-ordered life out of balance.

He took another look at her letter. He got it out of the file, touching it as delicately as a dried leaf folded into a book. The neat small handwriting made him feel like an adulterer. The letter was breezy and ignorant, full of disregard.

Dear Harry,

Don't faint. I'm writing to you, hope you don't mind. Since you may not recognize my married name, I'm Lena Fowler. Once we were a couple. You can't forget unless you're senile. That's unlikely (I tell myself) in view of your essay which I noticed a couple of weeks ago in the *Journal of Athena*. I don't usually read the *Journal of Athena* and I'm sure you didn't expect to reach me through it. But you weren't counting on my need for a root canal on a rear left molar nor on the intellectual pretensions of my skillful dentist who gives novocain so gently you don't know the needle is in. This excellently pretentious dentist subscribes to the *Journal of Athena* along with *Daedalus* and *People*. I never heard of the *Journal of Athena* but I saw your name on the cover and there you were.

So you're a professor of the history of science and here I am, daring to write in the hope that fifty years will obliterate misunderstandings and revive only nice feelings. That future we were going to share turned out otherwise. My name became Lena Fowler Armstrong. That means someone else came along as important as you, whose name was Armstrong. Homer Armstrong, who helped me produce other important people who didn't exist in your day. Unfortunately Homer recently left this world, leaving me free to mend old gaps if they are still mendable and I still wish.

Doubtless you have important people too. I hope they understand the sadness of the human condition well enough not to mind me. Everybody is dying out. The world looks different at seventy, it has a tragic hue. We are victimized one by one. Therefore, let's be true to one another like Matthew Arnold.

Harry if you have a sweet wife and children don't be alarmed. All I want is to say hello, glad I found you, and encourage you to send back a few gentle words to—I don't know how to finish the sentence.

Your old love,

Lena

The reason he hadn't answered that letter right away was a surge in his chest suggesting it was more important than it should be. After three weeks he realized the more indifferent thing would be to reply, which he intended to do once he finished his speech for the ladies. Then Oliver Quinn kidnapped Judy's baby. You can't write letters to old girlfriends in a crisis like that. Could he write it now while the crisis hung waiting? While David Leo was off to be a hero, and Judy at the office, and Connie Rice with no reason to come until late since there was no baby, Harry alone the long day in the house unable to think, unable to move, what could he say to Lena? Lena that time is dead. In order to replace you years ago I junked you. To junk you I had to see you as junk. The world moves on. Who do you think you are? Anyone looking at him would think he was composing in his head. He hoped sitting like that might fool his mind and start something.

Connie Rice came to cook dinner. Judy came home from work.

This is the third night, Connie said.

It's the fifth, Judy said. Friday. Jesus Daddy how can my baby live five nights without care?

That evening Judy went to the movies. Phyllis asked me to go, she said. Go ahead, Connie said. Take your mind off. How can I pay attention? Judy said. Pass the time, Connie said.

By going to the movie, she missed the spectacular news from David Leo, his call from Wicker Falls, not Wicker Falls actually but a motel not far from it called the Sleepy Wicker Motor Court.

I've found the baby, he said.

Found her? Harry high pitched and excited. You have her? No. You've seen her? No. Then how do you know? I know, Dave said, from the particular way in which they denied it.

Harry took up David Leo's story squeezed through telephone wires. Told by a junior English professor with a love for narrative, going back to fill in the events leading up to his conclusion with a care for how things felt step by step. The story told how he got to Wicker Falls in the middle of the afternoon after missing the side road and going all the way to the Canadian border before realizing. Found it on the way back, a small white sign to WICKER FALLS concealed behind a bush. A village on the side of a hill, a church, a white store with a gas pump, not all that different from Black Harbor except here there were no seaside nor summer houses in the trees. Rocky fields, woods close in, bumpy tree-covered mountains all around, Dave's interest in description. He went into the post office, which was a small white house with a single room and a counter, a postmaster who looked like an old New England devil. Fatherly, his eyes grinned most when his face was sober. When Davey asked him about the Miller Church he said, Well well well. When Davey asked what do you mean by that, he said why do you want to know? When Davey said because somebody kidnapped a friend of mine's baby the postmaster said that sounds like a serious interest.

He told Davey they call themselves the Miller Farm and have a place up Rib Rock Road a few miles from Wicker Falls. Rib Rock, is that what you said? Rib Rock Road. As for Miller, do you know who he is? Why, the postmaster said, He's God on Earth. God Himself, excuse me. When Davey responded with polite surprise, he laughed. The postmaster himself was a leader in the Congregational Church for the last forty years, as well as being a member of the school board, which made him a little skeptical of this Miller's claims. I'm not making jokes, the postmaster said. But he was struck by this kidnapping news because so far these folks been peaceful in spite of the rumors. What rumors? Rumors are rumors, the postmaster said, not believing in passing them on. He offered his advice. Try diplomacy first.

First before what? Davey said.

Strong arm tactics could be dangerous, the postmaster said. Getting ahead of Davey, who hadn't yet reached the point of strong arm tactics. Talk to them, the postmaster said. See what they have to say.

So David Leo called the Miller Church Farm from the pay phone outside the post office. The voice that answered, male or female, he couldn't tell which. Later he decided it was a woman but was never sure.

It was the voice of Miller Church Farm in monosyllables and when Davey asked about Oliver Quinn, is he there? the voice said, What you want with him? That is definitely what she said, Davey said, remembering the words, which gave him alarm at the time as he realized that he hadn't made any plans for diplomacy. He wasn't prepared. The androgynous voice came back saying, He ain't here. So David not giving up asked if she could tell him something about Oliver's baby, to which she said, What you want with her? Pay attention to those words. I want to know if she's all right, Davey told her, and she said, Wait a minute. The next thing was a more definitely male voice that said, Oliver Quinn? Never heard of him. You got the wrong number.

But they had already given themselves away, Davey said. She knew what I was talking about. She knew the baby was with Oliver and was a girl. I didn't get anywhere, but I did learn that.

David asked Harry, Now what do I do? He said the postmaster was afraid of violence. Davey wanted to look around some more. Maybe I should go out to Miller Farm, he said. Hold on, Harry said. Don't do anything dangerous. You've done a good job, he said. I'll tell the FBI man what you found out.

When Harry told Judy about David's call, she said, I'm going to Wicker Falls. This clarified everything and Harry said, I'll go with you.

You can't, she said. You have to give your speech. We'll keep you in touch, she said.

She called David Leo back, then the airline. She would fly to Boston around noon, then a long bus ride reaching Endicott around ten tomorrow night. David would meet her bus.

Later that evening Harry called Barbara in California. He told her everything except the letter from Lena. She was shocked enough without that. When he went to bed he heard Judy thumping around getting ready to go. He thought about David Leo in New Hampshire devising strategy. He thought what an adventure it would be if there weren't so much at stake. He wondered how any man could have the audacity to let people call him God, and wondered how dangerous that made him. He wondered if such a man could be interviewed for his book. Then he wondered how to extract the kidnapped baby from such a man. He imagined things getting out of hand and ending in a massacre. To get that out of his mind he returned to Lena Fowler and tried to compose a letter. The letter was about frauds and charlatans. He asked Lena if she had reconciled herself to death but he forgot the terms in which such a question should be asked and went to sleep without knowing what he was thinking about.

PART TWO

7

Judy Field

Five and a half hours by bus, afternoon into night. I pack a sandwich, cookies, a carton of milk. The rain turns to snow, the invisible mountains of New Hampshire in the dark. Snow flares in the headlights, park signs loom by suggesting the proximity of a notch or ski run or trail. National Forest. The bus wipers flop, the passengers sleep. The snow thins, I see the trunks of trees. There's a town called Gorham, its bus stop a gas station. We go on, the dark is absolute.

Here we are folks, the driver says, not too late considering. Another gas station. We step through the wind into the room inside, the floor sloppy with dirty water from boots. There's Davey to meet me.

Heavily wrapped, he lugs my duffel out to his rented car. The snow has stopped, the sky is black, invisible. It's a small industrial mountain city. He drives me in his humming new car out of town on a pretty good road up what I take to be a valley, no visible landscape. The road is already free of snow, the yellow stripe on the black pavement. Then another road, we go a distance, I don't know how far. The motel, the Sleepy Wicker, sits under big trees with nothing behind. I got you a room next to mine, he says, is that all right?

Fine, I say. He's thinking about questions we haven't discussed, the aura of illegitimacy in being male and female in a remote motel requiring separate rooms which happen to be adjacent. I know what he wants which he hasn't mentioned. I haven't decided what to do when he does mention it. Which he'll probably do before we leave.

But before we leave implies normal times. It ignores the catastrophe that brought us here. Catastrophe takes my stomach away. Hazel, I think, and my stomach disappears.

It's almost midnight, we're forced to wait until tomorrow. The anxiety can't wait. Talk. What did you do today?

Nothing, he says, I waited for you. Drove out Rib Rock Road for a look. Saw a mailbox at the edge of the road and a driveway across a field. No buildings in sight. Didn't go in because I thought I should wait for you.

Tomorrow. He thinks of three possibilities. I could make a telephone call if my feminine voice might make them more sympathetic. Or we could call the FBI. Or we could go visit Miller Farm. He favors a visit before calling the FBI as giving us more freedom. It scares me, who they are. Fanatics, believing their man is God, with their hands on my baby.

In the morning we go together to Wicker Falls, eating first at the Bonny Vista Café. Are we ready? The snow has moved on, the ugly cloud blanket is shredding with patches of blue and glimpses of sunshine brightening the new snow on the trees. Soon it will be clear and cold. Rib Rock Road goes up a hill from the so-called village of Wicker Falls. It winds twistily through hilly woods and comes out on back country fields, snow on everything. The mountains beyond the fields are speckly white, the snow showing through the bare trees like the bristly back of a dog. The road is full of snow but Davey is careful. Tire tracks on the road, but we don't meet anybody.

There's a white field on our right with a wire fence and a silver mailbox up ahead.

That's it, Davey says.

The mailbox says MILLER. There's a gate in the fence, closing off a white driveway that crosses the field to the trees where it descends out of sight. Recent tire tracks on the drive.

Is it locked?

I get out and look. How fresh the air now the snow has stopped, the sun coming out. No padlock on the gate, no sign of burglar protection or alarm, just a simple latch. Insulators on the fence make me wary. I try the latch cautiously, no shock, just cold.

We think it over in the car. What's to prevent us driving in? Davey is uneasy.

It's only Oliver, I say. I can talk to him.

I open the gate and he drives through. Across the field to the woods, slow and bumpy. I imagine us being watched from the woods. Just before the road goes down a jeep comes up toward us. Uh-oh, Davey says. The jeep pulls over to its right to make room and the two vehicles pass. In the jeep a man and woman in flannel shirts ignore us. So far so good, Davey says. The road turns at the slope, descends and opens onto a space with a number of structures. A large stone house, another house, a couple of sheds, an altered barn. An open place in the middle with three or four cars and a pickup truck.

Remember what we're going to say, Dave says. We're reporters, interested in religious organizations, sympathetic.

I wish I had a gun, he says.

No you don't, I say.

There are at least three white cottages in the woods around. On top of the altered barn a little pointed steeple is tacked on. A satellite dish next to the big house. A tractor.

A man comes out of the house to meet us. You lost? he says.

We're looking for the Miller Church.

You found it, what do you want?

We've heard about the Miller Church. Can we talk to somebody about it?

The looseness of the plan fills me with despair. The man folds his arms, looks in. He's elderly, his face has been out in the weather all his life. What for? he says.

Just curious, Dave says.

Curious? What's the nature of this curiosity?

We'd just like to know more, Davey says, forgetting his lines maybe.

Would you object, I start to say, and then I listen to myself amazed at my lying, would you object to a little article about the Miller Church from a sympathetic point of view to an audience of interested people?

You're journalists.

Amateurs, I say. Practicing.

You want an interview?

That would be fine. Or you could show us around and tell us about your group and beliefs.

A stocky woman from the house comes over.

Journalists wanting an interview, the man tells her.

She looks in. One's black, she says.

A sympathetic article, I say. We won't say anything you don't like.

Then you won't have no article because we won't like anything you say, the woman says. We don't want publicity.

That's right, the man says. We're not here for publicity.

We keep to ourselves, she says. Other people should do the same.

You don't want to spread your message?

There's enough of us already, the woman says.

We don't have to write anything, Dave says. We're interested for our own sake. We're looking for religious meaning.

Can't we look around a little? I say.

Look around, are you crazy? The woman says, You're standing on private property. We're not in the missionary business.

The man says to her, You can't say we're not in the missionary business.

Do you have a leader, a pastor? Can we talk to him ? I say.

No, the woman says.

The man says, If you want to talk to Miller, go home and call for an appointment. He might talk to you.

The woman frowns.

Who's Miller? I say.

He's a farmer, the woman says.

I'll make an appointment, Davey says. He starts the car. The prospect of leaving with so little makes me desperate.

Do you have any children here? I ask. Babies?

The woman squints at me. I match her fierceness and won't leave without results of some kind.

I have another reason, I say. I need your personal help.

She looks cold, like it better be good.

I have a friend in your group. I need to see him. His name is Oliver Quinn. He has a baby with him. The baby is mine.

The woman's eyes flare.

I need to know if my baby is here. If my baby is well.

You shoulda thought of that before, the woman says—which means I don't know what. She looks at Davey. You called yesterday, she says. We told you there's no baby here. You should have listened when we told you, you got no right coming back and pestering us. This property's private and we ask you to get off.

I'd like to speak to Mr. Miller, Davey says.

Go on, the woman says, get yourselves out of here.

We drive out. I blew it, I say. It makes me cry.

We did our best, Davey says. Now for the FBI.

It takes a while out in this remote neck of the woods, and yet they get a man to us by four, a lot sooner than I expected. He's awfully young, though, like an apprentice learning his job. He wears a suit, and he's polite, and his face looks like someone who just stopped being a child. His name he tells us is Bern.

He gets the story from me in my motel room with not enough chairs, leaving Davey standing up. Tell you what, Bern says. I'd like to consult my superiors before I do anything. Like we could get a warrant, he says. It would take me a while but we could do it. But you want to know the truth, I'm uneasy getting a warrant to search that place for you. Just yet.

Why's that?

This is not just another denomination of God-fearing folk. These folks are no saints, if what I hear. They got arms.

You think they'll resist a warrant?

Lady, I have no idea what they'll do. If what I hear, they're waiting for the end of the world. Waiting for the provocation that will bring the end of the world.

Bern notices my expression. I don't say it's true, he says. But what do they want with all those munitions?

The careful Agent Bern. He says, I'm thinking for example. What if we go out with our warrant and are refused admission, then what? Do you get my point? What I mean is, do we want to bring on the end of the world to make them accept our warrant?

You're afraid they'll shoot it out?

The FBI man is puzzled. You never know what to expect with these doomsday groups, he says. They're kind of desperate and don't care what happens.

Is this a doomsday group? Davey asks.

Don't ask me, Bern says. There's cults and there's cults. Fanatics, they're all the same when you get down to it.

No they're not, Davey says. They're not all alike.

Maybe not, but it's better to act like they are so we don't get surprised. That's a matter of practicality.

Does this mean you won't help us?

Sure we'll help you lady. We'll get your baby back. But I want to consult my superiors first.

We've got to do something.

I have to talk to my superiors, the FBI man says. We'll get back to you. First thing tomorrow.

Tomorrow? It makes me want to cry again.

So it's what to do with this evening, beginning with where to eat. We don't talk about the evening, it lies ahead unmentioned, but we do talk about where to eat. There's no place in Wicker Falls, the Bonny Vista's closed, I guess people in the smaller towns don't eat, but there's a café seven miles down the road in a town called Flynn. Dave drives under the darkened sky where the hills have disappeared. It's not exactly a great meal. Not much to talk about while we eat, either, and the words of the day, the man and woman at Miller Farm, the FBI man, Davey, go repeating in my head, and presumably in his head too.

When we're finished, Do you want to go back to the motel? What else can we do? Back in the car more silence. One thing Davey and I lack is an ability to fill up the time with chat. This doesn't mean we can't talk casually. Sometimes we do, sometimes we don't, it depends on the mood. In this case the silence is particular while the headlights illuminate snow along the edge, this empty road a white chute like luge in the Olympics. The particular thought, he has become my ostensible boyfriend. Though he was a longtime friend, who used to eat lunch with me before the baby and was always teaching me things, he hasn't been in the boyfriend position more than a few weeks. That means he would like to go to bed with me. He never said so. I can tell from his looks, his way of hanging around after my father's seminars and his incessant offers of help. He's shy and a little afraid, the worse because he considers my father his mentor on the faculty. He's also not yet sure what I feel (feel, not think—he knows what I think) about his blackness. So though he knows what he wants, he's reluctant to speed the time before either of us is good and ready. But now as he drives with me through the dark New Hampshire countryside after a snowfall, heading for a motel where we each have a room, and nobody who knows us is anywhere within a thousand miles (except my baby and the father of my baby, whom we are hunting), he thinks (I know what he thinks) of the ingredients—motel, alone with me, nothing else to do—that arouse. He thinks that and wonders what I am thinking. He knows I am thinking about how to get my baby back, along with questions about the police reluctance and the group we are approaching, and he wonders if at the same time I recognize the question that's on his mind. If it is possible for me to think that question in such a time of strain. If I would be repelled or find him insensitive, his heroism marred if he brought it up. I think about him thinking it back to the motel.

My problem is what to do if he brings it up. No problem if he doesn't, but if he does I should know what to say. No thank you, try again after this is over; or, Sure why not? with nothing to lose while we wait. I need to decide before it comes up.

At the motel, his lust fails. I presume it fails. Good night, we say, off to our separate rooms. We were in the lobby with our keys and he almost said something but held it back, I saw that. He intended but retracted the intention, too bad.

I'm in my room a half minute or less when Davey comes banging on my door. That's not seduction, that's news. Oliver, he tells me, message from Oliver. Come listen. The gaps in my veins go click. In his room, he replays the message for me.

David Leo, this is Oliver. (With audible breaths between his words.) I understand you want my baby. Hell man, you can have her, I showed her to Miller, that's all I want. Only you must talk to Miller, he's the only one can give the baby back. Come out here tomorrow ten o'clock, I'll introduce you. No one else, just you. I'll be looking for you.

There's a second message after the first, marked three minutes later. Hey man, Oliver Quinn again, I'm sorry, turns out not as simple as I thought. They's factions don't want to give the baby up. Don't worry, Miller's on our side. But you better come in the back way so people don't see you. Come through the woods where Rib Rock levels off. Go to where you can look into the compound and see the cottages and wait there. I'll find you. Nothing to worry about man, just a little precautions.

Hey hey, Davey says, like we won a basketball game. My quick balloon deflates as quickly. Too easy, I say, it's a trap. That surprises Davey, who wants to believe Oliver. We talk about it. An obvious trap. Davey doubts, why shouldn't there be factions, what reason would Oliver have for making it up? He wants to go in, meet Oliver, talk to Miller, do something. The more I think the more it looks like a trap, but the more he thinks, the less it does. I say if he goes I should go, but he thinks we should obey Oliver's instructions. I don't like that. Give him the benefit,

Davey says, if we don't respond and it's an honest offer; what then? He'll be careful, he assures me, he won't fall into a trap. It scares the hell out of me.

We get a long distance call from Harry, my father. How are things going? David tells him Oliver's message and his plan to go out there. I don't like it, Father says. I'm coming to join you. Davey tries to talk him out of it, but Father is firm. I'd like to know more about this man who calls himself God, he says.

Look, Davey tells me. We'll tell Agent Bern what we're doing and they'll back us up if anything goes wrong.

He's back in his room now. The other question on his mind, I saw it but it didn't come out. He thinks we've already rescued the baby and he'll be the hero.

8

Oliver Quinn

The waterfall drops through the gorge behind the compound. It leaps ten feet from the rim into a steep and narrow chute between rocks to the boulders in the mist forty feet below. When you look up from the bottom, the stream jumps out of the sky. You can't see the higher slopes of the mountainside.

The path zigzags up through the woods until it rejoins the stream at the top of the falls. Then it circles around the pool and returns to the crest on the other side before going on to Meditation Point. There are stepping stones across the top of the falls to where the path continues on the crest, if you want to take a short cut and aren't afraid of the rushing water. A shelter at Meditation Point looks out from a gap in the trees to the mountains south.

Miller told me through his deputy Ed Hansel to go up to Meditation Point and think it over the day after I arrived with the baby. He was displeased. I was supposed to study the discipline of accepting to live here the rest of my life. I saw the waterfall for the first time. I went up the path, the labor of the climb pulling my leg muscles and constricting my lungs to teach what a heart attack would be like. The top where the stepping stones crossed the lip of the falls was the best possible suicide spot in the world to look like an accident, to slip and drop forty feet through the rocks where the water swirls.

I crossed over on the stones. I watched the current like a liquid rope between my feet plunging off the rock into free-fall. It threw off spray on the way down and disappeared in the mist cloud over the rocks. Looking made me teeter and I almost lost my balance thinking that's how I'll go with the doom of the water in my ears. Instead I continued into the quiet pine-carpeted path to Meditation Point where I sat on the bench and thought what I was supposed to think. I caught cooking smells from the camp and looked at the gloomy cloudy mountainous view and heard the mountainous stillness and the slight creaking of the pine woods and allowed my gathering hate to flow. I thought how you could stand at the bottom and use that waterfall if you did it just right and no one would know the difference. If you did it just right with a proper luck.

Because I had come all this way and gone to all this effort. The baby was crying when we arrived. A more accurate word is screaming. Nick Foster and I gave up trying to stop it. An invention is needed, a patent would give the inventor a lot of money. We dealt with it by turning the radio to top volume, rap and heavy metal through the countryside, bringing to the ears of the trees and grass a new experience in sound. Also a new echo off the cliff faces of the mountains though we were too close to the source to hear it. Or anything else. If you vibrate the sound waves hard enough you can reserve all the frequencies leaving no room for a baby to cry.

Miller Farm at Wicker Falls, which I never saw before, with more buildings than Stump Island, so I should have been glad but the dark air was shivering in the currents curling off the tops of the trees, quivering in the cooking and grease smells from the kitchen behind the house, making me shudder, trying to make me get down on my knees, or do something. I felt it in the cold, the loud clear thought, here's where I die.

Radio off, the screaming of the child broke loose through the compound. I needed to find Maria, even Nick holding the child couldn't stop her now. A girl maybe fifteen runs out of one of the cottages. Who's this? Present for Maria, I say. The child shuts up when the girl takes her, prejudiced against males.

A couple of believers standing around. Miller here? I ask. Miller is God, so they say. The bad feeling sits on this place like poison gas. I go in to the Big House to report, Nick with me. Miller in his library, nicer than Stump Island, the quiet book-cases both sides of a Victorian window with tasseled drapes, he sits at the library table and invites me to sit too. I see him but he's too much to look at and I can't describe.

I remind him who I am. Tell him where I have been and why I came back. The child I brought. Why did you do that? he says. He frowns, God's frown, if he is God, which I am supposed to believe. I tell how I took the child, who was mine, from her mother. How Nick and I took care of her on our three-day trip and now I have given her to Maria.

I hand him the pamphlet. When I left home with Nick and the baby I brought this pamphlet with Harry Field's article in it. It was about the credulity of people believing in God without understanding science.

What's this? he says.

It's an article by the child's grandfather I say.

Why are you giving it to me?

Because it's blasphemy against you. I need to rescue my child from that influence.

His look stops me. God. He says, What does Loomer think about this baby theft?

Loomer? I got the idea from Loomer, I say, which I realize is true in a general though not a specific sense.

Then go tell Loomer, God says.

I left angry with God after all I had done for him. A woman named Lorraine, who looks like a pit bull, gives me my room assignment in Jehovah Cottage. The cottages bear the different names of God. I give over my car keys to Jacob the Mechanic. The car is no longer mine, the child is no longer mine, I am no longer mine. The only thing of mine is Nick Foster my disciple. My room is bare, clean and white with a maple chest of drawers, a cot with a blanket from the US Army, a straight-backed chair. My precedents are monks. I'm tired, I feel the Displeasure of God, I lie down on the cot. Tomorrow my work will be assigned.

Loomer comes in. What the hell's the matter with you? he says.

Why are you talking to me like that?

Who told you to bring that brat here?

Nobody told me, I thought of it myself.

Then why did you tell Miller it was my idea?

I got the idea from you.

The hell you did.

I'm too stunned to react and he goes out.

At dinner in the Mess Hall, everyone knows about me. This is the only baby at the Farm, and several women are pleased. It humanizes the place, Sylvia says. Thank you for bringing this little sweetness into our community. I look for Loomer.

Hear that? I say.

Bullshit, he says. I try to keep up with him, walking fast by the cottages not knowing where he is going.

I ask what's the matter? What more do you want me to do?

He's going to his pickup truck. Want you to do? I can see him remembering. He leans against the truck. Raskolnikov? he says. Then he laughs. You're kidding me.

I took risks to get this child, I say. The danger I faced, kidnapping, child stealing. I could have been caught, jailed for twenty years. Fugitive. The child could have died in my custody. We kept her alive, Nick and I.

You're stupid, Loomer says.

Why do you call me that? What's stupid about me?

He smirks. There's meanness behind that smirk, I see it clearly, it's always there. Is this your idea, he says, of what Raskolnikov would do?

The only thing I know about Raskolnikov is what they said in *Cliff's Notes*. He killed an old woman and her daughter to prove he could do it. I know that much.

You kidnapped a shitty baby to prove you could do it? You think that's the same league?

I shook a lot of people up. They're still shaking.

It's dumb, he says. Now they're looking for you and you're stuck with a baby around your neck.

Maria's taking care of her. She's Maria's now.

Robin Hood. You think Raskolnikov is Robin Hood? They'll find you, what will you do then? Have you given a thought to what Miller Farm will do then?

They can't find us, I say.

You hope, he says. Well Miller don't like it. Me neither. So we're giving you a job. You're to figure out the defense strategy for Miller Farm when the people whose baby you've kidnapped come after you. We'll be watching you.

On Friday a look around. Me and Nick Foster, escorted by Ed Hansel. It's more than Stump Island but I expect to hate it. The mountains and the closed-in feeling. The trees lean over us, the steep paths and woods full of death give me a deep cold feeling. When I think about the rest of my life. There's a service in the barn, led by Miller, God Himself. I ought to feel good but I don't. I tell myself intelligently that the look of a place comes not from itself but from the light my soul casts on it, and the gloom of this place is only the reflection of my gloom. If the gloom lifts, then the Farm, woods, mountains, fields will light up too (despite my hatred of woods mountains and fields) but until then. The question is how long.

All day I go around contributing to the community. I help in the kitchen. In the afternoon I get God's message from Ed Hansel, who shows me the waterfall and the path to Meditation Point. I climb the path and sit a long time on a bench under the bark roof shelter looking at mountain peaks in the south. I hear words in me hating this countryside despite the clear warnings of another voice that hating this country is equivalent to hating Miller. I grab the hating words in my hands as they issue through my windpipe, trying to twist them into something less blasphemous. I hate the unbelievers, I try to make them say. I hate the country out beyond, I hate the towns and cities, I hate the thinkers and the scientists and the bureaucrats. I hate the stiff religionists and old-fashioned fundamentalists and new-fangled modernists, their eyes and their beating hearts. I hate the military and the librarians. The accountants and stenographers. I hate the car salesmen and the pitchmen and the sports writers. I hate these to atone for the illusion that what I hate is this Farm and the life I am contracted to lead. Then it gets personal, who I hate.

I come back down to the compound and Maria brings the baby to see me in my room. Don't you want to see your daughter? she says. The baby looks at me shyly, like she has forgotten her grievances. That's your daddy, Maria says. She tries to hand her to me, but there's a mutual revulsion, the baby shying away in Maria's arms and I backing off. I put in my time, three days on the road and don't visualize holding the baby as part of my heaven now I'm here.

I changed her name, Maria says. I don't think George is appropriate for a little girl so I named her Holiness. Because that's what she is, just a little Holiness, aren't you, Holy?

No objection from me. The child can take back George when she grows up enough to decide for herself.

I'm cleaning rugs out back when Pearl tells me I'm wanted on the telephone. Oliver Quinn, she says, they asked for you. David Leo, damn him, the little black substitute, so they found us. Asked about the baby too, she says. Deny the baby, Miranda says. Deny Oliver Quinn and George alias Holiness no such names at the Miller Farm, never heard of them.

It calls for a meeting, though Miller stays out of it. Loomer is hot, I told you so, he says. Picking on me every chance. It's your doing, Loomer says, what you going to do about it?

I spend the rest of the day thinking strategy.

I find Loomer changing the oil on his pickup truck. I sit on the stump while he works. Raskolnikov is to kill someone, I say. Is that what you're telling me?

I ain't telling you anything, he says. What you think is up to you.

Raskolnikov is to kill somebody, I say. When you're done I want to show you something.

Had better be good.

You recruited me.

We all make mistakes.

Shit Loomer.

Sorry.

God is Hate, do you agree with that? I say.

You said it, not me.

It stands to reason, if God is Love, God is Hate.

Like you say.

He made me what I am. It ain't my fault.

Like you say.

He stood up, wiped his oily hands on his shirt.

What do you want to show me?

The path to Meditation Point. You been there?

I've seen it.

I'll show you another look.

We go to the bottom of the waterfall, where the path goes zigzagging up. We got guns here, right? I say. The Community of Miller Farm has its necessary stack of arms for self defense, am I right about that?

If you've seen guns, then there are guns, he says.

And here's this waterfall, you look up this waterfall till you see where the water jumps out over a rock that looks like a tiger's tongue? I say.

Looks more like a elephant's pecker.

Whatever it looks like it jumps out there like a stream of piss. You not been up there?

I been there.

Then you know this path that goes up, it cross up there to go over to Meditation Point. Did you know that?

It don't cross there, it goes back around the pool behind the falls.

The easy way is around the pool but if you want you can cross on the stepping stones right over the rim, right over the tiger's tongue, right there where you can see.

So what about it?

I tell him, my secret copyright idea for utilization of the waterfall. He laughs. I say he has no imagination.

I got a pretty good idea about your imagination, he says. Miller won't appreciate if you oblige this community defend itself with guns. That ain't Miller's idea what this community's for.

You let me down Loomer. I'm disappointed in you.

You're disappointed? I'm disappointed in you. I didn't know you were just a jerk.

You led me to believe. You made me think. I thought.

Thought what?

Forget it.

I guess they're in no hurry. A day passed with no news but then the next morning, visitors in a white car, Miranda says, one of them enamel foreign types in the mud right after the snow. The black man and a woman who claims to be the child's mother. Judy Field herself, what more could I ask. Judy herself, come for me. It begins to buzz.

Claiming Holiness as if she had never forfeited her rights. Robbed mothers don't go away, Loomer says, like he enjoys it.

They chase them off on private property, but then comes a telephone call from the police. Tell the so-called law that there's no such person as Oliver Quinn and no one-year old female child.

Next, Loomer says, they'll get a search warrant. You got a plan for that?

To make a plan I need to know how much the Farm will back me up. At the meeting Maria says we could give the child back. Yes, I say, and we could donate the Farm to the Nature Conservancy and our guns to the Army. I risked my life bringing her.

Nobody told you to risk your life, Loomer says.

Someone says police invasion, will the Millerites resist? You have all these machine guns and rifles.

It's not the time, Loomer says. It's not the cause.

What good is having this stuff if you never use it? I say.

Ed Hansel, for whom I have no respect, says, Realistically we'll have only one chance in our lifetime to use our guns.

So I have to keep my plans to myself.

They post guard duty while I'm thinking, and I have the first shift in the afternoon. Thaw time, snow melting, driveway full of mud. I sit on a stump with a rifle by the woods looking across the field to the road. I think and dream and sleep. I think about the future and dream about the waterfall. By dinnertime I know what to do. Nick Foster takes over on the stump. He has a walkie talkie. What do we do if the police come? We never settled that. Except Loomer telling the guards, whatever you do, don't shoot the police.

It's twilight and Nick's sitting on the stump and the woods are getting dark. Chunks of snow like ice cream melting on the clumpy leaves and boulders. Birds making a noise echoing in the woods. I don't know birds, though if I'm to live here the rest of my life I ought to learn them to add variety to the sameness, shouldn't I?

The one that says cheerily cheerilo is the robin, I remember that from school. What a disgusting thing to say every morning and night for the rest of your life.

My talk with Nick is a reminder. Nick is not yet assimilated into Miller. If I'm a disciple of Miller, Nick is a disciple of me. His job is to take his understanding of the world from me, and do my bidding. He sits on the stump with the rifle but not to shoot police. As a disciple, I tell him, you have come with me to renounce the world you have left behind. How far are you willing to go?

All the way, he says.

That's the way to think, I say. Don't shoot anybody. Bring them to where I can talk to them.

Okay, he says.

Is there anything of value that you give up by staying here the rest of your life?

The rest of my life?

The rest of your life. Everyone who lives here has made a sacrifice. I sacrificed George to get in the Raskolnikov Society. You'll never make the Raskolnikov Society, but you can be a soldier if you make the sacrifice. Is there anything you'll miss by living here?

Forever? Nick says.

That's the question.

I'll miss softball.

No you won't. You can play softball here.

I'll miss prime time television.

That's for your good. If you exercise you won't miss television.

I'll miss a girl friend.

What do you want a girl friend for?

You know.

Don't worry. Miller understands a man's needs. So what are you sacrificing?

I don't know.

Maybe you're not sacrificing anything. All the more reason to be loyal and do what I say.

By now it's completely dark and the birds have stopped. It's time to move, and I leave him on the stump and go down to the house to make my telephone call. He's not in, but I leave the message on his machine and the second message to make sure. Good thing I thought of that second message, it could have been trouble if I hadn't. Now it's up to the gods or whatever they are.

9

David Leo

Stupidly entering Oliver's intrigue. Where should I go in the woods? Judy drives my car to where the trees hang over the bend, I climb a leaning birch over the insulated fence, land in leaves, scramble through brush. A rough idea of direction.

Cloak and dagger, inside Oliver Quinn's mind, which is sickening. I have a knife but forgot to call the FBI man before I came. Maybe Judy will. Maybe she shouldn't. The trouble is, I keep assuming other people are as reasonable as I. The leaves are slippery under the remaining globs of snow. The woods slope down. A black slab below turns into a roof, a house under it, open space beyond, so here I am. Looking down on one of the Miller cottages. I descend quietly and bring other buildings into view. Here I sit, by a tree trunk behind brush.

Don't let nobody see you—Oliver's language is now my language. He'll find me somehow. I settle down to wait, watching the compound from a position so concealed that nobody can see me but Oliver Quinn, so he said. Two cars, two pickup trucks, a jeep. For a long time nothing happens, no people in sight, but I must be careful about eyes behind windows. Now two men work over a car. The hood is up, they lean in. A middle aged man comes out of the big house and goes into one of the smaller ones. It's well past ten o'clock. Is it that Oliver can't find me? A woman emerges from a cottage nearby carrying a baby. My thumping heart, is that the baby we are looking for? The woman wears a puffed up winter jacket, red and blue. She takes the baby into the big house. Think now, if that's Judy's baby.

My leg goes to sleep. I need to stretch it, don't let a clot form which could give me a stroke. I move it slightly, careful not to attract the attention of someone other than Oliver. Which is more important, not to attract someone else's attention or to attract his? The men with the car have left, I failed to notice where they went. A woman comes out of another cottage with a laundry basket, hangs up clothes. This is ridiculous. What else could I do? I could make myself known. Is that dangerous or does it just seem that way? There must be reasonable people here, women who hang up clothes, men who fix cars. Woman tending a baby. The guru himself, the one whose name is Miller with no first name (no Christian name). If Oliver wants me to meet him, I could step out and ask to speak to him.

Here she comes again, the woman with the baby stepping off the porch, a clear view almost facing me back to the cottage. Am I sure it's Judy's baby? The woman sits on the cottage porch and puts the baby down. Lets her totter around. Toys, red, yellow, can't tell what they are. The baby pushes something and it rolls. She sits beside a box taking things out. Judy's baby.

So now I know that, I can tell Judy and the police. Then what? Could the baby be kidnapped back? Figure that out, if she lives in this cottage with the woman. To come back at night when the guardians sleep. It would help to know the floor plan. Then to sneak in from the woods and slip into the unspecified room without waking anybody. Pick her up carefully enough she won't cry, tiptoe her out of the house through the maze of rooms with sleeping people. Then carry her, this quiet conspiratorially cooperative baby, back here uphill over fallen logs and pitfalls covered by leaves to the road where Judy is waiting.

It's eleven o'clock in the stillness of the morning, an hour beyond the time Oliver named. Should I walk around the woods to give him a better chance to find me? Or assume by now that he does not intend to meet me, that he has changed his mind or never intended to meet me in the first place? I look up behind me where I came, the woods rutted with stream beds between the trees. The man is ten yards back looking at me. He is not Oliver. He has straight black hair and he carries a rifle loosely in his hand. When he sees that I see him he comes forward.

Interesting place, ain't it? he says. He has a heavy shirt like L. L. Bean. A scarf. Face like a cowboy, not the young rowdy or singing type but the mature horse-breaking type. My scare shifts to hope if he's an outsider like me, one of the New Hampshire locals looking around.

I know that child, I say.

He looks. Yeah?

She's been kidnapped from her mother.

You don't say. So you come to take a look and size the situation up, he says. Friendly like.

That's about right.

Well in that case, let's go down and introduce ourselves.

So he belongs here after all. He waves his rifle slightly and I get up.

This way, he says. Directs me to a path on my right.

And I'm a captive. We come down into the compound. You been sitting a while I notice, the man says. You must have a lot of interest in that baby. With casual gestures of his rifle he directs me to the cottage porch where the baby is playing.

Hey Maria, the man says. This guy has an interest in your baby.

Well she's a sweetie, Maria says.

The baby is Hazel Field. She looks at me placidly, our acquaintance too slight for me to say she recognizes me.

Her mother's worried about her, I say. So is the FBI, I add, nervously.

Well, the man says, maybe you ought to talk to her daddy.

She's my baby now, the woman says. She says it calmly, not defiant but as a matter of fact.

Other people come around. Then Oliver Quinn himself, coming from one of the other cottages. Blue denim, red writing on his pocket, his name, Oliver.

Oliver has a round face, reddish hair getting thin, red eyebrows, a squint in the eyes. Greets me in the jovial way I always thought false. Dave Leo, he says, great to see you, what are you doing here? Hand out like a car dealer.

No mention of his message last night. I guess I know what happened. I'll go along provisionally.

I came about the baby, I say.

You take him, he's your problem, the cowboy man says to Oliver, talking about me. To me he says, Nice to meet you guy, and goes off with his rifle.

What about the baby? Oliver says.

Judy wants her back.

Oliver shrugs. Come with me, he says.

The people around have discreetly gone away. One guy with curly yellow hair still watches. Oliver takes me over to his cottage and the guy with yellow hair follows. Oliver sits on the step, I beside him.

You see why I couldn't meet you, Oliver says.

You mean that guy with the rifle?

I was tied up. I saw you all right.

I'd like to know what you have in mind.

Nothing much I guess.

You said I could talk to Miller and he would settle it.

Yeah, I said that.

Well what about it?

Shit, I don't know.

It's kidnapping. The police have an interest in kidnapping, Oliver.

This is between friends, Davey. You're not going to make a police issue between friends are you?

Funny to hear him call me friend. I never saw him except a couple of times in and out of the Field's house.

Why not? I say. You have the baby, she doesn't belong to you. Sure we'll bring the police into it.

He sits thinking a long time, stroking his cheek. The sun shines on his face, his overgrown red eyebrows, his rough skin. The thought moves through his face like he has been fighting in his brain all his life, his face like a mask semitransparent over another face. He turns into a stranger while I watch, making me wonder if he really is Oliver Quinn. If I mistook the rhetorical Oliver Quinn, the salesman, for real. Now I don't know what he looks like, with nothing to recognize him by, his amorphous face full of amorphous thought and mad.

He shakes his head and says, What is it you want again?

Judy wants her baby back.

It's out of my hands.

She's right over there.

She's not mine, she's in God's hands now.

That's the kind of thing you say about dead people.

She's right over there, I say again. But the woman has taken the baby inside.

I have no say in the matter, Oliver says. You could take it up with Miller.

Yes and you said you'd introduce me to Miller.

Yeah yeah. I'll show you where to go.

All right, I say, do that.

Don't talk down to me boy, he says, suddenly ugly. I ignore it, and he ignores it too. He gets up. So does the man with yellow hair, like a bodyguard. He has been sitting on the ground chewing a blade of grass.

Where are we going?

I'll send you up to Meditation Point, Oliver says. He looks up at the woody mountainside that looms behind the compound. That's where Miller meditates and looks at the mountains. Go up there and ask him, he'll tell you.

I mistrust this. He leads me to the woods in back of his cottage. A broad path goes up between the trees.

You go, he says. Take this path to the top of the waterfall. Cross over and keep going. You'll find Miller in his retreat just beyond. Tell him I gave you permission.

I'm to go alone?

It's you who wants the baby, he says.

Still I hesitate.

You want your fuckin baby, go up and ask him, Christ sake, he says. Like I was stupid.

Misgivings? Am I stupid? I start up the path, which gets steep in a moment. Look back at Oliver and the man in yellow hair watching me from where the path begins. I hear the waterfall, see spray, then the waterfall itself spectacular, a stream of frothing water falling from the jutting cliff into a long steep rocky trough. Above the waterfall I see only sky, which is blue now without clouds, the weather having cleared in my preoccupation. The path zigzags up the hill beside the falls.

The steepness of the climb, my muscles strain. It occurs to me, it occurred to me some time ago, I'm climbing into a trap.

Blindly doing what they say. Am I supposed to believe that this Miller magician, who is presumably not young, climbs this steep path every day to meditate? Or that Oliver would yield the baby so easily after eluding us so long? My brain is full of Oliver, absentminded and distant, whose words seem to have little to do with his head. I heard the sound of lying when he said Miller has his retreat up here. Certain lies you know by the tone.

It stops me. In the middle of the trail, half way up. Amazed I didn't recognize it sooner. If it was a lie, why am I here? It turns me right around. I look down the path up which I have come, teeter over it, then teetering takes over, to keep my balance I go running down bouncing like a ball or deer back to the bottom in a few seconds what took me minutes to ascend.

No one's here. The compound empty. I go to the cottage where Oliver was. He comes out from behind it.

Back already? Did you see Miller?

You're sending me out to nowhere.

You didn't find Miller? You didn't go far enough.

I came back. I don't believe Miller's there.

Did you get to the top? Did you cross the waterfall?

I turned back.

Why did you do that?

He looks at me a moment, then changes his tone. You want me to go with you?

(I think the knife in my pocket, in case.)

I should have gone with you, he says, introduce you. Okay, I'll go up with you.

It's a steep climb.

Too steep for you?

(The knife's in my pocket if I need it.)

I can make it, I say.

We go to the path. You first, I say.

He humors me, a broad shrug.

Back on the path opposite the bottom of the waterfall, the man with yellow hair sits on a rock with a rifle in his lap. Oliver calls to him. He clomps through the brush over to the man. They talk and he comes back. My assistant, he says. He hunts squirrels.

Where it gets steep I gesture him to go first.

Yes sir.

He clambers ahead of me. When he's setting the pace it doesn't seem as hard as when I was alone. Where the path is steepest he scrambles hands and feet. He is thick around the middle, his ass huge as he bends forward above my head.

The falls are loud. Sometimes Oliver's feet slip and send stones bouncing around me. Near the top, not as far as I had thought, the sound of the waterfall changes, receding downward and yielding to the sound of the stream above the waterfall.

At the top Oliver stands and stretches, relieved. I pull up beside him. I must describe this carefully. The mountainside above has come into view. The stream down its slope gathers into a pool which spills over the edge into the waterfall below. The path goes to the rim of the falls and then around the pool behind. The water pours fast through three smooth troughs between the rocks, and on the other side not far away the path returns and continues into the woods, level along the edge of the bluff.

Cross here, Oliver says.

He means us to cross over the racing channels on the rocks. The rocks are round and look slippery.

If you slipped you'd drop off the edge and if you dropped you'd die. I could be killed here if Oliver is in a murdering mood. I resist paranoia by reminding myself that I know Oliver, he was Judy Field's lover, a visitor in Harry Field's house, a civilized man. To fear him is to insult him. Nor should I suppose the people in the Miller Farm are dangerous though eccentric in their beliefs. He says we're on our way to Miller who is meditating up here. It's possible. Just be careful, I tell myself. Let Oliver cross first, and don't let him get too close when near the waterfall. My knife is in my pocket.

You first, I say.

He looks annoyed. You don't trust me, he says.

He shouldn't have mentioned trust, it shakes my trust.

I need to see how you do it, I say, explanatory.

Yessir, he says.

I watch his feet as he steps onto the first round stone between two channels of the river. Stretching a little he puts his other foot on the next stone so that he spans the second channel. This stone is big enough for both feet and he stands erect. The river pours thick and fast around him. His left foot reaches to the third stone, which will be the last before the solid ground on the other side. He slips.

It was too quick for me to know how it happened though I was watching his feet and saw no obvious errors. It looked simple and easy to do, I thought, and I couldn't see and can't understand what carelessness made him fall. The rock must have been more slippery than he realized. In the future (I know) I will often look back trying to remember more than I saw, which I can recount only like this. I saw the foot slip off the stone while the other was in the air. Then a flash of Oliver's denim in open space off the edge dropping out of sight like a weight into the place I had only just identified as automatic death.

Leaving me suddenly alone. I stood there in the shock of it. An accident. For a moment I tried to reverse time and when I couldn't I got a glimpse of chaos, thinking this is what we get for interfering. What who gets? Interfering with what?

I step toward the edge and grasp a sapling to look and see. He's not visible, the water drops out of sight into a cloud of spray, which continues to roil as if nothing had changed. I have a moment's suspicion lest this be a magic trick to enable him to creep up on me from behind. Stop that, I know what I saw.

My memory is half shuttered. I was looking at his feet. I was not watching his face. I did not see the look on his face when he slipped. But I would not have seen it even if I were looking because his back was turned. I'm glad I was watching his feet because that enabled me to see what happened, though I still don't understand why it happened.

By moving into the bushes on the left I am finally able to see a patch of blue on one of the rocks where the water foams. Oliver's blue, near where we started. There's a blasphemous relief to see him there which I censor in awe of death. Then the possibility he might yet be alive, creating an obligation to first aid. I must go down and look.

I tear down the path, again bouncing like a stone, falling like the water, like Oliver himself though my descent has more control, while his was pure physics.

Thinking as I go. The oddity that he, who knew this place, should be so fatally careless at this particular moment. While I was there. The path on either side of the brim is well-traveled. Many people including Miller himself have crossed there. I would have thought the only danger was the psychology of the edge. You don't fall off a subway platform into the path of an approaching train merely because you are standing there.

There's elation in my downward speed, some wicked thought saying let him be dead, now we can get Judy's child back. Along with new fears. I'll have to persuade people that what I saw was true.

Interrupted glimpses on my way down of the blue denim on the rocks, each view larger than the last, a man sprawled on a boulder around which the water divides, his arms spread, one leg out, the other curled under him, his head back out of sight probably in the water. It's at the bottom of the falls, just to the side of where the water hits, he dropped all the way from the top, and I am coming to collect the news that was given me there.

He's on the other side of the stream from the path with no easy way to get across. Is that what I should do, I don't really know. I need help, how do I get it? Run down to the compound, find someone. What do I say? How he went across first and slipped on the third stone and fell before I could look.

Someone is coming, stamping through the leaves from behind. It's the cowboy man again, still carrying his rifle. Following wherever I go. Men with rifles: this was where the man with the yellow hair, hunting squirrels, sat when we started up, the boulder right there.

The man with the black hair looks across the stream. That Oliver? he says.

Yes.

What did you do to him?

He fell. He was crossing and fell. He was two-thirds of the way across and he fell.

He wouldn't fall, he's not that dumb.

I saw him, I was right there.

Yeah? Let's take a look.

He pokes around and finds a way to get across. I try to follow.

Stay back, he says. There's no room.

He gets to the rock with Oliver's body and bends over him, inspecting him. There's some blood. I stand in a shallow spot where the water runs through my shoes and soaks my feet.

Is he alive?

Are you kidding?

He looks at the waterfall above.

Nobody just falls off that, he says. Someone pushed him.

No one pushed him.

You mean you didn't, he says.

Of course I didn't. He was taking me to see Miller.

Up there?

He said Miller was meditating up there.

That's what he said?

That's what he said.

The man with the black hair spends a long time examining Oliver. He studies his head, which I can't see, and opens his shirt and looks at it. He looks at his shoulder and his arms. I can't see what he is doing. Finally he comes back, and we return to the path. The man with the yellow hair, also carrying a rifle, has reappeared in the woods, standing back a little, watching. The man with black hair ignores him.

Come on, he says to me, I'll get you a ride into town. Where you at, the Sleepy Wicker Motel?

You're taking me there?

Ed Hansel will take you.

What about Oliver?

What about him?

Aren't you going to report his death?

It was an accident, you said so yourself.

Will you report it?

I'll do that, don't worry about it. On Miller Farm, we take care of our own.

It should be reported to the police.

He raises his voice a little. If I was you I'd keep it to yourself, considering your proximity to the case and what I saw.

What did you see?

I saw what I saw.

I did nothing. I was nowhere near him.

Then don't worry, we'll take care of it. We'll do the necessary legal work, which is none of your business.

I follow him across the compound, while the man with the yellow hair follows behind.

Get into the pickup truck. I remember my mission. My friend wants her baby back, I tell him.

Tell her to come and get her, the man says. Tell her to see Miller.

Up that path?

Hell, the man says with disgust. You tell her. Come tomorrow, come anytime. Come this afternoon.

This afternoon?

She'll get her baby back, he snaps. Wait here for your ride.

Suddenly he pats me on the arm, confidential, soothing. Hey listen, he says. Call off your FBI man, okay?

When we get the baby back.

Right, when you get her back. Best not mention that accident if I was you. FBI would get confused. We'll regard it as a accident if you leave us alone.

An old man comes and drives me into town, leaves me at the Sleepy Wicker Motel. I still shaky from the shock. What happen back there? he asks. Somebody died, I said. Who was it? Oliver Quinn, I said. The new feller? the man said. Accident? Fell down the waterfall, I said. That's a shame, he said like it happened often. Then we don't talk, as if there's nothing more to say despite all the questions in my head.

10

Judy Field

He came back from Miller Farm, banging on my door, shocked out of breath.

Oliver's dead, David said.

Oliver dead? What about Hazel? I said.

Hazel's fine. You can have her anytime.

I can have her, did you say I can have her back?

This afternoon.

He flopped into the chair. Shivering.

I waited a moment to ask. What happened?

An accident. Right in front of me. I saw him die.

What kind of accident?

He told me. That was the news, complete in seconds. The rest was talk. He described the accident and gave me the message about my baby, both things over and over. I couldn't get my feelings around them, there was something I couldn't imagine. I tried to liberate my joy from Oliver the enemy suddenly Oliver clumsy-foot, a harmless dead thing in the past. And God in whom I don't believe intervening with such excess it was like I killed Oliver myself. The punishment was imagining a man in blue denim under the waterfall when I wanted to think about my baby. Take this for selfishness.

Repeat this: I can get my baby back this afternoon?

Anytime.

Well let's go.

For the second time Davey drove me out Rib Rock Road. A man with a gun came out of the woods where the road starts down. I told him who I was and this time he let us through. In the compound a man came out of the big house. There he is, Davey said, and I saw what he meant about a horse-breaking cowboy. Cynical ruined movie face. Howdy, he said, like a cowboy. You want something?

I want my baby, I said.

Come with me. Your friend wait.

Hold on, David said. I won't leave you. I nudged him not to screw things up.

See Miller first, the cowboy said. No need to mistrust. Miller is good. You'll be grateful and full of happiness.

All right, take me to Miller.

I will not abandon you among these people, David said. The man was annoyed. Who do you think you are? he said. These is God-fearing folks, good people, don't insult them.

Please just let me do this, I said to David.

I followed the man into the Victorian house. A woman led me into a room with a tall window. A man sat behind a desk in front of the window. I couldn't see his face because the sunlight was too bright behind his head.

I'm Miller, he said. And you're the baby's mother.

They said you would give her back to me.

In a minute. Did you know your Oliver Quinn died this morning?

I heard about it.

Too bad, a tragedy and you his wife, he said. So would you do us a favor and stay overnight for his funeral tomorrow?

Overnight at Miller Farm? I didn't know what to say. I was scared.

Are you afraid of spending the night or is it a doubt about the funeral?

Can I be with my baby? I said.

Of course you can, Miller said. Please stay. It would be seemly, for the child's father and the good women who have been taking care of her.

I thought about them. All right, I'll stay, I said.

The cowboy took me back into the compound and I told David. He was furious. I knew he would be. I had to persuade him, urge him, finally insist on it. The cowboy said, Listen to the lady, man. You're just the taxi driver. Go back to your motel and pick her up tomorrow afternoon.

I felt sorry for him, angry and humiliated, going back to the motel and the night, all by himself. When he was gone, the man said, Do you want to see your baby?

Do I want to see my baby? as if that could be a question. Like suddenly noticing the soft spring day, and even the cowboy's dark glittering face was benign. He led me striding across the compound to a cottage under the trees, like Davey's description. And there she was, where I hadn't seen her before. My Hazy toddling around the cottage porch in clothes I never saw, but what do I care what she was wearing? The clothes were pretty and clean and there was a good sturdy woman sitting on the porch with a scarf around her head like a European peasant.

Thank you so very much, I said to the cowboy.

I'll see you at the funeral, he said.

What funeral? Hazel, Hazy, I called, my Hazy baby, it's Mommy, Mommy's back.

She stopped to look at me. Holding a rubber mouse. Did not smile, just looked. She was trying to figure it out. A week had passed since Mommy disappeared. She was only a little over a year, not old enough to remember a week ago. She saw I was familiar. I represented something of great importance, maybe the most important thing in the world, but she couldn't make the connection so who was I? It hurt.

She turned to the woman with the babushka, toddled to her saying something. Mama. She said Mama to the woman in the babushka.

It made me cry. I knelt down, held out my hands. Come to me Hazy I said, my voice failing.

The child stood by the woman's knee, silent puzzled curious. I was afraid to look at the woman, the opposition I might see in her face. I was afraid to let her see the tears on me if she should take that as an advantage. I couldn't look but I heard her voice speaking low to the child, That's your Mama, Holiness.

That gave me such a thrill, such relief, the woman acknowledging, not denying me, that I turned to her, how grateful I was, let her see me crying, I needn't be afraid now. Not only that, she called my child Holiness, recognizing her divinity and love. She was my friend and we were one, that woman whose name I assumed to be Maria and I.

Pick her up, the woman told me. She'll remember you in a minute.

I picked her up, stood on the porch with my reticent shy baby who didn't quite know what was going on. I hugged her to my cheek and shoulders and sobbed. Hazel, my sweet child.

I see what you mean, the woman said.

Hazel's arms went around my neck, forgiving me. She wriggled now, wanting to get down. I put her on the floor, she grinned her baby grin, she wanted to show me something, a toy kangaroo she gave me out of the box. She reached for it back, she wanted to play, my baby's way without the words she needs to tell me what's in her mind.

I sat on the porch floor while the woman named Maria sat in her chair and watched. Grateful that this woman did not keep the child from me. Why had she done so before?

You should take better care of her, the woman said.

Oh?

You let that man get hold of her.

Oliver? He stole her.

The woman was not hostile, she had a sunny middle-aged face like a saint. You shouldn't gave him the chance.

He tricked the baby sitter. Something inhibited me from admitting the baby sitter was my father.

You shouldn't have a baby sitter, the woman said. How can you turn over such holiness to a baby sitter?

I have to work, I told her. I have no choice.

She's my baby now, the woman said.

Watch out. I withheld my first words and spoke carefully. I appreciate the care you gave her. I can see it was good. I took a breath before the point: She was kidnapped from me and I have come to take her home.

Holiness is not the property of one person, Maria said. Nobody owns a child.

I know, but somebody has her care and somebody has her love.

The woman looked away. Others came around and spoke to me. What a lovely child. Sympathy for my loss, meaning Oliver. An old man named Ed Hansel. A woman called Miranda. I stayed the rest of the afternoon in Maria's cottage with the women and my baby and at dinner time we went to eat in the building called the altered barn. A big room under a pitched roof with sky lights and windows making it light and airy. Long tables and more people than I thought the cottages could accommodate. All kinds, all ages including children, in work clothes, overalls, jeans, jackets, boots. I thought, These are fanatics, committed to an absurdity, but they didn't look crazy, they looked like ordinary folk. Country folk, I thought, because I was in New Hampshire, though in truth I had no way of knowing that they weren't city folk from Baltimore or wherever it was Miller came from.

I sat at the end of a table with Maria and my baby in a high chair. The room was full of animated conversation and the dinner was hearty. Afterwards we went back to Maria's cottage. They set up a bed for me in the living room. They sat around and talked, ordinary talk. About the weather change and the advantages of this place over Stump Island and about Oliver, who I realized was largely a stranger to most of them. They discussed his accident, how surprising that someone could simply slip and fall down the waterfall, and they wondered if there was an unseen motive. They asked me if I saw anything suicidal in Oliver, any hints lately of suicidal intent, and was his bringing the baby here the first act of some elaborate suicide gesture? The way they talked it seemed like no one quite understood that he had kidnapped my baby from me. I reminded them. He stole my baby, I said. He kidnapped her. Yes, Maria said. He should have asked your permission. He shouldn't took her without your permission.

They turned out the lamps and we went to bed. I had my baby in bed with me, I had kept the milk up and could nurse her despite the interruption, I felt her warm and tickly snuffling and squeaking next to me in the dark. It seemed darker than any place I had ever been, though my eyes adjusted and I could see the window and the shapes of trees outside. I felt the New

Hampshire wilderness all around me, carrying me, the forest and mountains, and the silence of the compound. I and my baby miles and miles from home. Finally I remembered David Leo sleeping grumbling and discontented in the motel seven miles away.

In the morning, we had breakfast in the altered barn and returned to our cottages. A little later the cowboy came back. Time for the funeral, he said.

I had forgotten about the funeral. This too took place in the altered barn. Maria kept my baby while I mourned Oliver. At the entrance a woman spoke to me. Goodbye to your lover?

He's not my lover, I said.

No feeling between you? the woman said.

He was nothing but bad news, I told her.

Glad he's dead? Kiss him for me.

Though it seemed like a long time, it was only yesterday that Davey saw Oliver fall. The altered barn now looked like a church. Rows of folding chairs and a table in front. A television set next to it, also a piano, another table with electronic equipment including a large pair of speakers. The wooden box on the ground next to the table, that must be the coffin. It had leather handles.

Most of the seats were occupied. The man with black hair showed me to a seat. The woman next to me bulged and her excess pushed me through the ceremony. She couldn't help it and I forgave her.

Miller stood up in front. Big man in a red flannel shirt, good quality, and red suspenders, I had a better look now the sun wasn't shining behind him. He looked like pictures of Ralph Waldo Emerson but with long white hair like Franz Liszt. When he appeared people bowed their heads.

His voice was resonant in the microphone, though he kept it low. He spoke casually. His eyes were deep and shadowy, hard to see.

It's been almost a year since we've had a funeral and this is our first in Miller Farm, he said. We'll use the same format as Stump Island. Melissa will play something. Then some silence and anybody wants to make a speech and Melissa'll play a little more to wind it up.

Melissa looked nineteen. She gave a mistake-free rendition of *Für Elise* on the piano. She glanced at the Emerson man for approval. He nodded and she played the *Minute Waltz* by Chopin, quite fast. Then back to her seat hiding her face.

Now silence, the man said. Think what you like but remember why we're here. That's because Oliver Quinn died, so if you don't know what to think about, think about him. If you didn't know him, which is a lot of you, think about other people who have died. Let's go five minutes before anybody speaks. That will give you time to relax and forget about time.

I felt the people around me settle down. Some leaned back and looked at the roof. The woman next to me folded her arms and sighed. All through the silence she sighed as if breath were hard to bear. The man in front of me leaned forward and rested his face in his hands. For a while there was a quality of impatience in the crowd, squeak of chairs, cough, floorboard, the impatience of people waiting for something to end. Then it changed. Silence grew like dough and absorbed everything. The bodies disappeared, the noises stopped, I found myself alone. The silence was no longer around me, it was in me. It was full of my imagination wrapped in crystal or amber where you could see without hearing. The echo of Melissa's two piano pieces suspended the voices of David and my father and myself as well as the sounds of air and bus travel and Connie Rice and the cowboy. Also my baby and Maria telling me I should have taken better care of her, all these sounds crystallized in amber so I could remember and see but not hear them.

After a while I remembered that this was Oliver's funeral. I had not been thinking about him. While the others were grieving (if that's what they were doing) I had been rejoicing, not thinking of Oliver nor of his death as death.

So I thought about him now. I imagined him watching us but as he did he turned nasty. You came, he said, vindictively. You didn't want to but you came. He kidnapped the baby to force me to his funeral. He fell down the waterfall for that purpose. Was this a suicide we were attending? I hoped so, his deliberate death. Then I felt guilty. You did love me once, he said. Think of that.

I thought of it. I remembered his place, my place, and Cape Hatteras. I allowed myself to remember the motel off the dunes and a village called Buxton, an odd high striped lighthouse, the sand in the daytime room with the blinds closed but enough light through the translucency for afternoon nakedness in the noise of the wind and hushing surf nearby. Remembered the surge, the nuzzling and giggling, his grin and his boastful cock, the animal growling that seemed so cute at the moment and so strange later with screwing screwing screwing all afternoon and night and next day too while I invented an impossible future.

Not the real future, which was downhill like gravity. Down down to the kidnapping of my child which I will never forgive and his literal drop through rushing water into the sealed box in this room. It left me with no trace of love or sorrow so that even Cape Hatteras was only a madness remembered without feeling except that crude tingling surprise that must be what people call lust. My question later was how I could have felt even that. The reason was that I didn't yet know him, which enabled me not only to enjoy lust but to think it was love.

When I found myself pregnant he left, and I adapted. I excavated my head to cast him out, after which he returned barging into the hospital the night the baby was born claiming to be the father with a father's privileges. But I was cured of Oliver Quinn. He hung around, disappeared, came back, disappeared again. I thought he was gone for good thank God though I could have used some child support. Once again he came back and told me he had discovered God Himself living as Miller on a place called Stump Island, which made me wonder how I ever took him seriously. Finally he swiped my baby. He didn't want her to grow up under the influence of a black man like David Leo.

The least funereal funeral I ever saw. I heard a male voice speaking. If you could tell us, it said, how such a thing could happen crossing the waterfall where nobody ever fell before. Answered by Miller in the microphone: Accident. Accidents happen.

Isn't an accident an Act of God? the inquiring voice asked.

That's correct, Miller said.

Well?

A voice said, Rumor has it someone was with him when he fell.

If a rumor can be confirmed it is no longer a rumor, Miller said. If it can't be confirmed it is only a rumor.

More silence. I was sleepy. A woman's voice brought me back. She said, I didn't know Oliver Quinn. I have no reason to mourn except the general mourning, the universal sadness of God.

That's good enough, Miller said.

The man in front of me stood up. I have something to say, he said. He was thin, young, his face blemished, his yellow hair tight and curly. His voice was high and timid.

I have something to say, he repeated.

Someone said, You have something to say.

What am I supposed to do now?

No one spoke.

He tried again. What am I supposed to do now?

Don't do anything, a voice said.

I don't know what to do.

Sit down.

Don't tell him that, another voice said. Tell him to trust God.

Melissa went back to the piano. I was almost asleep. The first notes were shockingly loud but that was because of the contrast to the silence. She played *Clair de Lune*, not as slowly as I'm accustomed to. When she finished, Miller got up. That's enough, he said. The cremation will follow, down at the pool. Anyone can attend.

Everyone stood up and suddenly all around me voices chanted in unison. Three times, loud and deep:

Miller is God, he made me what I am.

Miller is God, he made me what I am.

Miller is God, he made me what I am.

That was the only thing during the whole ceremony that seemed crazy, yet it was so solemn it was hard not to join in myself. They dispersed. A group of men picked up the coffin by the handles, took it out and set it on the back of a jeep. Some of the crowd went with it down the hill, others to the cottages or the big house or up the road. I didn't see the black-haired cowboy. He was supposed to call David to come get me from the motel. Since I didn't see him I went back to the cottage to see my baby again.

11

David Leo

You wonder about me, why a normal guy like me should be interested in the white girl Judy Field. You excuse it by my background, my father a professor in Massachusetts with not many blacks in the college town where I grew up, and I living most of my life a little apart from my black cousins. Or you suspect me of not considering my people good enough. Either way, you find it a little unnatural, what draws me away from my own kind, and wonder what it means about me. I'll tell you.

Three years ago, my first on the faculty, I organized a writing group with Jeff Maybury. We sent out flyers to the departments and ten people came to the first meeting. None of them were black. Since I was the only black member of the English Department, I was used to this. Among the ten was Judy Field, a secretary in the Dean's office. She was pale and shy and nervous, and she peered out from under the dark hair on her forehead like looking out to sea. I was living with Charlene, and Judy was only a white girl with an interest in writing.

I did not know that I already knew her father, and several weeks passed before I realized who he was. I knew him at lunch. He was one of a group of professors who ate together. One was a geologist, a couple were historians, others came and went. We talked about the news and the university administration and the Tuesday science pages of the *New York Times*. We talked across the disciplines, and I felt more at home with this group than with the members of my own Department.

Eventually it came out. My daughter's in your writing group, he told me. She thinks you're wonderful. Wonderful? The powerful word stimulated me. The writing group met every week. Conscious of Professor Field's daughter watching me, I made vigorous critiques of the stories presented. When others spoke she looked at me, thinking me wonderful. It gratified me and made me eloquent. Her own stories were amateurish. We also discussed mine, which she admired. Her admiration gave me a thrill and I hoped her enthusiasm wouldn't wane.

I liked Professor Field, who was in his last year before retirement. I read some of his writings though I knew little about his field. He had a knack for making scientific questions easy to understand and he was interested in their implications outside of science. Since I didn't know anything about science I sat in on his class in Darwin. He was pleased that I wanted to expand my knowledge and he invited me to dinner with Charlene. There were four of us, Harry and his wife Barbara, Charlene and I. Not Judy, who was living in her own place. This was not a disappointment, for I had no expectations to be disappointed.

In fact I didn't know anything about her personal life. I didn't know that while she was admiring my critiques, she was seeing Oliver Quinn. I didn't want to know if she had a boyfriend. I hoped she had one to make her normal and I hoped she didn't for other reasons, but it was none of my business either way.

The next year Harry Field, now retired, held a private seminar in his home. Each week for the benefit of nonscientists he discussed someone like Newton or Galileo or Darwin or Freud. I realized I could learn from Harry Field and I attended these meetings. He was like a mentor, I a disciple. Joe and Connie Rice were also in the seminar. They were the more privileged disciples for they had studied under him formally. They were organizing a Festschrift in his honor and spoke of writing his biography. There was something fanatical in their adulation whereas mine was moderate and sane.

The writing group was smaller this year. We met less often. My critiques were getting stale and I wondered if Judy was bored. I wanted to revitalize her interest but didn't know how. One day I saw her eating lunch in the Student Union. I sat down with her. Two days later I joined her again. It became a routine. The writing group failed but I now had lunch regularly with Judy Field. I ate with her on Mondays, Wednesdays, and Fridays, and with her father and my faculty friends on Tuesdays and Thursdays. I thought of her as a friend.

In the fall she told me she was pregnant. I was stunned. I didn't know she was married, then realized she wasn't. She was calm about it, as if it were according to plan. I couldn't figure the plan out, though. She said the father, whose name was Oliver Quinn, was gone. Gone?

Scrammed. She told it like a joke, he run off from the pregnant woman like someone in Faulkner. I prepared to be shocked, thinking scandal in the old professor's family, but she refused to be scandalized and never dreamed that she was ruined. She chattered like it was a relief to tell me. The dastardly Oliver Quinn, I agreed. I wouldn't run away like that, not me. I thought of Charlene. I wondered, if I were free and Judy were black would I rescue her? Even then the thought occurred to me.

So she moved back to the Field house, and then she too joined her father's seminars while getting bigger week to week. I saw a lot of her now, three times a week at lunch and weekly at the seminars. It was so routine that any lapse alarmed me. I was afraid she would lose interest, without specifying what interest it was that I didn't want her to lose.

Well maybe I could specify it. I didn't want her to stop admiring my mind. My sharp critical insights, my logic, my lucidity, the clarity of my thought. Also my wisdom and sympathy at the lunch table. Judy's appreciation, her father's too, I told myself it was the whole Field family I cared about, like my own. I imagined them talking about me, appreciating me.

The baby was born in March. No one told me until days later. I wondered if I had a right (maybe even a duty) to visit her at home, I being not a female friend like Connie but an indefinite male substance in her life. I decided to wait until the natural course of events brought her back into view. This would not be at lunch. Nor the next seminar, which Harry moved to Joe Rice's house because of the baby at home. The seminar was tedious in Judy's absence. During the break Harry and Joe Rice talked about Oliver Quinn, who after months of absence had showed up at the hospital when she had the baby, requiring the parents and friends (which did not include me) to wait outside while he had the privilege of the delivery room.

Oliver's return prevented me from visiting Judy. She had her Oliver, I my Charlene. But the seminars returned to Harry's house. There she was, holding her extremely tiny baby and looking pretty. I didn't want to think of her as pretty. Intelligent, attractive, but not pretty. She greeted me like an old friend and turned her cheek to be kissed. That embarrassed me. I met Oliver one seminar night. A large man with reddish hair, who looked like a truck driver or furniture mover, holding her baby. He said the academic world was not for him, and I wanted to hit him. He made me think of police dogs and I wondered how Judy could be interested in a person with so coarse a face.

In bed that night while Charlene slept I raged silently over this discredited man. I need not have worried. He vanished again, and she never mentioned him. Meanwhile Connie, Joe, Harry, everybody talked about helping Judy, she with her baby and no time to herself. She had plenty of babysitters, her grandparents and all her good friends. I was one of those friends, a reliable family intimate.

Charlene and I were tired of each other and she moved out. I missed Charlene in the apartment but less than expected. It was strange to be without a woman. I thought I should look for one, but no rush. This too surprised me, how little need I felt.

I continued to see Judy at her father's seminars. The baby got bigger, three months, six months, getting close to a year. Connie and Joe and I, we took good care of Judy and her baby. When the grandparents went to the Caribbean I babysat so that Connie and Joe could take Judy to the movies. Later someone proposed that I take Judy to the movies while Connie and Joe babysat. I held her coat and opened the door to my car. Disgusted with myself for being nervous, like a kid, a date, love. Exactly what this was not, not date nor love and she a white girl. Only friendship and flattery, my status the same as Connie's and Joe's. In spite of which I was clumsy holding doors, walking beside her, getting tickets, sitting by her in the theater, so that it might as well have been a date.

This set me thinking at last, wondering if this preoccupation with Judy was a version of love. Not so, because there wasn't any sex in it. She was not what I thought about when I thought about sex. I had no naked fantasies about her nor any urge to touch. It was not her touch I wanted, it was her esteem.

That thought kept me steady. The barrier was racial, a natural recoil like an electric fence. I was relieved to discover the fence was still there because of the times I had feared I was turning white. I saw the black world from which my father had kept me mostly through the protected windows of the academic world, a feeling that though I came from them I was not of them. I felt ashamed of this sometimes, whether or not it was my fault, and I had plans to make amends, reconcile with my brothers, but not yet. My first task was to meet my father's expectations and get my career off the ground.

I called my obsession with Judy a platonic attachment. That made it noble, which was also a relief. You of course see the contradictions. On not wanting to touch her, well actually I did want to touch her. As I came out of the movie I wanted powerfully to put my arm around her and bring her close. Not sex though, because it wasn't as if I wanted to touch her. For a couple of months I had no desire to touch her while restraining my desire to grab. In truth, the instant I called it platonic, it ceased to be so in my heart.

Then Oliver kidnapped Judy's baby. A chance to be a hero. Why should I want to be a hero? Don't ask. When I boarded the plane to Bangor you would think it was some old chivalric love except that it wasn't. Pretense, practice. An exercise in as if. As if I loved Judy. If you don't believe in love or think it an illusion, then pretend the illusion. Suppose I flew to Bangor for love. Suppose I drove a rented car to Stump Island for love, stayed in the inn, went out to the island. Imagine that I drove from Stump Island to Wicker Falls for love, risked my neck out to Miller Farm for love, and watched the shocking death of Oliver Quinn for love. Never mind the resemblance, I said, it is only a favor for a friend.

At the Sleepy Wicker Motel I rented a room for Judy next to mine. If taking her to the movies a month ago simulated a date, renting her a motel room next to mine simulated an affair. I put her bag in her room. The sexual question was on my mind now, no doubt about that, but I fought it off.

It took this form. I thought: this is a class of situation, man woman and motel, full of conventional assumptions. You can't blame me for thinking of them, which is different from acting upon them, a thing I have no intention of doing, since my love for Judy is platonic.

That's what I thought Saturday while I waited for Judy's arrival and looked ahead to the next day and the strategy of coping with the kidnapping and getting the baby back. I thought about the stereotype. In the stereotype the man reserving a room for a woman at a motel would naturally invite himself into that room. Either that or invite her to his. She would accept the invitation, and the rest would follow. No matter what unrelated events took place during the day, the convention would take over at night making them like everyone else. This I added firmly does not apply to us. We're different, it's not what we want to do. I was in the middle of this thought when it occurred to me it was what I wanted to do. It was exactly what I wanted to do.

That's how I discovered the sex missing from my love. I did want it, the whole thing, in bed with Judy Field as if I had wanted it all along. If you are shocked, so was I. It was like discovering I was an adopted child. I fought it with denials. I do not want to have sex with this white woman, I said. I am not attracted. I am not perverse. If once I let myself into her spell what other unnatural charms and lures will I be open to? Yielding to this white woman would make me vulnerable to all white women, and who knows what ugliness would follow? What strange and alien attractions? Relatives, aunts, cousins. Old women, grandmothers and children. Freaks, women with mustaches and lizard skin. Men too, pretending to be women, pretty boy thugs. A chaos of rampant sexuality, how could I ever trust my feelings again?

The reality of her presence at the bus stop restored my calm. I was glad to see her after all, I reveled in the pleasure of her winter jacket, the grace of her movement around the puddles on the bus stop floor, her familiar smile of recognition. It was not just any attraction I was feeling, it was this particular one. It had nothing to do with relatives or women with mustaches. The only thing was that she was white, and suddenly this was irrelevant. My sense of the difference between us which originally had been sexually almost like a species difference had been worn down by disregard and proximity until now I couldn't find any trace at all. Instead just this sudden consciousness of sex on my mind, like the approval of someone in authority. As I drove her through the darkness of this country which I had discovered and was now introducing her to, I kept thinking sex sex sex. Like my clothes disappearing around my hips as I drove. Which livened and braced me even though it put new distance between us since I didn't dare say what I was thinking. I postponed. Not tonight, let the time ripen. That was all right because we had business to do, a problem to solve, a job ahead of us. She was preoccupied. The evening was overshadowed by the morning to come. It was not until the next evening, Sunday, after a day of effort and concern, after we had driven out to the Farm and been turned away and had talked to the policeman and gone to the Hijack Café in Flynn for dinner, not until then that I felt in my hips again the question, has the time ripened? Driving back in the dark from the Hijack Café, Judy beside me on the country road with headlights flashing the bushes and tree trunks in the musing silence and I now stripped of all inhibitions not caring that she was not black, indifferent to that once primordial fact, restrained now only by my fear of what she would think. Yet not quite clear, not even yet. If it had been inconceivable to me until now, why wouldn't it be inconceivable to her still?

The only way to find out was try. If I had the courage. Thinking a false move would spoil what I now considered the most important friendship in my life. Quite apart from the racial question, she was preoccupied with her stolen baby. She would think me insensitive, coarse in feeling. We stood by her door before goodnight. I thought I saw an invitation in her eyes, but when I hesitated it was withdrawn, replaced by thank you, a hearty handshake and goodnight.

I'll try tomorrow, I said to myself, though I knew the invitation would not be repeated. When I got to my own room there was the red light flashing and the startling pair of messages from Oliver Quinn. I summoned Judy to hear them, and for a few minutes she was actually in my room, but it was different now with a project to think about. An adventure, with risks. A relief too, the opportunity for more heroics. Judy was worried about a trap, I pretended not to care. We called her father, who also thought it dangerous. That added to the glory though I foresaw that his joining us tomorrow would be another impediment, reducing my hope. I thought that was probably just as well, for this was serious business, this rescue of Judy's baby, and it was selfish of me to be so preoccupied.

You know what happened, how in the morning I went out to Miller Farm, met Oliver and climbed the mountain path with him and watched his unexpected terrible death. After which in an anticlimax they told me Judy could have her baby back. When I drove her back to the Farm to pick up the baby, to my amazement she decided to stay overnight for Oliver's funeral. I went back to the motel alone to wait for Harry. I was angry, do you blame me, though the integrity of my anger was shaken by the recurring image still in my head of Oliver's legs kicking out in the unsupported air before his plunge. This left me unsure of everything.

This was my mood just before I made my decision, which I made that evening, to marry Judy Field when this was over. Clear the brush of both my prejudices and hers. Raise her child and have one of our own. People would notice, let them. I foresaw the enlightened community that would welcome us, a university or college town like the one I grew up in. I foresaw traveling in a car and going into restaurants and stopping at hotels. We would have wonderful friends. We would buy a house and prosper and live happily to a good old age.

Meanwhile I waited for Harry, who would replace Judy as my company this evening. As I waited my cheerful idea faltered in the chill of the room or some mood working at a deeper level. I began to seethe without knowing what I was seething about. The longer I waited the more I felt as if my heroism had been silly and the whole trouble was punishment for breaking some law. What law I didn't know, I could only guess.

12

Harry Field

Wakened by the alarm at five-thirty, he shaved, packed, drove to the airport, ate in the food court. In Boston, he changed to a smaller plane, crossing the tarmac in the wind to get aboard. His legs bothered him. Even a short distance made them ache and he would slow down or stop and rest. Soon he would have to carry a cane and put a handicap sign in his car or worse.

The smaller plane took him to a small New Hampshire airport halfway up the state. He had come to this airport for his father's funeral twenty years ago. It was on a flat shelf cut into the hills above the town. The plane made a steep turn before coming in, giving Harry a view of the slopes with trees like bristles on the back of an animal and white driveways like thread curling up to toy houses from the narrow road.

At the country airport the sun came and went, and clouds clung to the bulging mountains. There was a small waiting lounge with a food counter, a Coke machine and some benches. He rented a car and tried to call the Sleepy Wicker Motel, but David and Judy were out. He drove down to the town, then out across the state on the rural roads of New Hampshire. He passed fields and went through woods under trees. Climbed twisting roads and crossed flat stretches with hills on both sides.

With broken layers of clouds and open sky, the ground patched with sunshine and shadow. Old barns and isolated houses and a closed boys' camp on a lake with trees leaning over the water. From a plateau with small farms an abrupt vista of the higher mountains north, a jagged horizon a great distance away. Stopped to eat in a resort town, mostly closed this time of year, then continued to the higher White Mountains of New Hampshire. He crossed National Forest boundaries marked by brown signs. The weather darkened, the clouds closed in and truncated the mountains and turned their roots black. It made the countryside sad, while his windshield wipers squeaked.

He reviewed the question of why he had come. He came because he couldn't stand the waiting and suspense. Not a good enough reason for his daughter and her boyfriend. He came to help out, what kind of help could he give? He came because of the last straw, last straw of what? Anxiety. The strangeness of Oliver's telephone message to David as reported by David last night. Come out and see Miller to get your baby back. Come David, not Judy. Not the front way, sneak through the woods. Intrigue, the flame of Oliver's lurid and vulgar imagination. Harry didn't like it. If you dwell on it go crazy, the psychopathic possibilities. If you think in such terms, Oliver's message to David had all the look of a trap. He imagined that trap. He imagined it in many versions. David captured, David killed. Then Judy all by herself in the New Hampshire wilderness exposed to madmen. That's why Harry came, he had no choice. He tried not to think about it, his own lurid thought rebuked by the impassive New Hampshire countryside through which he drove.

The mountains were full of his father, who in the early years of the century used to climb and map them, and when Harry was a child brought him back trying to recreate them for him.

They were full of menace from deep out of the past despite the serenity of Harry's childhood. Everything he saw from the car window reminded him of things. Clouds steaming on the slopes of the decapitated mountains shivered him with loneliness. A path up into woods from the road recalled a path up to the cabin with his parents. He remembered the cabin, the cold uncivilized mornings, damp dropping out of the trees, the hiking expeditions through leafy wet ground, the slippery boulders along the path. He entered now a famous White Mountain notch, climbing for miles through white birch and pine and fir, the upward view blocked by the leaden sky until surprisingly it cleared exposing high cliffs, a sheer rock face in the sun. Followed soon after by a vista of the great mountains across a valley, full of American history and literature, peaks named after presidents, tan and beige and white with snow in the sun and rich with glinting rocky detail. His emotions followed the mountain weather just as in childhood, elation in the sunlight on the peaks, melancholy and depression when clouds closed down.

The mountains were full of death stories, people dying on the slopes of Mount Washington Father of our Country within a few yards of the summit hotel that they could not find in the blizzard. They were full of Nathaniel Hawthorne, whose traveler one stormy night took refuge with a family in a house in the notch. After an evening of talk in which the traveler boasted of his future, they heard the rocks descending and ran out to the avalanche shelter. The rock stream parted, sparing the house but crushing the family and its ambitious guest in the shelter. He read about them in the mountain cabin in an old volume with a red cover and engravings, while his father, mother, brother, and sister also read under the kerosene lamp and the rain pattered on the roof and the wind moaned. The reading and readers and story and time of reading formed a unified knot in Harry's memory. Now this trip to help his daughter would join the combination. Everything merged, his father's climbing, the views from the summits, the rain on the cabin and the aura of death. As a child he kept his mountain gloom to himself, thinking it a weakness, but he knew now that for his father the gloom was as important as the joy, the deathly past as indispensable as the living future, and no experience could stand by itself.

Driving made him dreamy and for moments he forgot his anxiety. He remembered Lena Fowler; whose letter from the past he still had not answered. He considered the distance between Wicker Falls and Anchor Island, where Lena lived. From the northernmost tip of New England to well down below Boston. The possibility of a quick trip to Anchor Island before going home, if they were able to solve this kidnapping problem. Big if. Reality questions, if the if iffed, what would they do when it did? David would take his rented car back to Bangor and fly from there. Harry would return his to the little airport where he got it, bringing Judy and her baby with him. A detour to Anchor Island would require him to leave them at the airport, a drastic move needing an excuse, for which nothing came to mind. But what if the if didn't?

How could this strange adventure have been avoided? Judy's foolishness, getting pregnant by Oliver Quinn. Stuff of classic Victorian tragedy, how shocked his mother would have been, which to Judy was just silly. Her lack of history, despite her college education. She thought she was in the vanguard of something, a single mother, heroine, supported by celebrities and characters on television, whereas it looked to Harry as if she were only making the best of a mess. But it wasn't the pregnancy or ensuing baby that made it a mess, it was Oliver Quinn, revealed as a madman. Whose fatal madness was perhaps only an extension of the madness of a guru named Miller. The question was, what kind of group is the group at Miller Farm? How did it compare with groups in the papers and magazines? Moonies. Buddhist monks. Cults that brainwash middle class children and live in communes singing chants. Doomsday groups in the back country waiting for Armageddon. Suicidal followers of fanatical leaders, Jonesville, Waco. Hate groups, white supremacists, neo-Nazis, Aryan nations, the Ku Klux Klan. Armed militias preparing for civil war or race war. Survivalists to outlive Armageddon, with deep cellars and guns to keep everybody out. The Manson family.

Be sane about what to expect. He was curious about this man who called himself God. What kind of charlatan or quack would go so audaciously among people? How would he make them accept him and why he would want to? In other circumstances Harry would like to interview such a person, ask him real questions, get into the machinery of his mind to see how it worked, and his followers. He was still seeking clues to the endless gullibility of people. He did not think such an interview possible. With nothing but Miller's name to go by, Harry's image of him was a balloon. A bloated oratorical man. Fill in the picture with greasy swollen cheeks, grinning pig eyes. Follow me, suckers, I'm your God. Harry knew how the interview would go. Miller would act his Godly part, and questions would slip away on the oily sluice of language. Impervious. It would be just another promotion, and Harry would feel ashamed for helping.

He followed David's directions through the papermill city of Endicott on the Androscoggin River, took a secondary road into the wilderness and got finally to the Sleepy Wicker Motel. The motel was beside the road, which was not well traveled, under large deciduous trees still bare and steep wooded mountain slopes on both sides. It lay now in gloom as the evening settled in low. He checked into the motel, got a room, called Judy's room, no answer, then called David. You're here, wait wait, David said on the phone, wait till you hear what happened. I'll be right over. He sounded wildly and uncharacteristically excited. He came into the room looking mad.

Where's Judy? Harry said.

She's staying the night at Miller Farm, David said.

What?

She has her baby back, but she's staying at the Farm until Oliver Quinn's funeral tomorrow. Oliver, he died this morning. It was an accident.

The deep relief and the shock. They talked it over and over. The news was violent, apart from the events. How defensively David described the accident. Right in front of his eyes, not ten feet away. He didn't push him, he wasn't even close, I'll swear he wasn't. The man who suggested he pushed him, well thank God he dropped that, because how could David prove anything when it was just the two of them alone? It made even Harry feel guilty. Why should that be? The mere hint that someone might suspect David of pushing Oliver on the waterfall even though quickly withdrawn seemed to Harry to implicate immediately not only David but Judy and himself, perhaps especially himself in some transcendental guilt that dyes events regardless of their causes.

They talked, then lapsed into silence while time cooked. That was time's job. It cooked the most outrageous and impossible happenings into a cake called history.

Finally Harry called Miller Farm. He asked to speak to Judy and after a few minutes heard her voice. Hi Daddy. Are you all right, he said, are you safe, are you free?

I'm fine, Daddy. I've got Hazy back and I'm so happy.

And you're spending the night with those people?

They want me to stay for Oliver's funeral, Daddy.

Do you want to do that?

It's the least I can do considering he's dead, she said. Daddy, they're nice people. I like them. I even talked to Miller. He's nice too, you'd be surprised.

Miller is nice?

He's a sweet old man.

He claims to be God.

He doesn't act like God, she said. He acts like a nice kindly old man.

This roused Harry's interest, if Miller should be different from what he had supposed. How would he like to be interviewed? he said.

Oh Daddy, for heaven's sake, Judy said. She laughed.

A half hour later the call came to Harry in his room. The bell startled him like out of a sleep. Professor Harry Field, the man's voice said. This is Miller at Miller Farm.

Miller?

I hear you want to interview me.

Really? Harry said. Would you be willing?

Why not? the man said. His voice was softly resonant with precise elderly enunciation. Harry thought it was a New England accent but then realized it was not that specific.

I should tell you a couple of things, Harry said. I'll approach you from a skeptical point of view and I don't expect you to persuade me of your beliefs. I make a point of exposing frauds and charlatans. Not that I regard you as one.

Relax, Miller said. I know your writings.

You do?

I'll talk to you tomorrow when you pick up your daughter. You can ask anything you want. You don't scare me.

You don't scare me either, Harry wanted to say but didn't. He couldn't believe Miller knew his writings, but he felt flattered anyway.

13

Nick Foster

Oliver looked out the window. Hey Nick Oliver said look at this.

I looked. I couldn't see anything.

Look in the woods behind the house. Above the big rock.

I saw a face.

Look at him. He's a black man. See his black face.

His face looked brown. It didn't look black. But Oliver said it was black so it was black.

Do you know what that man wants. He wants to take your baby away.

I didn't like the black man to take my baby away.

That man is the devil Oliver said. He's black and wants your baby. Don't you want to stop him.

I want to stop him I said.

Let's take a walk Oliver said. Out the back where he can't see us. I have a job for you. Will you do a job for me.

I always do a job for Oliver. That's my job.

He got a gun out of the closet and we went into the woods where the path goes up to Meditation Point. You been practicing with a rifle he said. Do you shoot pretty good.

I shoot good.

Show me how good you shoot.

We went to a rock at the bottom of the waterfall. We looked up to the top. See that he said. That's where the path crosses over to Meditation Point. See the tree branch like a horse with a crest on its head.

I saw the horse with a crest on its head.

Shoot the crest off.

I pointed the rifle at the branch that looked like a crest and squeezed the trigger bang. The crest popped off and a bunch of leaves floated down the waterfall.

Good. Now listen I want you to remember what I told Loomer yesterday.

I couldn't remember.

When me and you and Loomer were here at the waterfall Oliver said. And I told him if I want to shoot somebody I can stand here with my rifle from the Miller Ammunition Pile, and I can hit somebody crossing over the stepping stones up there.

I remembered that. I remembered Loomer said if you wanted to shoot somebody with a rifle you could pop him sitting down at the dinner table. Oliver said if I shot someone crossing the stepping stones he would fall down the waterfall bang them rocks and nobody'd know it was a bullet. Loomer said a perfect crime. Particularly if you happen to be standing here with your rifle at just the moment when he happens to be crossing over on the way to Meditation Point. Oliver said the point would be to know when he is going to cross over to Meditation Point. Then everybody would think he slipped. Loomer said particularly if he just happened to cross that way instead of taking the easy path around the pool if he just happened to like stepping stones. Oliver said the point would be to make sure he does cross by the stepping stones.

Do you remember that Oliver said.

I remembered.

All right Oliver said. Now Nicky. If the black devil who wants to take your baby crossed the path to Meditation Point could you shoot him in the head.

I squinted to make a picture of the black man crossing and I made a picture of the rifle pointing at his head. Yes I said.

So if you see the black man crossing on his way to Meditation Point would you shoot him.

No I said.

Why not.

Because thou shalt not kill.

But if I told you to shoot him would you do it then.

I thought. I always do what you tell me I said.

But if I told you and you shot him what would you do about thou shalt not kill.

I don't know.

You could say it's not really killing because the black man is the devil. Thou shalt not kill except the devil.

It's okay to kill the devil.

Good. The black man wants to take away your baby. He wants to marry the white woman and raise the baby as a black and white baby. That's offensive to good people.

The baby shouldn't be a black and white baby.

The baby isn't but the black man wants to take the white woman away and marry her. That's black and white. Does God like black and white.

God doesn't like black and white.

Get it straight. God likes white and he likes black because he made them white and he made them black. What God doesn't like is black and white.

God doesn't like black and white.

I have a job for you the most important job in your life. I want you to wait on that stump with the rifle. When Loomer catches the black man I'm going to send him up to Meditation Point. When he gets out of sight on the path come over to this rock and watch. When he crosses over to Meditation Point I want you to aim carefully and hit him in the head.

You want me to shoot the black man in the head.

He looked at me and I looked at the ground.

You want me to kill the black man.

Do you have any objections.

No.

Why don't you.

Because he's the devil and you're supposed to kill the devil because he wants to take my baby away.

Are you worried the police will come and put you in jail.

I was scared. Will they do that.

Not if you do the job cleanly. This is why it's important to shoot when he's exactly in the middle across the waterfall. Look up see the long shaped rock where the water divides that looks like a tiger's tongue. Do you see the rock that looks like a tiger's tongue.

I didn't know if I saw a tiger's tongue or not. I thought I saw it.

Take another shot to show me you see it. Hit the tiger's tongue.

I shot the tiger's tongue. A puff of dust popped off the tiger's tongue but if Oliver hadn't told me I would have thought it looked more like a puppy's tongue.

That's the place he said. Shoot him when he's stepping on that. Do you know why it's important to shoot him then.

No.

Because then he'll fall down the waterfall and it will be an accident. When he falls and hits the rocks nobody will look for a bullet.

It takes a while but I see what he means. It makes me laugh and shake Oliver's hand.

If there is a bullet I'll be here with rocks to bang him up some more. Then nobody will ask did you shoot him because nobody will think of it.

I laughed again.

So what are you going to do.

I'm going to sit on the stump and wait for the black man.

And when you see him what will you do.

I'll watch and when he crosses over I'll shoot him.

And what exact moment will you shoot him in the head.

I'll shoot him when he crosses the tiger's tongue.

And what will happen.

He'll fall down the waterfall and nobody will know.

Because it's an accident. You'll be at peace because you have carried out the will of God and done a great service.

I followed him back to the house. Loomer was there looking out the window.

That your man Loomer said. Think I'll round him up.

I watched. After a while I saw Oliver talking to the black man and then they went to the beginning of the path and Oliver told him where to go. The black man who looks brown except Oliver says brown is black went up the path. When he was out of sight in the trees I went over to the rock at the bottom of the waterfall where I could see to shoot him. I waited a while. Loomer came up behind me. He scared me. He had a rifle too.

What are you going to do he said.

Shoot squirrels I said.

Is that what Oliver told you to do.

I didn't say.

Black squirrel maybe.

Brown I said. I felt smart saying that.

He told you to kill him Loomer said. When do you do it.

When he crosses over to Meditation Point I said.

You're supposed to shoot him then.

I didn't have time to answer because there was a crashing noise and the black man tearing down the path like a bunch of bees. He was going so fast he didn't see us.

Look like he changed his mind Loomer said.

Now what do I do.

Guess you wait to see what Oliver tells you next.

Loomer went off into the woods and I went back to the stump.

After a while Oliver and the black man came up the path together. They saw me and Oliver came over.

He looked in the eyes like a snake.

Get this straight he said. I'm going up with him. When he crosses over do it like I said.

Okay.

When he crosses the tiger's tongue be sure you get him and not me okay.

That's silly I said. I'd never shoot you.

He went back to the black man and they went up.

Loomer came back. You still supposed to shoot him he said.

Yes.

When he crosses the waterfall.

Yes.

So he'll fall down and they won't blame you. Are you nervous.

No.

Not afraid you might miss or make a mistake. Not scared he'll fall the other way and not drop down the waterfall after all.

Not if I hit him when he's crossing the tiger's tongue.

What's the tiger's tongue.

The rock up there that looks like a puppy's tongue.

He looked up. That won't work he said. If you shoot him there he'll fall back and land in the pool. He'll just float around bleeding in the head and when they find him they'll see the bullet hole and know what you did. Then you'll have to face not only the police but the wrath of Miller.

Oliver told me.

The right place to shoot him is when he steps over the elephant's pecker.

What.

The rock to the left of the tiger's tongue where the water is spouting out. Looks like an elephant's pecker.

I saw the elephant's pecker. It looked more like a spaniel's pecker. My spaniel had a red pecker that stuck out when he sat on the ground thumping his leg.

Why does he want you to kill Leo Loomer said.

Do you mean the black man.

The black man. His name is David Leo. Why does Oliver want you to kill him.

Because he's the devil I said. He wants to take the baby away.

The baby yes and the mother and the whole damned she-boodle. Fuck him.

What.

Do you think it's a good idea.

What.

It's a bad idea. Oliver's crazy. He's bringing trouble to Miller Farm. Don't you think so.

I don't know. I didn't know what to do. I was scared of Loomer.

You wouldn't know if Oliver didn't tell you right.

Oliver takes care of me.

Right. So now he wants you to kill David Leo. Tell you what Nicky. I'm a better shot than you. Let me do it.

Oliver said I'm supposed to do it.

I'm superseding him. You go back to the cottage.

You'll do it the right way.

Exactly.

You'll do it when he's over the tiger's tongue.

Not the tiger's tongue the elephant's pecker.

Will you tell Oliver why you did it and not me.

I'll tell Oliver. Go shoot some squirrels. Shoot a lot of them. Make a lot of bangs.

I didn't see any squirrels. I couldn't hear anything because of the waterfall noise. I walked around but I stayed where I could see Loomer because I wanted to be sure since this was the job Oliver gave me. After a while I heard a rifle shot. I saw him standing on the rock at the bottom of the waterfall lowering his rifle. I guessed the rifle shot came from him. I couldn't think of anywhere else it came from.

Loomer came back to the stump. He saw me. He's coming down Loomer said.

I heard crashing running down the path again. It was the black man again. He ran to the stream and stood at the edge looking at something.

Think I'll go help him Loomer said. Stay behind a little.

I stayed behind and saw Loomer go up to the black man at the edge of the stream. I wondered where Oliver was.

Loomer crossed over the stream to the other side stepping on rocks. He bent over something. I came closer and saw it was blue a person lying on the rocks. It was the same color blue Oliver was.

I wondered if it was Oliver. I hoped it wasn't Oliver. Oh how I hoped it wasn't Oliver. Loomer talked to the black man.

After a while Loomer and the black man went down to the compound. I went to the stream and looked across at the man in blue. I wished Oliver would come back and tell me what to do. I tried to cross over like Loomer but it was too hard I slipped and got my shoes and socks and pants wet. I wished Oliver would show up. I hoped the blue man wasn't Oliver oh how I hoped it.

A bunch of people came up from the compound. Loomer was with them. I didn't see the black man any more. The people went into the stream and picked up the blue man. They put him on a stretcher and covered him with a green plastic sheet. They carried him down to the compound. I tried to catch Loomer. I followed him to the big house.

I said what happened.

He slipped Loomer said.

Who.

Oliver.

Is Oliver dead.

Yep.

I said you shot him.

Don't make up stories man this was a accident.

You shot the wrong person.

I don't make mistakes. He slipped.

I saw you shoot him.

No you didn't.

I heard the gun.

Things aren't always what they seem. You didn't see what happened up there. He was careless and his foot slipped and down he came. It's just as well too.

Just as well.

Better he die than Leo. Shoot him and bring in the FBI the end of Miller Farm. You wouldn't want that to happen.

Oliver wanted him killed I said.

It didn't happen and it's just as well. A accident. Do you know what a accident is. It's an Act of God. Ordained of God.

God. I thought how Loomer looked. You mean Miller.

Miller was meditating in the Big House he said.

Then it wasn't God.

Unless God made his foot slip.

What am I supposed to do now.

Do what you always do whatever that is.

I can't.

Why not.

I need Oliver to tell me.

Well Oliver's gone looks like you need someone else to tell you now. Shit. You want me to tell you. You want that.

I didn't want to answer.

You want me to be your guide you do what I tell you. I'll be your guide. Do you agree.

I felt sad.

Don't cry he said. The bastard wasn't worth it.

That night alone in the room where I used to share with Oliver I thought about him. I cried again.

The next day they had the funeral in the Barn. They had Oliver in a box and everybody came and mostly nobody said anything and Miller talked. There was a woman somebody said the baby's mother. I wanted to talk to her about the baby but I didn't know what to say so I didn't. I often want to talk about something but I don't have anything to say about it so I can't. I wish you could talk about something without having to say anything. I wanted to talk about Oliver being dead but I didn't have anything to say about that either.

After the funeral they took Oliver down to the pool to burn him up. They put the box on a stand of logs and poured gasoline and lit it. There were flames and smoke went up. It took a long time. I tried to see Oliver through the holes but I couldn't see anything. It made me sad to see Oliver burn up. I couldn't see him though.

Loomer sat beside me. This is called cremation he said. Now if they's any bullet holes nobody will know.

I thought they wasn't any bullet holes.

I said if he said. If they was not they was.

I remembered. I saw you shoot him I said.

No you didn't. You don't know what you saw.

It's not fair to kill Oliver.

What's fair.

Fair is I couldn't say I thought I knew but I couldn't say.

Fair is it's not fair to kill Oliver and not somebody pay. You want to punish someone. Is that what you mean?

That's it I said.

I understand. Actually I didn't tell you the whole story. Between you and me okay. What if David Leo killed Oliver.

The black man did he.

Don't tell anyone. What if they were crossing and David tripped him. If he didn't like Oliver and pushed him when he saw the chance bye bye Oliver.

He pushed Oliver.

Before I had time to shoot him. What could I do.

That's not fair. He should have given you time.

That's bad. Thou shalt not kill.

I got mad.

Let's keep this to ourselves Loomer said. A secret between us. According to everybody Oliver slipped and fell. Better far better to leave it that way. Do you know why.

I didn't know why.

Better for Miller Farm. Not to have police folk and FBI types snooping around. Who knows they might even accuse you since you were in the woods with a rifle. We don't want no police in here and if we keep our trap shut we won't get none. We take care of it ourselves our own funeral and cremation and nobody else know anything.

He shouldn't have pushed Oliver I said. It made me sad and some other feeling too.

What you want is justice Loomer said. You want fair. Somebody should pay. Do you agree.

Somebody should pay.

What should he pay.

I don't know.

Well how does the world decide these things.

I don't know.

They have a trial Nicky. Would you like to give the black man a trial you and me.

That would be nice.

Ourselves no police no lawyers. Would you like to be the law in this case.

I liked that.

We'll give him a trial and charge him. If we find him guilty he will pay the price. How much would you like him to pay. A little. Some. The maximum.

Which is biggest.

The maximum. Should he pay the maximum.

He should pay the maximum.

All right then we'll give him a trial with the maximum penalty. Do you know what the maximum penalty for killing is.

Kill him back.

Something like that Loomer said. I'll have to look it up. Someone as important to you as Oliver you kill him back. It would make you feel better.

I'd feel better.

Only one problem.

What's that.

If we're going to try him we need to catch him.

I bet you have a plan for that I said.

Smart Nicky. It means going away a while. You willing to help me catch the black man and give him what he deserves.

It's only fair I said.

You owe it to Oliver.

I owe it to Oliver.

14

Harry Field

Harry's preoccupation with death seems as fresh at seventy as in his teens. What happens to his I when he dies? Arguing with nature. How can you destroy this sight and knowing and this world which lives only through this knowing? With nature's rhetorical reply, You'll never know you're dead, why worry?

He thought often of Gus Wessel, his wife's father who had been Harry's professor and who died last fall. Old Gus was content to be obliterated. In his nineties glad to die with no residue of feeling, no breath of memory left. Harry couldn't understand. The foreverness of time. The eternity of death making it as if he had never lived.

Old Gus used to talk, repeating what nature told Harry. Are you afraid you'll be forgotten? he said. Vanity. The same soup drowns us all.

This old father-in-law was the only person Harry told about his fears and then only in his old age. The old mentor became a new mentor by authority of the shadow of death. They argued playfully, Harry pretending to be as afraid as he really was. Old Gus was a man of winks and jokes. His memories never changed, the same lost anchor on the sailboat, Professor Paul and the plums, running out of gas while driving up Cadillac Mountain.

When Gus died it was peaceful and normal. And terrible. This was a death (of all deaths) that they could not discuss and Harry could only invent what Gus would have said. It was the reduction of Gus's consciousness from real to imaginary, like his father's death, his mother's, and all the others to come. The insult of Gus Wessel's nonexistence.

Harry thought he knew what made death terrible. It was the idea of permanent good, gained from a lifetime of education and opinion. What mentors taught: things are good, some things transcendently good, some things worth more than life itself. Life saturated with value like a body soaked with gasoline. Art. Morality. Love. Then death kills you and me and it goes up in flames. Good and bad, beautiful and ugly, all you have been taught, flamed out into the eternal blank of death. Harry forgot to mention this idea to Gus Wessel and now he never could.

Outwardly he took the scientific view and wrote articles. Inwardly he still longed to rediscover the reconciliation he had before his granddaughter's kidnapping, lost like a gift stolen before he could open it.

At Miller Farm, Harry Field interviewed God. Nothing allowed Harry to hope this fraudulent pretender could answer his question, the idea was insulting. That's why this narrative can't be in the first person. As they drove to Miller Farm in David's car, Harry in the first person looked forward to jousting with Miller as a celebration of the baby's release. In the dark peripheries outside his first person, who knows what hopes remained unuttered, inadmissible, ashamed?

The sky was sullen, gray and blank revealing nothing. A woman came out to greet him. She directed him to the big house and sent David to wait with Mrs. Field and the baby.

The house was a cavernous Victorian space. Stained glass panels in the door. A broad central hallway with a staircase and balcony. He saw through to the back and the house was full of light. An actor's voice invited him up.

A man stood on the balcony, tall with white hair, a red flannel shirt and jeans. Later Harry would hear Judy's description of him as Ralph Waldo Emerson and Franz Liszt, but to Harry he looked more like Walter Huston as Old Scratch.

Harry had an embarrassing need to pee. Bathroom? he asked. Over there, the man said. Harry knew, more men die of prostate than of any other cancer. It was foolish not to have it checked.

Now here was Miller, who claimed to be God. They went into his study. A computer and a yellow cat washing itself among the papers. Glad you came, God said. Harry sat by the window in an upholstered chair with a high back. The man faced him in a similar chair. He looked benevolent until you noticed his eyes. There was something wrong with them. It was hard to tell which eye he was looking out of. One seemed fiery, the other was shaded.

They looked out at the compound, the altered barn in the center, the cottages at the edge of the woods. I'm Miller and you're Field, God said. What can I do for you?

Mainly I came to get my daughter and my granddaughter.

They're free to leave. This is an interview you requested. What do you want to know?

What did Harry want to know? I suppose I want to know what you really claim to be.

I looked up your essay on religious credulity, Miller said. I'm on your side. I'm glad when pseudo-scientists and con artists are exposed.

Is that so?

I also looked up your essay on science and religion.

He stared at Harry, though Harry couldn't tell which eye was staring nor whether the look was benign or malignant. The light from outside cast a shadow across his face in the Walter Huston-Old Scratch way. You know what they call me, don't you? Miller said. In the presence of madness Harry shivered.

They call you God? Harry said. It sounded too ridiculous to be uttered, which made Harry timid.

Some people do.

And you encourage it?

Miller closed his eyes, folded his hands, leaned back like William Buckley. This is an interview, he said. Let me tell you about my life. Would you like that?

Fine, Harry said.

Miller talked. Once I was an ordained minister, but too many people loved me and I had to leave. I started my own church in a Philadelphia apartment. Now here we are.

His talk was like a practiced oration. I had a religious experience. We call it The Revelation and it's the Constitution of the Miller Church. I was in a Philadelphia park on a bench thinking about something that had just happened. I heard a voice telling me who I was. And who do you think that was?

A response was expected, but Harry waited. Miller nodded. Thus was born the Miller Church. I started with five from my original mission, meeting in the Philadelphia apartment. Now we have more than forty. We moved from Philadelphia to Cape Cod, living in tents. We grew. A benefactor let us use an island in Maine and last year we came here and became the Miller Farm. My disciples. We're self-supporting. We live out of the wilderness. We grow our food and make goods to sell, clothing and wood carvings for small change. Reclusive and exclusive. We don't seek members.

All my people have been rescued from lives of personal despair. They are remade by their deliberate belief in the thing about me that most shocks you. They are stripped of ambition, freed from self. They don't care for doctrine. They shrink from authority voices demanding them to choose, choose, choose. We give them shelter and leadership and relieve them from responsibility. I do good, man, I do good. Look out the window and see.

Harry saw two women talking on a cottage porch and a fat man carrying a laundry basket.

You rehabilitate people? Harry said.

Not if you mean sending them back to the world, Miller said. I remove them from the world. My people are estranged from the world. They are allergic to institutions. The threat of penalty in every blank to be filled in. The enemy is society itself like a great schoolmarm. The scolding press, the tax collectors, the criticizing neighbors, the chiding church. I remake them into the ambitionless world of Miller Farm. Nothing can touch them here. We're a sovereign community.

You tell your followers you're God and they believe you?

That's what rehabilitates them. Believing in me frees them.

Do you yourself believe you're God?

Your own essay explains it.

It does?

There's the objective world where the sciences prevail. And there's subjective consciousness where the universe is mind, nature its embodiment. Wise people hope to reconcile the two worlds and believe both at once. You said that in your article. Well here I am, Miller said, the answer to your wish.

What?

The intersection of nature and mind. If the universe is mind then mind is divine. I am conscious, therefore I am divine. Therefore God. What do you think of that?

It made Harry laugh. Why then, he said, if you're God, so am I. We're all God. Is that what you mean?

Miller laughed too, like watch it, the waters are deeper than you think. There's a difference between your divinity and mine, he said. Your consciousness partakes of God. But you and your consciousness together do not constitute God. I do.

How do you know?

Like this. Would you ever go among your fellow beings and announce in all seriousness that you are God?

Of course not.

Well I would. That's the difference.

You really are an old fake, Harry said. He liked Miller.

Not at all, Miller said. What I really am is God.

Meaning you're a liar and I'm not.

Not at all. I know I'm God. You don't. Knowledge is faith and religion depends on faith. I know I am God, you know you are not, and neither of us needs proof.

Is this what you tell your followers?

I teach people to forsake ambition, break free from self. Defy the taboos that constrain their souls like the blueprint of an old castle. Familiarity is death, leave it and seek the strange, accept the unacceptable, think the unthinkable. This does not mean go out and seek adventures. It's an inner change. My people live quietly on Miller Farm sharing their lives with the birds that sing and the animals that hunt and rest and mate and sleep.

Believing you are God.

When you've left the world it comforts you to have God near.

And you snicker at them.

Never. It's a serious matter being God.

I'll bet it is.

It's a trust. I embody the spiritual God. Divine incarnation, most religions have it. It makes divinity, otherwise dispersed through the sentient universe, communicable. It brings God to people, so they can talk together like you and me. They like to see me confined by the same bodily limits that confine them. In my incarnation I can only do what the human machine I inhabit is able to do.

You can't work miracles?

I prefer not to. Likewise my human knowledge is limited.

You don't know everything?

This is the divine amnesia, temporary for the duration of the incarnation. Knowledge in God is sight, the direct perception of what is. What you see depends on where you stand. When I occupy my human body my sight lines are blocked. Mock away. I have an offer for you. In your article you said you had a lot of questions for God. Well, here's your one-in-a-lifetime chance to ask God everything about the universe you always wanted to know.

This is a joke. You'll answer?

If you don't believe I'm God, just pretend and ask as if I were.

You like games.

Yes, God likes games.

Here's the scene, question and answer, Harry Field's once-in-a-lifetime chance to ask God everything he always wanted to know, while Miller leaned back in his chair with his arms in the red flannel shirt behind his head, grinning, like Walter Huston as Old Scratch with reminiscences of Ralph Waldo Emerson and Franz Liszt and something wrong with one of his eyes. All right, Harry said, I'll ask you a question.

Question (Harry): Have you all the human body parts?

Answer (God): Yes, shall I enumerate? I have a pancreas, a liver, a spleen, an appendix, a gall bladder, shall I go on?

Q: Are you immortal?

A: Miller will die. God lives on.

Q: Have there been previous incarnations?

A: Many.

Q: Who controls your incarnations?

A: God does. There is no God over God.

Q: Yet you discovered, you did not ordain, your incarnation.

A: That's the divine amnesia.

Q: Well then, God, what's your relation to nature? Are you the creator or an overseer? Is there an opposition between you and nature?

A: Nature is my general body. Miller is my particular body.

Q: Did you create your body? Did you create yourself?

A: That's a language problem. Creation implies before and after. Eternity transcends time. I know myself without creation and there's no knowing beyond me.

Q: Well. I was going to ask if having started things up you just watch or do you sometimes intervene? But if you get rid of time that question has no meaning.

A: What you're asking is, do I suspend the laws of nature? Miracles, ghosts. My reply: God never violates God's rules. On the other hand.

Q: On the other hand?

A: Here I am. Everything that happens is an Act of God.

Q: What shall I report to the scientists as your latest word on the origin of the universe, the big bang, the beginning of life, the evolution of species, the inner structure of the atom, the strong and weak force, antimatter and quarks?

A: Tell them to admire me.

Q: You take the credit?

A: Your scientists are probing me. They make mistakes but they're on the right track.

Q: What exactly are some of those mistakes?

A: To tell would be tampering. They'll find out.

Q: You don't know, do you?

A: Ask me another.

Q: Is there life after death?

A: That's what everybody wants to know. You'd think it was the most important question on earth.

Q: Do you have an answer?

A: Depends what you mean by "after." If you stay within time, then by definition there's no life after death. Outside of time, "after" is meaningless. There is no after and life is eternal.

Q: There you go outside time again.

A: Consider two ideas about time. In one, time moves constantly forward. Since everything eventually ends, eternity is death. In the other time is a field. The only movement is your consciousness scanning the field, arranging things into an illusion of sequence. From this point of view all moments are eternal and you live forever within your life.

Q: That sounds like my article.

A: That's where I got it.

Q: You don't know any more about it than I do.

A: When people ask me the death question, I tell them what they want to believe. If you die believing you'll go to heaven you'll never know if you don't.

Q: That's my article too. What did you tell people before you read it?

A: There are many religions on the face of the earth. I appear differently to different people.

Q: What made you choose this remote place to incarnate?

A: It's not my only choice.

Q: Are there other incarnations? At the same time?

A: Why not, if time is a field?

Q: Here's another question. Many religions around the world regard the others as false. Do you prefer some to others?

A: It's possible.

Q: Which do you prefer?

A: That's my secret.

Q: Tell me then, why are you so brutal and cruel and unjust? God smiled. A: Are you speaking of God or Miller?

Q: I thought you were the same.

A: So we are. I'll answer you. Life eats life and dies as food. That's what's known as flux, to make the universe work. Otherwise there's nothing for you or me to be conscious of.

Q: How mean. People think you are full of grief over the evil things they do and all the while you're getting ready to give them the whammy.

A: Some people blame it on the devil.

Q: What? Is there a devil?

A: You think I'm the devil, don't you? Call it my two-part structure, the principle of antithesis, fundamental to all creation. You suffer pain so I may live, old sadist that I am. But don't think you're more virtuous than I, you hypocrite. Whence came your idea of virtue? And your love for the earth and your life which I gave you? You're no different from me, except that you refuse the responsibility. You see the suffering in the world and feel safe because you can shift the blame to me and let my mysterious ways take the blame.

Q: Are you calling me a hypocrite?

A: If that's what you heard, that's what you heard.

Q: Let's talk about something else. What's your relation to Jesus Christ?

A: My son. I was very fond of him.

Q: Did he rise from the dead?

154

A: Don't ask me to comment on doctrines. That would be to intervene.

Q: I think you are a sly devil. Do you believe in God?

A: I believe in myself.

Q: I think you're either a charlatan or a madman.

A: I don't mind.

I have a more personal question, Harry said. Why did Oliver Quinn kidnap my granddaughter?

Because he's a fool. He thought it would impress me. But he died.

Why did he die?

That was an Act of God.

An Act of God?

An accident, you know the expression. People call it an Act of God because they see God's hand in it.

Did you have a hand in Oliver's death?

I have a hand in everyone's death, Miller said. I willed it. What else do you want to ask?

Harry thought.

Q: I understand you have a large collection of weapons. What do you need them for?

A: Some of my people are afraid of the end of the world. Don't worry. I keep them under control. Nothing is more savage than religious war. Nothing equals the power I have over people's souls and hearts. That's why I advise you to show respect.

Q: Respect for you?

A: Respect for the fanatics. They'll kill you if you insult me, even if you think them contemptible.

Q: That's your lesson to me?

A: You may write about this if you wish.

*

At the end of the interview Miller rose and went to the door. The unasked question on Harry's mind still pressed for an answer. Tell me, he wanted to say. What was the reconciliation with death that I have forgotten?

But I'll be damned if I'll let this fraud know that much about me, he said to himself. At the door Miller put his hand on Harry's shoulder as if he had heard the unuttered question and this were his unuttered answer.

They went down the stairs. Do you need to go to the bathroom again? You should have your prostate checked, God said.

They went to the compound. Get the woman with the baby, Miller said to the man on the porch. The man loped across the yard like a cowboy. He had black hair swept back from his forehead.

While they waited Miller talked about his people. Maria Garn, he said, who's been taking care of your grandchild. She's a mother of kids, beaten by her husband. She heard me speak one day. I invited them to join me. The kids are grown now but they have stayed on, Jack, Paul, Nancy.

Miranda Abel. Drugs and sex, abandoned by her friends. I told her to forget her friends, consider herself dead, and the new Miranda is newborn in a different world. Living with us she doesn't need drugs, sustained by her belief in me which I can always replenish according to her need.

Ed Hansel, my oldest aide. An old plumber, he stayed with me when I left my church, and stuck by me when I had my revelation in the park. It was he who discovered the rehabilitating power of belief in me and how to utilize it to help people.

There coming out of the cottage was Judy holding her baby with David Leo followed by the man like a cowboy and a couple of women. Laughing in relief, together at last. Judy hugged Harry. He took the baby, who looked with eyes of wonder. He shook hands with David. His daughter thanked the women and they all went together to David's rented car.

There was another young man by the car, really just a boy. He had a tight mat of light curls on his head. His eyes scowled. He watched Judy get into the front passenger seat. When Harry went to hand the baby to Judy, he got in the way. Stop, he said.

He was looking at David Leo though it was Harry he blocked.

What's the matter? Looking on, Miller remained benign, unchanged. The blackhaired cowboy took a step toward the boy.

You need a car seat, the boy said. You can't drive a baby without a car seat.

I know, Judy said pleasantly. We don't have one. This is a rented car. I'll hold her carefully.

Wait, the boy said. Don't move.

He went over to the other cars. David Leo got in and Harry handed the baby in to Judy. David started the engine. The boy turned around and yelled. I said wait, he said, wait.

What's the matter with him? David muttered.

The boy reached into one of the cars. It took him a while. Let's go, David said, go, go, but he couldn't because Miller was in front of the car. The boy extracted something from the other car and brought it back. It was a car seat.

Here, he said. Use this.

So they all got out and put the car seat into the car. Thank you, they said to the boy. The boy watched as they went up the drive back to the road.

A happy ending, Harry said.

How amazing, Judy said. That boy had tears in his eyes.

He looked like he wanted to kill me, David Leo said.

He was looking at the baby with tears in his eyes, Judy said.

PART THREE

15

David Leo

We saw different things. Judy saw tears in his eyes. The glare I saw wanted to kill me. Just a kid, Judy said. He was the one with a rifle by the waterfall the day Oliver Quinn died. He and his rifle, and the cowboy with his. How quick the cowboy moved toward the kid when he stopped us at the car.

It was celebration time after nine days of ordeal. She crooned and chuckled her child in the car seat all the way back Rib Rock Road to Wicker Falls and the Sleepy Wicker Motel, free free from that awful place and those awful people.

What next? We have our two rental cars from different places, I'll take mine to Bangor, where I'll fly home, and Harry his to Lebanon where he'll fly. Judy and the baby go with him, too bad. There's a little side trip Harry would like to take to a place called Anchor Island down towards New York. An old friend he hasn't seen in fifty years. Therefore he'll put Judy and the baby on the plane at Lebanon, then take the bus to Anchor Island and be home in a few days. Do you mind?

Not at all Daddy, Judy said, but who is this old friend? Forcing him to admit friend was girl friend, sex and old times neutralized by old age. Oh boy an adventure Daddy, and she teased him all the way back to the Sleepy Wicker. It isn't what you think,

161

he mumbled, just a polite call while he's in the neighborhood (some neighborhood) and she said fine as long as you don't dump Mother, which was the farthest thing from his mind.

Meanwhile tonight the mood is party, though there was nobody but the three of us and no place but the bleak motel. I suggested we go to Endicott for dinner with champagne but Judy reminded me the baby was too little for a fancy restaurant. We couldn't celebrate the baby because of the baby. Any party would be the party of doing what we had to do. We went to the motel and decided to party at the Hijack Café in Flynn instead.

In my room there was a message to call Loomer at Miller Farm. Uh-oh, Loomer the cowboy who brought me in to the compound from the woods, who looked at Oliver Quinn's body on the rock, who sent me home after suggesting I had pushed Oliver. That death was stuck back there in Harry's happy-ending story and we weren't rid of our problems yet.

I called back as requested and spoke to Loomer. Just want to make sure you called off your FBI man, he said.

I'll do that, I told him.

Another thing, he said. That car seat my friend give you.

That car seat?

Miller needs it back, he said. No big deal. You can rent one in Endicott at Jefferson's. Get one for the professor's car and bring ours back to Miller Farm tomorrow. I thought damned if I'd go back to Miller Farm and we talked back and forth, he polite yet fishy and finally he suggested I leave the car seat at a gas station named Jake and Jim's outside of Endicott. Rent a new one at Jefferson's and leave the old one at Jake and Jim's in the morning. It won't delay you that much, he said.

It seemed fishy but I agreed to it because the car seat was their kindness and I couldn't figure out what the problem was.

Disciples

We gathered again and went to Flynn, I driving with Harry in front and Judy again in back next to the baby in the car seat. Judy refreshed and clean in a plain white shirt, her brown hair slanted across her forehead and eyes looking out at the world under her brows. I wanted to touch her like a demand of the air which everybody felt though she was preoccupied with her baby now as she had been preoccupied with its absence before and I still had to wait. When I opened the car door for her she looked at me suddenly full of lilies in her eyes, and said, How can I repay you, Davey? What can I do for you? Clear and pointed. Startled, with her father standing by, I knew my answer which she also knew, which I could not speak. I grunted, and she added less pointedly, I'm forever in your debt.

How repay me? Said with such luminosity in her eyes that the unspoken words were audible in the light: I'm yours and all you need do is ask. The baby recovered, the kidnappers gone, time for the reward. A promise. Still I was careful and in a moment relapsed into doubt. Because of the baby, the baby, the baby in her room. The case was hopeless. How could she think of me when she was wrapped up in the baby?

I went through this in my head all the way to the Hijack while I drove. Also while we were there and Harry talked about his conversation with Miller, who must be insane because he calls himself God and yet according to Harry is intelligent and even sophisticated, talk which I followed and participated in even while I continued to review the Judy question in my head. Trying to think into her real thoughts, how she expected to fulfill her promise. To be honored right away or vaguely at some future date—tonight or later. I could wait if I had to, a long time if required. The important thing was to let her know I had received her message, understood it, welcomed it. Otherwise she would think I didn't want to, and that would be the end.

Maybe, was it possible, she'd be willing even with the baby in the room? If we were quiet? If we could avoid the additional complication of her father, how to approach without rousing him? Her room was between mine and his. The walls were so thin you could hear television two rooms away.

That father, my mentor and great man, had turned into another person whose relation to me I couldn't judge. In this part of New Hampshire he was mostly just the father of the girl, a position naturally antagonistic. Not that I felt antagonism, not that. But he didn't seem like a great professor any more. He didn't seem like a name in bibliographies associated with the Field Approach or Fieldean Analysis, phrases I have seen in print. He didn't seem like the man in cool charge of the seminars I remembered. He was as nervous curious and surprised as anyone else. Nothing mentory about him when we had talked about approaching Miller. On that subject my ideas had been as good as his or better maybe, yes better. His celebratory wonder now reminded me of his previous helplessness, for he was a little naive about everything. You could say Harry Field had lost face in this crisis if you cared about face, which he tried to regain on the dark country roads by talking about the man who thought he was God. Regaining face by talking, while I had status by driving the car as well as by having witnessed Oliver's death, balanced in turn by Harry's money financing everything. Whatever the balance, if Harry's daughter let me into her room between Harry's and mine while baby and Harry slept we'd be very quiet.

In the midst of these thoughts I reminded myself how much I had done for both Judy and Harry. I had flown to Bangor. I had gone to Black Harbor and visited Stump Island. I had driven from Stump Island to Wicker Falls. I had gone back and forth in the Wicker Falls area from motel to post office to Farm. I had scrambled through the woods like a spy, had been taken prisoner by a man with a rifle and was sent up the steep woods where I watched a man fall to his death down a cataract. I was subjected to innuendo as if I had committed a crime. All this I had done for the Field family. It was right that Judy should come to me at last. The trouble was, this contrary fear that I was over-interpreting, that in reality neither Judy nor her father cared what they owed, that it embarrassed them and they'd be glad when enough time had passed for everyone to forget.

We stood in front of Judy's door between Harry's and mine on the porch, clarifying plans. Get up at seven. Go to Endicott for breakfast before going to Jefferson's at nine for the car seat. Everybody got an alarm? I gave Judy a meaningful look which she ignored. She took the baby and shut the door. Thanks for everything, Davey.

I wondered if she expected me to come back after her father had retired. If I could knock on her door without his hearing, if he would be good enough not to look out his window and see me. I lay on my bed next to the wall where her room was on the other side. I knocked on the wall. I knocked again, louder. I thought what a fool, blushing in my room where no one could see.

I owed it to my heroism to make an unequivocal attempt. I got up at last and went out to the porch. The light still showed around the edges of her drapes. Light also in Harry's window. I knocked softly. Again. I heard her voice, Yes? I didn't want to speak, so I knocked again. She opened the door a little violently in a bathrobe holding the baby to her breast.

What do you want? Impatient with no hush at all.

Can I come in?

She went through a display of shifting expressions beginning with anger but slipping fortunately into others before finding words. I was relieved she got through her anger before speaking.

She shook her head. My baby, she said. It's too soon. I'm sorry Davey.

Too soon? Too soon means later, as good as a promise. She was so apologetic in her rejection that I was reconciled, more than reconciled, elated, and I went back to my room elated with nothing else on my mind but getting up tomorrow at seven.

Loud knocks in the morning to make sure of it (that was Harry the Enforcer), then loading the bags and leaving the keys at the office, and all the while Judy and I talking small without looking at each other to cover our embarrassment. Then driving, Judy in my car with the baby, Harry leading alone in his, the vacant feeling in our stomachs like a tunnel from our bellies into the earth to China. We ate in the coffee shop in Endicott, waiting for Jefferson's. Judy with a slight shrillness like a diversion from something else teased her father again about his trip to Anchor Island. We went to Jefferson's at nine. Car seats for sale but none to rent. Loomer's mistake. To hell with it, I thought, go ahead with our plans. Which we should have done. But Judy was too scrupulous. I'll buy one, she said. I'll take it home with me. I lingered with them on the sidewalk after they put the new seat in Harry's car and the baby Hazel in the new seat. Saying goodbye. Judy was in a good mood from ragging her father, which made him gruff. Suddenly she put an arm around me. The other arm held the baby. She gave me a kiss, a look in the eye when the kiss was coming, full of acknowledgment and an emotion I'm afraid to name lest I overstate, with the kiss that missed my cheek and landed on my lips for one second, her two lips distinctly felt, and brimming eyes full of the promise I knew now that she had indeed made.

So I left happy, all previous reneging canceled and back to Go. Back to my car with the car seat empty full of reminding.

With cheer now to make the long trip to Bangor happy all day.

I found Jack and Jim's Garage where Loomer said it was, with an orange and white sign. Pumps on the apron in front, the garage back from the street. I went behind the pumps to the garage, a small office, an old man behind a desk. I told him I'm supposed to leave a child seat for Miller Farm and he said, Put it out there.

I leaned into the back of the car to release the car seat. As I lifted it something pressed me in the back. I looked around and saw Loomer leaning over me. Help you, he said. I don't know how pushing me in the back was supposed to help. I brought the seat out while he pushed, I couldn't tell which way. Put it there, he said.

I put it on the ground while they crowded around, more than one person, it seemed like three or four. There was Loomer. There was the kid with the yellow hair who had given us the car seat. They eased me into the passenger side of my car and the door slammed. Loomer got in on the driver's side. The others got in back, though when I looked there was just one, the yellow-haired kid, and if there had been anyone besides him, I never found out. Loomer took the keys out of my hand before I realized he had them. He started the engine.

What's going on?

Relax. The car jerked forward while I looked out and saw the garage man inside at the telephone not noticing us and the car seat on the concrete outside the office. We pulled into the main street of the town and kept going in the direction I had intended to go.

What are you doing?

Relax.

The yellow-haired kid leaned his elbows on the seat back looking at me. I wondered was I being kidnapped and what was holding me? We stopped for a traffic light. Should I jump out? My bag was in the trunk but if I was being kidnapped it was more important to get out. I reached for the door.

Uh-uh, Loomer said. The kid touched my shoulder, the grip strong. Just relax, Loomer said. In the moment it took to confirm that nothing was holding me, in that moment the light changed and Loomer started up and accelerated fast on the road out of town, and now I really was confined in the car.

What are you doing?

We just want a little conversation to clear up a few points.

You're gonna pay, the kid said.

Shut up, Loomer said.

My heart dropped a dead weight, knowing the story wasn't over. I thought of them in Harry's car ignorantly enjoying the happy ending. By the time they found out, it would be too late and they would never know what became of me. No one would ever know, as if I had never lived.

16

Harry Field

At the back country New Hampshire airport, he delivered his car to the agency and Judy and her baby to the gate. Taxi to the bus and bus to Boston, then another bus. He settled into the bus not knowing if he was an adventurer or an idiot.

The problem loomed on the horizon of his stupidity like a New Hampshire mountain. This Lena whom he was going to see didn't know he was coming. He had never answered her letter. This mountain of stupidity, what would he say when he got to Anchor Island if she wasn't there? Or didn't want to see him? Or worse. Worse was possible.

The bus lumbered out to the highway, then high speed through the thick gray day to Boston, taking him away from sanity like a kidnapper. Saying to himself, I am not insane. Hey old man, goes the question, what brought you here? With plenty of leisure in the dead rumble of the bus to think about it. What brought him? Impulse. A moment in the exhilaration of yesterday's happy ending when he was free to do anything he liked. Absolutely anything, Harry. Here you are, alone in the wilds of New England your mission finished and fresh from an interview with God, what would you like to do? The answer jumped from ambush: go to Anchor Island and look up Lena.

Suddenly enough to make him tell Judy and David without reflecting, for reflecting would have made him unfree again. I think I'll take a little side trip to Anchor Island to see an old friend, he said, do you mind? Whereupon he was committed and his freedom vanished anyway. Lost in cause and effect. Leading to here I am Lena, brought by your letter like a missile cross country, fast as I could. Oh God in the bus pounding on the interstate with the sea haze ahead already whitening the sky over the tree line, that wasn't what he meant.

So why hadn't he answered her letter? Not to be too eager, he happily married, she long forgotten. Now instead of a letter or E-mail or fax, he was going to see her in person, looking more than eager rather than less. Plus another problem: he hadn't told Barbara. Having forgotten to mention Lena's letter when it first came. This could be misinterpreted. He should have simply said, Well what do you know, a letter from Lena Fowler after fifty years. Then she could say who's Lena Fowler and he could tell her and she could tell him to answer the letter and they could even discuss whether to make a quick stopover at Anchor Island next summer if they happen to be near. Instead he'll have to tell Barbara there's nothing to be afraid of. He'll have to emphasize like undoing a lie that Lena Fowler means nothing, only old time curiosity. Just a detour since he happened to be in the neighborhood only three hundred miles out of my way, eight hours by bus. What are you curious about? Only what fifty years will do to a person you remember as young. The same years hijacking Lena Fowler into her seventies that hijacked you and me.

With the necessary changes the bus rides from Lebanon to New Dover take the rest of the day. New Dover at nine, then the ferry to Anchor Island. He didn't know the ferry schedule and maybe he'd have to spend the night in New Dover. Maybe in New Dover he could change his mind. Get another bus to New York and take his punishment from Judy. I was mistaken, Judy, a bad idea.

Uncomfortable in the overheated bus, unable to do anything but wait, he tried to remember Lena better. There was a stain on her memory if he could remember it. Two summers of love in Sherwood Forest between college years—one and a half actually because of the breakup. The rest of the year they lived at their respective colleges, writing love letters and being faithful. Her family was new in Sherwood Forest and she was new, they were new, the summers were new, full of aura. Full of electric sex that he called love and she passion, as yet unconsummated moving step by step on a certain inevitable course until she broke it off short for reasons old Harry could not remember. The stain was what he couldn't remember, something about how she broke it off in a huff but no memory of what the huff was about. She left in the middle of the summer without warning, a trip to Europe with her mother on a week's notice or something like that, which made him mad. To old Harry her trip seemed understandable (if her mother wanted to take her why shouldn't she go?) making young Harry look petulant, though in fact it was the end, since afterwards she went straight back to college where she met this lab instructor who was really something. Clark. That was his name, Clark, disclosed in the apologetic letter she eventually wrote. When you say the word fickle, the person Harry thinks of is Lena.

In the three weeks since her new letter his stale old memory twitched into life. Associations brought things back, like how she cried about having to go. They sat in her mother's big old-fashioned parlor with the antique chairs, and she burst into tears. I have to go to Europe with my mother. I'll never see you again. She can't go without me. I have to go because it's the

171

opportunity of a lifetime, Lena said while she sobbed, because how can you pass up the opportunity to see Notre Dame de Paris and the Eiffel Tower with your mother when you're only nineteen? She got huffy only when he complained. What, are you saying I should pass up this opportunity just to stay here with you? So what did she mean about never seeing him again? Irony, exaggeration, frustration, that's all, except it turned out to be true, she never did see him again, because of Clark.

The idea occurred to him even then that she was being whisked off to get away from him, because things were getting too hot. It seemed plausible then and fifty years later it still seemed plausible. In the bus the old narrative woke up like a sleepy tiger, remembering a promise she made. The night before her departure, parked in her car off a country road at the edge of woods in middle Westchester. Things got worked up and she said, If you go to the drugstore tomorrow I promise. Tomorrow night, she said. His memory was distinct, it's the kind of thing you don't forget, and it happened on the night before she went to Europe. Then she reneged. Now that's odd. How could she make such a promise on their last night if there was not to be another night? So it was not the last night but the second to last. Then how did she renege? Apparently—yes—she canceled the last night, the promised one. She couldn't go out with him that night, why? because she had to pack of course, what did you suppose? She had to pack, therefore no last date, only (remembering now) a short trip over to her house in the middle of the evening to interrupt her packing and say goodbye, which he remembered as awkward in the entrance hall of their big warm clock-filled house. Forgetting the promise made in the forgetting that before you go to Europe you've got to pack.

That was the end of the love affair between Harry and Lena. Postcards from London and Paris, sometimes a letter. Back to college, and the letters grew scarce. A letter told why she wasn't coming home for Christmas. Another told him about Clark. She stopped answering his letters, then wrote a long emotional one hoping Harry would find another woman with whom he could be as happy as he had been with her.

Her mother and father, who had moved into Sherwood Forest two years before, moved away. He didn't know where Lena went. If she had married Clark or somebody else or gone into an asylum or died. Fifty years later she found him accidentally in a magazine in the dentist's office, pure luck. It was crazy to go to Anchor Island on the basis of so little.

But the bus goes where it says it goes and there is no way to stop it. Kidnapped. Who's kidnapping me? he thought. Hijacked by the choice he had made in a moment of impulse, by his own mind implemented by the bus driver. The driver chose what routes they took, how fast they went, which cars they passed, when to slow down, shuttling Harry across geography as he willed. Kidnapped by Lena, who had been kidnapped to Europe by her mother and hijacked by Clark. He had kidnapping on his mind. It occurred to him in everything that came up.

A few minutes before nine Harry got off at a steamboat dock smelling of fish, with the lighted island steamer coming in to land. Making it impossible to change his mind now. Though there was a bus to New York waiting on the dock the impossibility was as strong as manacles and chain. The boat was coming fast. Ignoring the pain in his chest and arm, he went to the telephones, found the Anchor Island phone book. He hoped she was not listed but there she was, L F Armstrong, the same address as her letter. He paused to breathe deeply, if this was the heart attack scheduled for him. He put in his quarter. The wind blew the sound of automobiles and baggage wagons around the

173

dock. He punched the buttons, heard the ringing of Lena's phone, while the angina subsided.

Somebody's voice, Hello?

This is Harry Field.

Harry? Harry Field? My God, Harry Field. Where?

At the ferry dock in New Dover.

You came to see me?

Well. He was passing by, just wanted to give you a call.

Will you come over on the ferry? Will you stay here?

Better to stay in a hotel if there is a hotel.

The Anchor Inn, I'll get you a room. I'll meet your boat.

The voice had a masculine edge he didn't remember. Age. He couldn't remember Lena's voice.

He boarded the ferry and went to the forward upper deck to look out. Black dark with lights allocated according to a code of some kind, he couldn't figure out what he was seeing. In a few minutes the true Lena would replace a fifty-year old icon whose paint had peeled. Proximity ignited the still mostly moribund memory like the phoenix, he was surprised how it leaped up. The country road, the parked car tilted on the soft dirt shoulder towards the woods. His hand under her skirt, warm thigh and a hot spot, and her fingers finding him, all in the dark. I can't stand it. Me neither. If you go to the drugstore tomorrow. Tomorrow? I promise. Forgetting that she had to pack.

Remember now how they met, going to summer school in New York, the same class, a coincidence. A literature class taught by Professor Oblong, the name comes back. They commuted on the local train, changing to the elevated at a station called Marble Hill. He noticed her in class before he realized she was from Sherwood Forest. She sat in front, looking young and shy with soft brown hair and a white collar lapped over her sweater. He couldn't remember where he had seen her before. Then when he saw her on the platform at Marble Hill he realized where. You're in Professor Oblong's class. And you live in Sherwood Forest too? My name is. Henceforth they went together on the train and subway every day. They talked about Professor Oblong. His analytical mind, his well-articulated insights, his kindness. Professor Oblong was the first bond between them.

She looked clean and well tended, more short than tall, a thin face with a thoughtful look. She wore a gray flannel skirt and a sweater, changing to white shorts on afternoon outings. He would climb the hill to her house, big on the hillside under two oak trees, and they got in her car and went places. The beach. Bear Mountain. Hikes in the woods, she in her shorts. Her parents belonged to a country club, they threw parties. A new world for him. Summer dances with a band, trumpet and saxophone riffs in the dusky air over the parking lot around the pavilion. Her evening dress, black with a frill, the red corsage he gave her from the florist, and the act of dancing, her forehead on his chin. He wore white pants which his mother ironed and a navy blazer with gold buttons. The glamor dried up long ago but it came back now from thinking. The center from which it radiated was the upstairs playroom of her big house where they spent afternoons left to themselves. He lolled around reading magazines, listening to records. She played Chopin on the upstairs piano, the easier nocturnes and preludes with nostalgia for times before he was born and people never known, mourning the tragedy of life. Her playing was clunky and schoolgirlish, but who cares? The tragedy of life was full of the excitement of approaching sex, one careful step after another. The sex peeped out through their shared admiration for Professor Oblong. After Chopin, Harry lay on the floor of the upstairs playroom, she lay beside him and they talked about Professor Oblong. They signed up for another course from him the second summer. He was even more amazing than before, so amazing they temporarily vowed to make literary study their career.

This devotion to Professor Oblong proved they were serious. It enabled them to do things to each other without feeling crass or wanton. Later, after Harry became Professor Field, it was hard to remember what was so great about Professor Oblong. He became obsolete, but originally he justified their curiosity about what was inside each other's clothes. Their shared admiration of him made that curiosity respectable. They called it love, passion, as they found the things they were looking for bit by bit, not to rush anything. They didn't go all the way, but they talked about it and meanwhile went part way. Then a little further. They went in outdoor places, or in her car, or in the woods or in the upstairs playroom. They went further until there was not much left though it was still not all the way. They talked about where they were going. Talk to me about what you want to do. But we better not. Later maybe. Then came that night in the middle of the second summer, beside the country road where I can't stand it, and she said, Tomorrow, I promise.

Someone was against them, that too came back in the memory surge, though he couldn't remember who, only the vague remembered feeling that he had enemies struggling to possess the mind of Lena Fowler. Then her mother whisked her away to Europe before she could fulfill her promise, which either proved or did not prove he was right about enemies.

The ferry trip was short. A cluster of people on the floodlit dock. A woman waved, greeted him at the gangplank, he didn't recognize her. She had flaring dyed red hair and a long horse-like face, ravaged. Lena?

Harry? You haven't changed a bit.

He was surprised he had never noticed the horsey potential when she was Lena. She was wearing a white T-shirt with a lion on it. She came up to be kissed. She smelled of onions and the kiss was brief.

You came.

Passing through.

She took him to the Anchor Inn where he checked into a room light and plain like a room in the country. It had a view of the harbor lights, where the ferry in its dock blocked out the darkness. She took him to a seafood restaurant for a drink and late snack. He looked for the Lena he remembered in the Lena she had become. She laughed more than she used to. She wasn't shy any more. She was full of opinions. She said how good his horoscope was for this meeting, which shocked and disappointed him thinking, That's the end of you Lena, but he was ashamed of that thought and did not speak. How widely they had diverged. It made him uneasy to be looked at so admiringly. She murmured, I remember, I remember. He indicated that he was happily married. My wife, he said. Barbara. She's in California helping her mother get used to her father's death. I've just been to New Hampshire with my daughter and her baby. I'll tell you about that.

He had an odd feeling she wasn't listening. I remember, I remember, she said.

What do you remember? Lots of things.

I'm a widow, she said. Homer died five years ago. I've developed an interest in everything. She took his hand across the table. Faithful to Barbara, he took it back. I remember, she said. You were my first lover. Boy, were you good. She looked old and wild. Guess what I'm remembering.

What?

Guess.

I don't know.

I'm remembering how good you were.

What do you mean, good?

You were my best lover. Homer was nice, a good husband but he didn't have your touch.

Harry was amazed because it hadn't occurred to him her memory could deceive her on this of all points. It was never consummated, Lena, he said. He tried to say it gently.

What are you talking about?

It never happened.

What do you mean it didn't happen? You were great. All my life I've remembered those nights.

He didn't know what to say. He saw her disappointment like the ferry going aground in the dark.

You say it didn't happen? He didn't reply.

We must rectify that, she muttered. Almost inaudible, is that what he heard? No, he thought violently thinking Barbara's worst fears, but not sure what to say since she said it so low.

She turned her face and smiled and said, Oh well, thereby turning into Lena exactly as remembered except for the bulldozing of her face. What happened to us? she said.

Don't you remember?

I met somebody. Clark, that's who. He was good too.

You went off to Europe in the middle of the summer and that was that.

So I did. Europe, I remember that, she said delighted like a child. You were furious.

I got over it.

She sat there looking at her past, and it made her laugh. Alice Trent, she said. I haven't thought of her in years.

What, Alice Trent? That was a name like an explosion out of a crypt bricked up by Edgar Allan Poe. Unpleasant associations, full of menace though nothing specific yet. Who was Alice Trent?

She's the reason I went to Europe. That was so funny.

Funny, was it funny? He remembered Alice Trent, her mother's musical friend. The short trim woman in her forties, with dark eyebrows, a rouged complexion, a cigarette, a knowing look, who played the piano. Who was always there. While they enjoyed each other in the upstairs playroom they would hear her music floating up from the downstairs piano. Sometimes the music would stop, which made them nervous. She appeared unexpectedly through doors and whenever she looked at Harry there was a bit of a smile not wholly friendly like I know what you're up to. Once she discovered them more exposed than they should be. Button up kids, she said, the folks are on the way. This would make you think she was on their side, but she made him uncomfortable. He didn't think she was on his side.

Actually he hated Alice Trent, mainly because Lena thought she was so wonderful. She's the model of what I want to be, Lena would say. He was ashamed of his dislike because he thought it came from his vanity, wishing she thought him as wonderful. But then she told him about the advice Alice Trent was giving her and it was mostly against him. She says we must not let ourselves get more steamed up than we already are, Lena said. Well for Christ sake how steamed up did you say we were? I told her the truth, Lena said. You told her we did this? Uh-huh. And Alice Trent advised us to stop? Well what else could she advise? We should exercise, ride bikes and go on hikes, outdoors, things with friends. She's not a pill, she's a sophisticated woman of the world, she knows a lot more about life than you do, and her advice was take my time before getting too entranced over any man including you. As for sex, according to Alice Trent, what young girls think is going to be so great, it ain't what it's cracked up to be. It's a crude exercise, Alice Trent told her. You'll be happier if you postpone it. Some women

never need it at all and it's natural to feel disgusted and humiliated. Especially humiliated, Alice Trent told Lena (and Lena
passed on to Harry). It's different for a woman from what it is
for a man.

One day near the end Alice Trent got tough. You're heading
for trouble girl, she said. You've got to stop it. Curb his selfish
appetite. More, worse. She told Lena that Harry didn't love her.
Never mind what he tells you, a young man that age is not
capable of love. The sex urge is too strong, he can't think of
anything else. What he's got is lust, what he wants is sex, that's
what you mean to him, and you mustn't believe him when he
calls it love.

No wonder he thought of her as his enemy. He tried his best
but he couldn't prove it wasn't lust because it was. He fought for
his self-respect, trying to find a way to fit lust into self-respect,
and when Lena made her promise that very night after telling
him of Alice's warnings, he thought he had won, and when she
reneged the next and final night, he was bitterly not surprised.
All of which he remembered now that Lena herself admitted
Alice Trent was the cause of their breakup fifty years ago. I
knew it, he said. What's funny about it?

The futility, Lena said.

What futility?

Everybody trying to protect somebody from the malign
influence of somebody else so they can exert their own malign
influence. It's a universal truth.

What malign influence do you mean?

Why I went to Europe. You knew why, didn't you?

Knew what? Why you went to Europe?

You didn't know that while Alice Trent was trying to protect
me from sex, Daddy was trying to protect Mother from Alice
Trent?

What?

This was exciting, the possibility of learning news fifty years old with Lena polishing the gleam of gossip that made her shine like the horsey old sun. And even though it was fifty years dead the narrative tension (or something else) made Harry's weak old heart pound as he waited to hear like the news of the day. What are you talking about?

My father sent my mother to Europe with me to rescue her from Alice Trent, Lena said. Alice Trent had my mother under a spell like Svengali, is that who I mean, Rasputin, is that the one, Diaghilev? Alice Trent was having an affair with my mother is what I mean. (Really?) When Daddy found out, he blew his stack. His gasket, whatever it is men blow.

You never told me about that.

I was embarrassed in those days. But that's why we went to Europe if you didn't know.

Why did that make you go to Europe?

It's like Henry James all over again. Daddy told my mother get away from that woman, take the keys and take our daughter to Europe. Cool off like healthy exercise. He didn't put it like that, he put it nicely. A gift my mother couldn't refuse.

You could have told me that's why you went.

No I couldn't. I had to protect my mother's reputation. Do you want to know the joke?

What joke?

Alice Trent went with us. Daddy paid our way and she paid her own and joined us in London. That kind of pissed Daddy off.

I guess it would.

When we got back, Mother went to live with Alice and Daddy married Lily Moon from Las Vegas, which I see no reason to tell you about.

Meanwhile, Harry said, you went back to college and found what's his name.

Clark. He was really good, but then I married Homer. Now I've found you. Thank God for that. I've got you back and I'll never let you go again.

Wait a minute.

You're married. Kids and grandkids. All I mean is, we're reconciled. Is it all right to say that?

Sure.

I'm lonely, she said. Everybody's dead.

It's too bad.

Homer died. So did Rosalie. My mother. My father. Clark. Even Alice Trent. Everybody but you.

Do you have children?

So I'm told. I hear from them at Christmas.

I'm sorry.

Have you ever been unfaithful to your wife?

He tried to remember if Lena in the old days asked blunt questions.

No.

Good boy. Will you spend the night?

No. I should go back to the hotel.

Will you stay a while and let me talk? I have a lifetime of things to tell you. Don't you?

Maybe. Do you remember Professor Oblong? he said.

Who?

Professor Oblong? Our teacher in summer school.

Never heard of him. Did we go to summer school?

That's how we met.

I thought we met at a party.

We met in Professor Oblong's summer school class.

If you say so, she said. Aren't you curious to know about Homer?

Tell me about him.

She talked about Homer and he lost his way following. At midnight she took him to his hotel after telling him all there was to know about Homer and Clark and her daughter who died and Anchor Island and the Anchor Island Senior Society and annuities and retirement plans. Also her membership in the Society of Mystics and her classes in astrology. He kept his opinions of these things to himself and wondered what she would think when he told her. He wondered if there was anything he wanted to tell her. The incentive had disappeared. There was one thing. He wanted to tell her about the kidnapping of Judy's baby, and maybe she would be interested to hear about the man who called himself God. Save that for tomorrow.

He had forgotten to call Barbara. Too late tonight, he thought, forgetting that it was only nine-thirty in California.

17

Nick Foster

Loomer said if we want to catch him we must get up good and early. It was shiny on the tree branches and foam on the bushes and we ate in the mess hall and got into the pickup truck. We went to Jake's and Jim's. A man with a white beard. Loomer said gonna leave our truck here a few days. Guy come in a few minutes delivering a child seat. Tell him put it on the sidewalk.

Tuneup your truck the man said.

Nah.

Takin up space. That'll cost you.

I'll pay. Miller Farm you know what that is.

Never heard of it.

You will some day.

You want to leave it put it over there.

I think we'll sit in it a while first Loomer said.

We sat in the pickup truck over there.

Two things can happen Loomer said. He come with the woman and old man and baby and the other car or he come by hisself. If he come with the other folks we chase him later down the road. If he come alone we catch him here.

Catch him I said.

Do you know what to do. When he come back to the car crowd him. Make him get in the other side. You get in back to watch him.

Crowd him I said.

We waited a long time. Bastard Loomer said. He looked at his watch. The white car drove up and parked in front of the office. The brown man got out and went in. Black bastard Loomer said.

He looked brown. Oliver said he was black too so I must be wrong.

Brown or black Loomer said. Black brown yellow red they're all black in the eyes of God.

He came out of the office and opened his back door. He's getting the car seat. Let's go. Don't get excited just amble.

We ambled. The brown black man name David Leo pulled the car seat out of the back. He put it on the ground. Loomer opened the door and we crowded. He looked around and we pushed. Loomer slammed the door and I got in back. I leaned forward with my hands and Loomer got in the driver's side. He started the car.

What is this David said.

Nice going Nicky Loomer said.

I did a good job. It feels good when I do a good job.

I looked back and saw the car seat on the concrete in front of Jake and Jim's office. I couldn't remember who was supposed to pick it up. I asked Loomer.

Forget it he said. Somebody will find a use for it.

The car seat on the sidewalk made me sad. I felt like crying.

Loomer drove and I sat behind David. I was supposed to watch him and grab him around the neck if he made a move. I kept watching him to make a move. I grabbed his shoulders. Once he leaned forward and I caught him by the neck in my elbow. Jesus he said.

You're not supposed to make a move.

We're going sixty what could I do.

We drove fast on this road with not many cars. There were trees and a valley with mountains and the road had a yellow line in the middle. The mountains stopped and there were fields and ditches and towns. The towns didn't last long. Sometimes in a town there was a traffic light. There was a brick building with square towers and rows of windows that Loomer said was a factory. In a town there was flags hanging from a rope across the street.

Loomer said I didn't need the handcuffs so I didn't. The handcuffs were in my pocket. Loomer said he had the handcuffs from his police days. He had his gun from his police days. I don't know where the gun was. He said he took it when he quit. He had a radio from his police days. Also the black stick. I don't know where the radio was. He had the stick when we crowded David. I didn't know where the stick was now.

David said you can't do this to me. He said it a lot.

Shut up I said.

Loomer said you did call off your FBI man didn't you.

I wish I hadn't David said.

Don't you worry Davey boy it's all for the best. For justice and to satisfy Nicky here. You met Nicky. Say hello Nicky.

Hello I said.

We're taking you to trial Loomer said. It's known to the legal world as a sub peony it's a game of tag. The bailiff give you the sub peony and if he find you you gotta go and if he don't find you you don't gotta. You heard of that.

Sounds familiar David said like laughing. Not happy laughing some other kind.

Well you're the unlucky this time we caught you and now you gotta go. If we didn't catch you don't gotta go but here you are bound by the sub peony because we're taking you to trial.

What trial.

Your trial man. Your opportunity to answer the charges against you.

What charges.

Tell him Nicky.

I don't know I said.

Come on boy. He's a little hard of remembering and a little shy too Loomer said. He thinks you killed his mentor Oliver Quinn so that's what the trial is about.

I didn't kill Oliver. I had nothing to do with it.

Nick don't believe you. That's why we need a trial. He say you did it you say you didn't. The trial is to ascertain the true facts as opposed to the other kind.

It's ridiculous. I didn't kill Oliver I was nowhere near him.

Exactly why we need a trial.

You want a trial get me some real police and a lawyer. This is kidnapping.

Your trial is perfect to fit the crime and the charge. You couldn't find a fairer trial in the world.

I'm glad to hear that. Are you going to tell me where we're going. Miller Farm's back that way.

Ain't going to Miller Farm. Too crowded. Change of venue you know that term. A neutral venue quiet and secluded. Wouldn't you rather have a neutral venue for your trial.

Who's going to be the judge in this trial of yours.

Trial of yours. The judge. Why Nick and me a two-man panel we'll judge you two for one make the trial twice as fair.

You're the accusers. You can't be the judge.

A fair-minded person can be anybody trust us. I'm not accusing you Nicky is.

David turned and looked at me.

Why are you accusing me he asked.

I didn't like it when he looked at me.

Tell what you saw Loomer said.

When.

When you was in the woods when Oliver got killed.

I saw you I said.

Who Davey.

I saw you. I meant Loomer I saw Loomer.

Not that. Tell how you know Davey killed Oliver.

You told me I said.

Whoa hey I didn't tell you you saw it yourself. What did you see.

I couldn't remember what was right to say and what was not. I forget I said.

No you don't. You saw Davey push Oliver over the waterfall and down he fall. Never mind. We'll have your testimony tomorrow and then the judges will get together to decide who's telling the truth. Davey or Nicky. The sole witnesses. Ain't that fair.

A car came up behind with its siren going. Uh-oh Loomer said. Hang on to our prisoner. He slowed down.

No monkey business he told David. Nicky's got a gun in your back and he's not afraid to shoot a cop if he has to.

What gun I said. I don't have no gun.

Shh. I forgot. Nicky don't have the gun I do. It's my old police gun and I'm the one who ain't afraid to shoot a cop if I have to. You don't want that on your conscience do you. If you have any doubts I give you my solemn word of honor and oath your trial will be as fair as a trial can be.

The cop came to the window.

Let me show you my ID Loomer said. Miller Church Farm

Wicker Falls New Hampshire. As you can see I'm an ordained minister. I was hurrying to help someone in my flock.

The cop peeked in the window and looked at us.

Sorry Reverend the cop said.

When he was gone Loomer said they always let me off with a warning. How about that Nicky don't you think that was a manifestation of the power of the Lord. The principle of narrow escape. Too bad Davey, look like you run into the principle of reverse narrow escape because if we hadn't connect just right back there we'd be having our trial without you and you'd never know what you escaped.

We drove on. Sometimes we talked sometimes we didn't. Once they talked about me.

Loomer said this Nicky who's watching to make sure you don't get stupid this Nicky's a sweet gentle kid ain't you Nicky.

I'm not a kid I said.

What I mean he loves babies wouldn't hurt a fly unless the Lord tell him right about that Nicky.

Right about that.

I heard your Oliver tell me when you was bringing that baby to Miller Farm three days and nights on the road you took as good care of that baby as any mama that right Nicky.

I liked that. I took good care I said.

A man of instinct Loomer said. I recommend him to you Davey if ever you need a man of instinct. He tended that baby and changed its diaper and rocked it to sleep just like its natural mama right Nicky.

Right.

So ever you need a mama for your kid if your real mama too busy just call up Nicky he be glad to obliged.

Glad to obliged I said.

Sometimes we didn't talk. Then we talked again. Loomer asked David what you think of Miller.

I have no opinion I never talked to him David said.

But your friend did. Fieldsy. They had a long talk. So what did he think of Miller.

He thinks Miller is intelligent and original but insane.

What. After talking to Miller half the day a privilege his truest disciples are seldom granted Fieldsy thinks Miller's insane.

I noticed Loomer's words were surprised but Loomer wasn't. I notice that with Loomer. He doesn't sound like what he's saying.

Christ David said. The man claims to be God.

If anybody else claimed to be God he'd be insane. Not Miller because Miller is God.

You believe that too.

What's belief Loomer said. What's love. What's goodness. What's justice. What's God. Those words have big meanings man.

We stopped talking and then we talked again. Who's your guru Loomer said. This Fieldsy is he your guru.

I have no guru.

Bullshit man your leader teacher mentor. You judge each man by his guru so who's yours.

Professor Field is a fine teacher I owe him a lot but he's not a guru.

Everybody needs a mentor. If you don't have a mentor what happens Nicky.

I don't know.

Nicky don't know. Nicky never know. He wouldn't know a damn thing without a mentor to tell him. Neither would you. Nobody would. You gotta have a mentor how you get from being a puppy to a grownup dog.

A puppy would turn into a grownup dog mentor or not no matter what you do.

That's instinct. Two sides. Instinct and mentor. Nick's got instinct and needs mentor. Otherwise he don't know what to do. Do you Nick.

No.

The world need mentors and it need disciples. If they wasn't disciples the world go to hell. Everybody against everybody doggy dog. Chaos and murder and Nick going around not knowing what to do. That's the point of Miller a good strong mentor. The strong mentor he bind people together what to think. The disciples learn what to think from the mentor all think the same gives them strength. Strength from unity e pluribus unum you break sticks one at a time but not in a bundle. What do you say Davey man.

That's a fascist philosophy.

Whoa watch them names. It's simple common sense and religious truth if you ain't willing to submit your self to a mentor greater than you and look up to him like God you're a rat in the sewer liable to swept away in the garbage and human waste.

In the academic world we teach people to think for themselves David said.

That's dumb. You don't control nobody that way.

I don't want to control anybody.

That's because you're the natural disciple type. Me I'm watching for Miller to falter. He ain't young and one of these days he's going to be replaced.

I thought you said he was God.

He's God like on lease before time run out. Incarnation eventual he'll be replaced. My disciples will be a somewhat more active bunch than the present ones.

You're going to usurp the throne.

You ain't listening. Not usurp. Take over when Miller is ready peaceful. You want everybody to think for theirselves that's dumb you ask me. Could Nick think for himself. What do you think Nicky would you like to think for yourself.

No.

See. If all the Nickys of the world learned to think for themselves what a mess. What we need is a strong God to keep everybody in their place. If Miller ain't up to the job here I am. I strongly advise you to break your ties with Fieldsy before it's too late.

The trip got long. It got longer and longer the longer we drove the longer the trip got. I was getting tired looking at the back of the black man's head all the time. Sometimes the world folded over. It turned and folded inside itself so you could pull the inside and put it on the outside. My head tossed around. Loomer and David changed places David driving Loomer in front of me and I looked and they were back the way they were before. There was a big airplane noise and the planes were coming down to land one on top of another with the sirens going and I looked and the field outside was just like it was before the airplanes and I don't know where they all went.

Your man has fallen asleep. I heard David say that. He was on top of the house looking down where I was trying to crawl under the front porch. I could take advantage of you now couldn't I he said. I'm not asleep I tried to say from under the porch but I couldn't make the words come out. They were hard words and I had to push hard to make anything happen though I thought the words clearly. I thought them loud but I couldn't make the sound come. Wake up Nicky don't be an idiot I heard Oliver talking only it wasn't Oliver it was Loomer and then the car was exactly the way it was before we were going fast through a village with white houses and a gas station and a flag and I don't know what happened to the porch and the roof. I looked to see if the black man was laughing because I thought he was but I couldn't see when I looked.

Where the hell are you taking me he said.

It's called Stump Island Loomer said. It's an outpost.

Christ I've been there David said. He laughed. Loomer laughed. I don't know what they were laughing about.

The road ended. There was water in front of us. There was a dock and a gas pump and a building with windows and a porch. We got out. Keep your hold on him Loomer said. He went from the upper dock to the one below. He talked to a man.

Bring him down he said.

We got into a rowboat with an outboard motor. I had never been in a boat before. I hoped it wouldn't sink.

He pulled at the outboard motor. He kept pulling.

Don't show the gun just keep it. Ribs is best. You won't try to escape will you Davey.

He pulled the outboard motor. It began. It made a noise under the water and over it too. It was not as loud as a lawn mower. I used to pull the lawn mower. It was hard the same way.

The sky was the color of my aunt's silver polish when I helped in the kitchen. The boat went. We went way out. There were bunches of trees sticking up in the water with rocks around them. The waves went up and down. The boat went swish through the water and the water turned white and green. It had big white eyes looking up at you.

We got off at Stump Island. I had never been to Stump Island. We walked through the woods to an open place with a house and another building shaped like a great big slinky except straight. We went into the house. We had a picnic.

It was time to sleep. It's your job to watch him Loomer said. Don't fall asleep a sentry never sleeps.

I sat down in the corner of the room with a gun Loomer found. It was a rifle. I sat it across my lap while David curled up in a corner and went to sleep and I tried to watch him in the dark and not fall asleep.

In the middle of the night the rifle went bang and jumped me up. A match lit and David sat up like a raccoon in the garbage and Loomer in his underwear with a lamp. What happened.

I don't know I said. The gun went off.

What made it go off.

It went off by itself I said.

Be careful with it Loomer said. Trial in the morning. We don't want anybody miss that.

18

Lena Fowler Armstrong

Harry says we didn't and I thought we did, so who's wrong? He sleeps in his hotel a few blocks away while I wait in bed until it's time to get up. Even after fifty years, how could he forget the trellis, the car, the front room when Mother was out?

My mistake. Merging Harry all preparation with Clark all fulfillment. First one, then the other. Plus Ted before either of them. I remember now. It was because I never told Harry about Ted, allowing him to believe me virgin like himself. No such drag on Clark, who knowing all went zip to the point. Imagine forgetting that Harry was Harry and Clark Clark. I suppose I never did tell Harry about Ted, so to this day he thinks. Never mind. My, how memory returns when you look at it.

If he didn't know about Alice Trent and Mother no wonder he thought I panicked because of sex. He wouldn't have thought that if he knew about Ted. But his own panic about rectifying the omission makes me wonder why he came, taking all that trouble which I didn't ask for.

The brightening sky, the house on the harbor bluff which I can see from the bed. Plan the day for Harry, at least he'll stay over a second night. If I don't scare him again.

When he walked off the boat, I looked for a ripened facsimile of the guy I remembered. It didn't occur to me he'd look like a seventy-year old man, though I knew he would. I recognized him and thereafter couldn't remember what he used to look like. The old Harry who was young swallowed by the new who is old. He had more trouble recognizing me. So have I changed more than he? My red hair. My adornments. In the restaurant I saw him searching me for the sweet shy child we both used to know. I don't know where she went. Truth is, I don't remember him very well either. Mainly I thought he was nice and we got along all right. I thought I was in love but I don't remember why.

Seven-thirty at last and I call him at his hotel. Woke him, I guess, his voice froggy and confused. Sorry, Harry. I wake so early these days, then lie in bed waiting for the rest of the world. The reason for my call, to invite you to breakfast.

He comes to the house looking good for seventy. Out of breath from walking, not so good. We sit on the sun porch. He's embarrassed, I must relax to relax him. He notices my silverware in the sun, the view of my trellised garden, the mirrored globe, bird bath, feeders. I see him thinking. It occurs to him I'm rich. He wonders would he have been rich if he had married me?

My robe is red, my furry slippers peek out under the hem. I see myself in his thought as he looks at me and murmurs politely. Too polite to tell me how grotesque I look. The paleness of my face against my lipstick like a clown. He keeps looking for old Lena. My hair flares out, my body hangs like canvas on my bones.

I was the girl with the soft brown bangs. My large blue eyes go pop. I used to lean forward familiarly, charming, now my face looks like a horse over the stable gate. There's a hump in my shoulders, not conspicuous, but he sees it. I was hoping he wouldn't. I would like to smile at him. Harry, I say. My voice sounds like a man's. It was a mistake to bring him here. Why has age treated me so much worse than him?

The thought makes me mad, a familiar irritation. I am infinitely superior to when I was twenty.

What will I do with you today, Harry? Our horoscopes are auspicious. He winces, warning me, be careful about something. All the things that may have happened to Harry that I know nothing of. First I'll drive you around the island. You can read the *Times* while I get dressed. Do the puzzle if you like.

Upstairs naked in the mirror I squint to blur the view. My face is more battered than the rest of me, otherwise you might have trouble guessing my age. If you ignore my breasts and shoulders and arms and legs and hump. Dim the focus. The dark is best for both of us.

Lena the good hostess. Down I come to him on the sun porch, dressed in white pants and a Mexican cape of spicy colors. Turban around my hair and red rimmed sunglasses. Car to the village. Along the shore in front of the affluent beach cottages to where the road crosses to the other side. The sandy parking space for the beach out to the point. The houses behind us and the dunes, almost out of sight. Step out and walk? Foggy over the water, and though the opposite shore is not far you can't see it today. The beach is cold this time of year, the wind blows, Harry pulls his jacket around him. It doesn't affect me. I'm probably healthier than he. Shivering on the sand in his jacket, he bulges. Old men are bigger than young, their necks are thicker. He'll probably have a potbelly like a pregnant woman when I get him out of his clothes, if I do. He'll be at least as embarrassed about that as I'll be about my paps unless his male vanity blinds him. If it does, educate him. Show him his ugliness first, then show it doesn't matter.

I don't care. He follows me onto the sand. It seeps into our shoes. He shivers and huddles, I swing my arms and stick my head up addressing the shrieking terns. I charge him where he stands reluctantly in the sand. He thinks I'm going to grab him and dodges like a quarterback avoiding a sack. He laughs but doesn't like it, I see it in his face like a moralist. Too old to be playful, he puffs. Too cold for you? Back to the car.

Come, I'll show you the town. The Whale Shop with posters and scrimshaw and fish nets. Pots and model seagulls. Introduce Marjorie Billings. Meet Harry, I say. My old boyfriend, he precedes not only Homer but even Clark. So glad to meet you, she says. Harry tilts his head cute, like Dopey or Bashful.

Fifteen Minutes of Fame, shop full of blouses and sweaters and silk things purple violet and orange. Pennants and turbans. Meet my first love, I tell the girls. Think of that. When your first love comes back fifty years later, I say, remember us.

On the sidewalk he remonstrates. Really, Lena, he says, it's not as if I were free.

Well, we'll think about that. I take his arm and sweep him into Gordman's. Sporting goods. Girls, my oldest and dearest friend. Linda and Lucille look at him shrewdly. Isn't he sweet? I say. Well young man, Linda says, take good care of Lena, she deserves all the good care she can get. Aren't friends nice?

Library, beauty salon. Art store, where I get my supplies. He doesn't know I paint, so I tell him. Oils and watercolors. I also weave and embroider. I quit the piano, arthritic fingers.

Suddenly it's lunch time. Mrs. O'Bannon's Tea House, with the gazebo view over the harbor, where the ferry comes in, loads, and goes out again. I explain vibrations and emanations. Radiations which no scientific instrument has picked up because science hasn't yet discovered the medium in which they travel.

His skeptical look is normal for one who has worn the blinders of science for fifty years. The question is whether this has ruined his open-mindedness. We're talking about the spiritual realm, I explain. It's outside science because science is physical whereas spirit by definition is non-physical. It has its own science, spiritual science, which is what interests me.

He eats his eclair with a funny look on his face. I hear a word that sounds like "bullshit." What did you say? It couldn't be that. He stitches a hem into his voice with a look saying, You don't really believe that stuff, do you?

Harry, I tell him, it's my life.

Oh dear. See how his eyes disappear into his forehead, gesture sweeping away flies, expression like despair. Oh dear, how are we going to get around a little chasm like this?

No words for a while.

Are you one of these science bigots? I ask.

Bigots? he exclaims. That stirs him. The flare of rage out beyond rage snorting like dragon fire, what can I do but laugh? The laughter quenches the fire and he sinks.

Has a gap opened between us in the last fifty? I say.

How can an intelligent woman like you believe that stuff?

What stuff are you calling stuff?

What are we talking about? Astrology?

Absolutely.

What else? Crystals?

I maintain an open mind.

Spiritualism? Mediums? Trances, sessions around a table? Lena, he says. I can't begin to tell you what I think about such things.

You don't have to, I know what you think. You used to have more imagination, I say. I'm sorry this has happened to you.

He draws his breath to explain the basis of science but stops, seeing it won't do any good.

We don't have to agree if we love each other, I say.

He brushes at the flies in his head. He's just been interviewing a man who calls himself God, he says.

You mean his name is Mr. God or he thinks he's the deity?

His name is Miller and he thinks he's the deity. He lives at Miller Farm with his followers, who agree with him that he's God. I ask how he snookered them into that and Harry asks why I believe my crystals but not Miller. I need to see for myself, I say. So how did this Miller get his followers to follow?

There are enough fools around for every charlatan, he says.

At the table in the bay window of Mrs. O'Bannon's Tea Room while the other guests disperse and waitresses clear their tables, Harry tells me about a man named Oliver who stole Harry's granddaughter and took her to Miller who calls himself God. Also a young black wooer who went in pursuit and saw Oliver fall mysteriously to his death down a waterfall. Then Harry himself went to Miller to get the child back, and Miller gave him the opportunity to ask God all the questions he ever wanted to ask.

It sticks in my mind like a crippled kite on the wires, the idea of asking a man who claims to be God everything you ever wanted to know about God.

The Daisy Girls meet at three-thirty. I leave Harry to entertain himself. Tonight I'll cook him a wonderful dinner. When I go, he's on the couch in my west-facing living room where the sun is bright on my furniture and curtains in shades of white. Go ahead, he says, I'll be fine.

My mind wanders through Mrs. Manchester's paper. I can't tell you what it's about while I think about sex like a girl. Not quite a girl. For the record, if we didn't do it then, make up for it now. To complete the list. That's how men think, right, Harry? Like having a trip to Europe in your history to look back upon. You've seen plenty of pictures of the back of Notre Dame, so it isn't as if you don't know what it looks like. But the record says you were there, and that's what counts.

At some point he'll talk about his wife. Her name, Sheila, Beatrice, escapes me. There are two possibilities. His marriage is breaking up and our old engagement is about to be fulfilled. Or we've reached the age where sex no longer matters. Marriages as old as his like an oak tree indifferent to games in its shade. His wife Sheila Beatrice Barbara (it comes back) has been away a few weeks. She won't care as long as we don't chop down the oak. Which is it? By tonight I'll know.

We can avoid the chasm by not mentioning it. Censor myself for a night. After censoring myself for Homer all those years.

Back from the Daisy Girls I find Harry asleep in the chair, his mouth open, the *New York Times* sliding off his knees. He looks old and dead, so why was I fancying romantic thoughts? The crossword is unfinished, he fell asleep in the middle. He pops awake, startled, apologetic. I laugh.

I cook dinner while Harry sits on a stool in the kitchen. Hustle like my mother, though I'm more organized than she. Harry on his stool is a child, converted from an old man. It's the route to death, a U-turn you make somewhere in old age to zip childward back to the universe gate.

He talks about a paper he wrote attacking everything I believe in. You're too old for me to educate, I tell him. We have lots in common anyway. If we can make our memories agree. Our good nature and tolerance of difference. I don't mind if you're a science bigot as long as you don't argue with me. He laughs at that. As long as you don't convert me, he says.

While we talk I wait for his news, the real reason for visiting me on Anchor Island. The break in his marriage or some other break. It doesn't come. I catch his unspoken thought. He's holding back his news until he can unite an old image with what he sees of me now. He remembers the summer haze trembling in the hot tar at the Marble Hill station. He remembers the summer afternoons buzzing in my mother's living room and a certain girl timorously interested. He remembers the rich summer foliage of Sherwood Forest-on-Hudson like a green stain in the air. I see it in the old man's head while he sits on the stool.

Meanwhile I work, demonstrating what an able woman I am. I tell him my life. The heart attack that killed Homer and liberated me. The three world-traveling children, with achievements for the annual xeroxed Christmas letter. I tell him my cooking skills, my dinners, entertainments to conceal from the snoopy public the state of things between Homer and me. Harry says I have turned into a different woman. Though he doesn't elaborate, I know what he sees: the seasoned woman of life I've become, hearty and sensible. I see the shift in his emanations. He is surprised to realize he likes me. Not the magic girl of long ago but the present me, the woman he sees before him. He likes me.

At last he talks about his family. Barbara, Judy, Baby Hazel, Barbara's old mother in San Diego. Still the news doesn't come. A perfect home, ideal children and wife. I approve, admiring whom he admires, how happy to have such nice folks.

He boasts about his career. Tedious but a good sign. His vita, his awards, his books. Promises to send copies. I lose details in the proliferation, he'll think I wasn't listening, and in truth I am too busy not burning something on the stove.

He has his vanity, but he is milder than Homer. Life with him would have been less tempestuous. We would not have had the fights, at least not the shouting and screaming. Life with him would have been duller, but I would have welcomed the peace, unless I needed to go through Homer in order to appreciate it.

As he talks I detect the melting of his resistance. Not from his words, just my intuition picking up a warmth in the old man that he hasn't felt in maybe years. He is converting the magic girl of memory into me, with a spontaneous erection as he sits on the kitchen stool amazed at his luck.

I don't actually see the erection. It's concealed in his clothes and I couldn't see it unless I made him stand up. But I don't have to see to know there's an erection in the room.

Dinner's ready. I light the candles. We sit on two sides around a corner of the table. He compliments me on the elegance. The tastiness too, yum yum. Lena, this is really good.

Don't ask if it's better than Barbara's.

Eat and talk, all energy now, free enough even to joke about our astrological differences if we don't follow up. His conversation with Miller God and my collection of Angel Voices. He doesn't believe in voices and I ask are Bernadette of Lourdes and Joan of Arc liars? All the visions of Mary, and he says something disrespectful, but it doesn't matter now. I wonder if I can count on him to make the first move. If he doesn't I'll have to. I need to think up a move since time is roaring now.

Dinner done, clear the table, while time shrieks like a dishwasher. Load it up, do the pots and pans, put things away. Back and forth in the kitchen, dodging collisions, avoiding opportunities to touch because it hasn't been brought up yet. We are now crossing a field between the woods, after which.

Living room, sit down. My God I'm trembling. How calm he looks, more than before, a bad sign if it means he has given up the idea. Leaving it to me. Why am I trembling, I with my rich and rewarding love life? Is it all behind me now?

How to do it? Old and wise, the simplest way just ask. Else surrender to death which is on its way. We're on the couch. A snifter of brandy, another tactic. Harry beside me where I patted the seat when he tried to sit in the opposite chair.

Take a breath. Do it.

Harry, I say. Will you go to bed with me?

Pop eyes. Shock, fear. Oh dear.

Oh my, he says.

Tragic though it be, I laugh. No? I say.

Back off, divert the embarrassment before it's a flood. That's all right, I understand.

I'm an ugly old hag. The emanations of his disgust, automatic repugnance. It burns me up. If I'm an ugly hag, he's a scarecrow. Who the hell does he think he is, to think he's more attractive than I? He didn't say that, be fair. If I asked he would say it's his wife. So much for finding out what brought him to Anchor Island.

He's worrying about my feelings. Before he leaves he repeats: Don't think I wouldn't want to.

So I try again. Don't want to change your mind? I say, bright and smiley. I shouldn't have said it. The terror which is impossible to conceal, with its humiliation for me.

Pretending nothing happened, off he goes to his hotel, that is, I drive him there. We'll see each other once more only in this life, which is tomorrow at breakfast. I'll have breakfast with him at the hotel and drive him to the ferry.

In the night I take it back. Perhaps he knows he's a scarecrow and thinks I'm a bird. Sea bird. The egret of regret.

At breakfast, I apologize for being impetuous and embarrassing him. I was foolish, I say. He mumbles, still no more articulate than last night though he can talk about anything else.

Actually during the night, it was not Harry on my mind but Miller who calls himself God. The boldness hooks me under the gills. The very idea makes Harry look like a dead fish. Harry, I say. What would Miller do if I paid him a visit?

Harry's bewilderment. You want to visit him?

People like that interest me.

He's a fake, Harry says.

Fake or not. He's a shaman. Gifted with spirit. So full of spirit he doesn't know how to contain it. I want to see him.

You're the epitome of tolerance, Harry says. You accept everything with no discrimination at all.

No I don't. I want to know everything. How does Miller confront the great religions of the world?

He ignores them.

Because I care about God, I say. I love my God. Don't you?

Harry is puzzled. How can you love something so abstract?

Gratitude, I tell him. Isn't it obvious.

Gloomy Harry, God is so cruel, he says.

That's what Jesus is for, I say. Now I want to see Miller. I want to find out what he knows. Why should you be the one to talk to him? I'm the one who can learn from him.

Well, Harry says. I wish you luck.

19

David Leo

They took me back to Stump Island that I never hoped to see again. Going to my trial. Late in the afternoon under a sky full of high gloom in a boat with an outboard motor almost swamped in the black resisting sea. Windy. Cold. I held my knapsack in my lap not to get it wet in the bottom of the boat. The cold made holes and crawled into my windbreaker.

We ate on the island, burgers from shore. Kerosene lamps in the empty house. Then only sleep because Loomer didn't want the trial until tomorrow. I in a sleeping bag in an empty room guarded by Nick, who had a rifle in his lap. I considered how to escape. Outwit my captors and dash through the woods to the boat. Best bet, wait until Nick fell asleep, then grab the rifle. They'd come after me with guns, and I'd have to get that engine going. I was tired of heroics, sick of adventure. I thought these people are insane, I am going to die, and nobody knows, nobody cares. How could I have been such an idiot as to be here, how could I have avoided it? I thought Loomer had something up his sleeve, but it wouldn't help me. I gave up trying to wait out Nick, who was still awake when I fell asleep.

In the middle of the night the rifle went off. It was nice in the dark after the bang with Loomer yelling before he could light the lamp, and Nick yelling back and Loomer cussing when the match went out. Loomer was pissed off but Nick was cool. He said the rifle went off by itself.

In the morning Loomer cooked eggs on a wood fire, a stack of firewood next to the house. Best breakfast I ever had in such conditions. After breakfast he sent me out to shit, we'd have the trial when I was done. The outhouse smelled like summer camp, the pine needles and the soaked dead leaves on the ground, which would have been nice except for the conditions. The trouble with the conditions was I had nothing to compare this with and therefore no idea how it would come out. A game. My death. They did give us the baby back. I wondered why.

They had the trial in the building that looked like a wind tunnel, a corrugated aluminum cylinder with a big open space inside. Dead farm implements. A box of crutches in the corner.

A gouged table in the middle. Loomer sat in an old armchair at one end, Nick and I on wooden folding chairs, Nick next to him and I across. Rifle leaning on Loomer's chair.

Oyez oyez, Loomer said. Davey, you're charged with killing Oliver Quinn by pushing him off the waterfall on the path to Meditation Point. How do you plead?

Ridiculous.

You plead not guilty. Nicky, we'll open with your testimony. Then Davey's defense. You start, Nick.

What do I do?

Tell what you saw. Why are you accusing Davey?

I don't know.

You need a lawyer to guide you through your testimony.

I don't have any lawyer.

I'm your lawyer. I ask and you answer. Start at the beginning, Nick. On the day Oliver was killed, you and Davey and Oliver was in the woods. What were you doing there?

Is it okay to tell?

Tell everything, Nicky.

Oliver. He wanted me to shoot Davey.

Wait a minute. Careful, Nick.

Shoot me?

Shut up, wait your turn. Shoot Davey, did you say? When were you supposed to do that?

You mean like when he crossed the waterfall? The tiger's tongue.

Is that right? So what happened?

I don't know.

Never say I don't know, Nicky. It makes you seem indecisive. Did Davey cross the waterfall?

He came back down.

He came down? Then what?

He went up again.

With somebody?

Oliver went with him.

Then what? Did somebody else come along?

You came along.

Did I really? And what did I do?

You said let you do it.

Do what, Nicky?

Shoot the black man.

Come on, you're kidding. Shoot Davey? I? I said I'd shoot Davey, is that your testimony?

I guess. What's testimony?

Testimony is what you say, Nicky. Well did I shoot him?

I don't know.

Well what did you see next?

I saw Oliver on the rocks.

Did you see anything before that?

I don't know.

Remember what I said about I don't know. Did I shoot?

Yes.

What did I shoot at?

I don't know. Squirrels? You shot at squirrels.

Did I get any?

I don't know. I guess. You're a good shot so you got a squirrel.

And then you saw Oliver on the rocks? Was he dead?

You said he was dead.

What did Davey do?

He talked to you.

He came back down first. So why are you accusing Davey of killing Oliver?

I don't know.

You don't? Didn't he kill Oliver?

Yes, he killed Oliver.

How do you know?

You told me.

I? What did I tell you?

You said Davey pushed Oliver.

Did you see Davey push Oliver?

No.

Think again. Did you see Davey push Oliver?

Yes.

Where were you when you saw him?

I don't know. I was with you.

You were at the bottom looking up?

Yes.

You saw Oliver cross and Davey right behind him and when Oliver was over the elephant's pecker Davey reached out and give him a shove. Is that what you saw?

Yes.

What did Oliver do then?

I don't know.

Never say you don't know. Did he fall?

Yes.

What happened to Oliver when he fell?

He died.

So who killed Oliver?

The brown man did. Him. Davey.

Okay now we've established that—

You haven't established that, I said.

Loomer ignored me. What do you think we should do to Davey?

I don't know.

Should he pay?

Yes.

Why? Because he killed your teacher? Your best friend. Do you miss Oliver?

I miss Oliver.

You'll never see Oliver again. Does that make you sad?

Nick started to cry.

Does it make you mad?

What kind of trial is this? I said. You're stirring him up.

Why he's got a grievance man, release his bottle up feelings. Okay Nicky, it's Davey's turn. Let's see what he got to say for himself. He looked at me. What's your defense?

I didn't kill Oliver. I was nowhere near him. I was on the ground and he was three-quarters across—

Over the elephant's pecker or the tiger's tongue?

I don't know what you're talking about. It sounds to me from Nick like you killed him yourself.

Easy man, it don't help the defendant to accuse the judge.

Nick looked at Loomer, a shocked expression in his eyes.

Nick says you shot the gun. What happened, did you miss me?

Nick says I shot a squirrel, Loomer said. He was calm like he was expecting everything we said, like he was drawing it out of us.

What are you up to? I said.

Shit man, Loomer said. I just want to get this business over with. So it's your theory Oliver slipped on those rocks he had crossed a hundred times in his career since the short time Miller Church moved to Miller Farm? He just simple stupid slipped?

It's my theory somebody shot him.

That would be easy to check if we had the body. Unfortunately, the body's burned. All we got is your word against Nick whichever the judges deem is most plausible.

And what Nick said, I said. He saw you shoot and Oliver fall.

Did you say that Nick? Did you see me shoot and Oliver fall? Is that what you saw?

I don't know.

You ought to stick to your story. You can't go around changing your story all the time.

Okay, Nick said.

Listen man, Loomer said to me, your chances in this trial ain't good if you go around saying I shot a man on the waterfall.

I don't intend to. If I get out of here alive, I won't come within a hundred miles of you or Miller Farm long as I live.

Had enough of us?

Damn right.

That's a point to consider. Let's see what you and Nicky's testimony has produced. There's the question if I shot a gun when Oliver fell, what I was shooting at? Nicky knows I wasn't shooting at Oliver, don't you, Nicky?

Nicky thought and said, Yes.

I was supposed to shoot you, but evidently I didn't.

Unless you missed, I said.

I don't miss. Does the evidence suggest I was trying to save your life?

He looked like I should answer this and I felt a little roller coaster thrill. I didn't want to assent but he stared me into it. It might, I said.

Would that be because maybe I thought it wouldn't be good to let you get killed on your first visit to the Farm with your connections and your mission? Or could it be that I am basically good and don't approve of killing?

It might be.

But goodness knows, I wouldn't shoot Oliver would I? Not if I don't approve of killing. Do you understand what we're talking about, Nicky?

No.

Don't worry, it's just high I.Q. chitchat, it has nothing to do with you. So what on earth could have made Oliver fall?

Maybe you hit the wrong man, I said.

Hell man, he said. I'm the best shot on the Farm. Is it possible I was shooting to scare you just before you pushed Oliver. Maybe the bullet went bang up whiz between your hand reaching out and Oliver's shoulder waiting to be reached, zip between you and him to prevent you pushing at the very moment Oliver lost his balance and fell. Is that a good compromise?

Not very.

Never mind what you think. Is it plausible for Nicky? That's what counts, ain't it, Nick?

I don't know.

Never say that. Maybe the shock waves of the shot trotted Oliver down bouncing off rocks until he were dead. Would you buy that, Nicky?

I don't know.

It's the same difference to you because it's still Davey's fault if he started to push and it was the shock waves to stop him that sent Oliver over the edge. We're talking about this from Nicky's point of view. Nicky's version which ain't necessarily your version. That's for the judges to decide, which version. Is that all? You got anything more to say for yourself?

Why would I kill Oliver? I said. I don't kill things. It would be insane to kill Oliver in the midst of you people.

You wanted him dead, Loomer said.

I thought of denying it and decided not to. That's not the same, I said.

Loomer shrugged like I had proved his case.

Take a break, he said. Defendant, need to pee?

He led me over to a corner where the floor ended, so I could pee in the dirt. He leaned near me and looked back at Nick at the table. Relax, he said. I'm getting you off.

What?

Don't tell Nick. I'm saving your life again.

I was glad to hear that but not sure I believed it.

Nicky wants you strung up and shot dead because you took his baby but I'm fixing so you'll get off and live your life in peace. Be grateful man. Thank me.

Thank you.

We went back to the table. Now we come to the punishment part, Loomer said. It's up to us, me and Nicky the judges, to decide what to do to you the defendant.

The accuser can't be a judge, I said.

Don't interfere with the way things is done, Loomer said.

He turned to Nick. What kind of punishment should he get?

The maximum, Nick said.

Wow where'd you get that word, from me? What do you mean by the maximum, Nick?

You know, Nick said.

You mean like tit for tat? Like he should die.

Nicky's eyes shone. His lips tightened, he clenched his teeth. Die, he said. I wondered how Loomer figured this was saving my life.

Death penalty? Loomer said.

Death penalty, Nick said.

Execution?

Execution.

Hanging?

Hanging.

Firing squad?

Firing squad.

That what you want, Nick?

Yes.

So there you see in bold relief the terrible burden of the judge, Loomer said with a sigh. Defendant, what should your punishment be?

You should let me go because I didn't kill Oliver, and you should persuade Nick too.

I saw a question unclenching Nick's teeth.

The judge's burden, Loomer said. Between the death penalty and letting you go. We need to find a compromise.

Come on, Loomer, that's not how cases are decided.

You don't think cases are decided by compromise? Look at the conflicting evidence. He say you pushed him, you say you didn't. The rifle shot by me suggest a different scenario in which your intent to push was thwarted but the consequence was the same. The argument is, we don't have the proof of guilt we need to convict. Neither do we have the proof of innocence we need to acquit. Therefore we must compromise and find a punishment satisfactory to both sides. To satisfy your blood thirst, Nicky, and to satisfy Davey's feelings of innocence, which need to be respected no matter how guilty he is. Do you follow me?

No, Nick said.

Never mind. What I decree is exile. Exile on this island to spend the rest of his days foraging for berries and catching the spawn of the seas, birds if he can. He have the house and hangar and woods and sea. What do you think of that, Nicky?

You're not going to kill him?

No, Nicky. Exile's right because this guy think he innocent. So who kill Oliver? Must be somebody behind the scenes pulling strings. Davey's only the innocent stand-in. We can't get the absent killer so we punish the stand-in by absenting him. Okay Nicky?

Nicky looked bewildered almost crying again.

Would you like some counseling on that matter, Loomer said.

Yes.

Tit for tat, but it wasn't as if Davey killed you. If he killed you then it would be right to demand his life in return, but it wasn't you it was your guru he killed. So who's life should pay for the life he took? Think of it this way. Your guru for my guru, that is, Davey's guru for yours. The one who pull the strings, reflect on that. Don't worry, everything's for the best. We're going now. Get our stuff, Nick.

No, Nick said.

Get our stuff I tell you.

I'm mad, Nick said.

The hell you are. Get our stuff.

Nick's face wrinkled and he started to cry. He went to the house. Loomer said, I'll send a boat to pick you up. Don't forget our agreement.

What agreement?

Jesus you already forgot. I saved your life. I saved it twice, do you grasp that fact?

So you did.

So don't go around making trouble.

I said, what are you going to do with my car?

Ho, your car. It belong to Hertz, Bangor, right?

Right.

I'll take it to Bangor for you, he said. So you see it all come out right in the end. Guess we'll go now. Take care.

I went down to the shore and watched them go, the little boat reducing to insect size past the big island across the channel and out of sight. I sat on a rock by the dock and waited for the boat from shore. I was thinking how to get home. Thinking fortunately I had my knapsack and wallet with cash and plastic. I had an unreserved air ticket from Bangor which Harry had paid for but how could I get to Bangor from Black Harbor without a car? I doubted there was a bus from Black Harbor to anywhere. I could hitchhike. But if I could hitchhike to Bangor, I could hitchhike home, which would save Harry the ticket refund. I wondered if Loomer would actually take the car to Bangor, because if he didn't I would have to press theft charges against him.

Meanwhile I waited for the boat. I sat on the rock and paced on the shore, exercise. I thought of going around the island but didn't because the person in the boat might not know where I was or which island and I would have to wave to him. I got into the question of payment for the person in the boat. This raised the question of cash, of which I would certainly need more before getting home. I could get this out of an automatic teller machine, thanks to modern technology, though I doubted I'd find one in Black Harbor.

Meanwhile the boat didn't come. My expectations shifted. Whereas before I expected the boat to come and hoped my fear it wouldn't was paranoia, now I expected the boat not to come and hoped my contrary hope was not foolishness. Another of Loomer's tricks, he being a man of tricks. Exile after all. If no boat was ordered for me, I would have to use my ingenuity to find a way to shore.

A lobster boat went by. It came suddenly around the point moving fast. I waved and shouted, though they couldn't hear me over the engine. The lobsterman waved back. He got smaller like Loomer's boat and disappeared around the big island.

Before it got too dark I went up to the camp to see if there was a boat in the wreckage. There was a canoe with a hole in the side. Also a large aluminum rowboat. It was so heavy I could barely move it. When I lifted it I saw a gap between the metal and the spine along the bottom. I couldn't find any oars either. I thought if I looked long enough I might solve the oar problem. The only way to get the boat to the shore would be to roll it on logs. To do that I would have to widen the path through the woods. I could do that with the axe in the hangar. But I couldn't think of a way to seal the gap in the bottom and if I didn't the boat would sink. I thought if I had to stay here a year I could probably devise a way to get ashore without help. I wondered if Harry and Judy would file missing persons reports.

I slept cold in a blanket in the house. My night was full of ways to get off the island and what then. I invented adventures in hitchhiking. Loomer came after me again. I tried to figure out his reasons for things. Why he wanted me to know that Oliver had intended to kill me and that he had prevented it and that he had in fact killed Oliver. I worried about his hint to Nick that his real enemy was Harry, and I wondered if I was marooned here to clear the way for an attack on Harry, though I couldn't think why they'd do that. I reflected how easily the Miller people had given up the baby after such resistance and wondered if they were setting more traps, and I told myself not to be paranoid, but how could you help it when you were deliberately stranded on an island for no reason you could figure out?

In the morning I went back to the shore. I took a can of lunch meat and ate on a rock. There was fog in the distance, but the nearby islands were clear as binoculars and it looked like a nice day. Another lobster boat came around the big island and went through the channel. I waved again. I took off my shirt and waved it, but the boat went on.

I gathered sticks and built a fire. Maybe I could attract attention with it. I built it into a sturdy bonfire. The fire on the shore reminded me of burning Shelley's body after he drowned in Italy. Even a good swimmer would not be able to swim ashore. This was the Maine coast in early spring and no one could survive in this water.

The sun approached noon and moved into afternoon. My fire died, I didn't see much point in it. I thought of inventions to attract the attention of lobster boats. Flags. How to make a flag convey the notion of emergency, help. I thought how stupid to die here the victim of Loomer's games.

Around three o'clock, a little motor boat came around the other side of the island opposite where the lobster boats had gone. I waved my windbreaker back and forth trying to look frantic. I ran to the end of a point of rocks jutting into the sea. The boat kept going. There were two or three bumps sticking up, a little outboard motor not much different from Loomer's. One of them waved. I waved my windbreaker back and forth.

The boat stopped. It turned. It approached. Thank God, I said. I ran back to shore leading them to the dock. The boat hovered off the dock, cautious, where we could shout back and forth. It was a white haired man and woman and a black and white dog.

I'm stranded, I yelled. Can you take me ashore?

Their name was McCaskill and they lived on Fig Island. I remembered seeing their boat on my previous trip. It was hard to explain why I needed a lift and they were reluctant to come to the dock until I had done so. Finally they took me aboard. I sat in the bow with the dog. It was a heavy load for their little boat and we lay deep in the water. We chugged our way to Black Harbor. I could see they were skeptical. I can't imagine anybody doing such a thing, Mrs. McCaskill said. But if they did it, Mr. McCaskill said.

I was thinking what fee to give them, but when we got to shore I was so grateful to have my destiny back that I forgot. Later I decided that was just as well. They were doing a Samaritan deed and might have been offended if I put a monetary value on it.

PART FOUR

20

Nick Foster

We landed at the dock. Loomer paid the man and we got in the car and drove to Bangor. Loomer drove. It's better that we didn't kill him Loomer said. He's only a puppet of someone else's will. Exile on an uninhabited island. He's paid his penalty we saw to that.

He paid.

We drove through towns with white houses and big trees. We passed fields. We passed mailboxes at the ends of driveways across the fields.

Look at the pretty country Loomer said. Elite country high class. Women's country. Look at the antique shops on the country roads. Make-believe farms look at the cute views.

I looked at the yellow fields and the bare branches. The road was bumpy and had holes in it.

Land where the good old USA began. Then it went west and left this behind. Changes are coming.

The road went straight and flat across a field. It dipped around a farm house. At the bottom there was a blue stream under the bridge. It looked like the rest of the country to me.

Changes are coming to Miller Farm and changes to the good old USA Loomer said. When we get to Bangor I'm going to buy you a bus ticket and send you home to Cincinnati.

It sounded like he was talking to somebody else.

Did you hear me he said. When we get to Bangor I'm going to buy you a bus ticket and send you home to Cincinnati.

I thought what he said and I said what.

Yes he said. The time has come for you to go home and resume your life.

No I said.

What. What did you say Nicky.

I don't want to go to Cincinnati I said.

Yes you do Loomer said. You have no reason to stay at Miller Farm now your guru is gone. It's time to be independent grow up and be a man.

I am a man.

Okay then.

I didn't know what to say and cried. I want to go with you I said.

You want me to be your new Oliver do you. That's real flattering. However we need the work you can do back home.

What kind of work.

Well now maybe you can keep an eye on things. Like you can tell me if David Leo escapes. Don't look so shocked. If he's clever he'll escape.

You said he would be there all his life.

We exiled him. That ends our obligation. What's next is up to him.

I thought.

Know your enemy Nicky. Who sent Davey Leo to Oliver. That's the question. A man is but the puppet of his guru. Who sent this otherwise harmless black man or brown if you insist to chase your guru. For whom was he acting is the question. Whose will was he obeying.

I thought. The lady I said.

What ho the lady. Judy Doodie with the baby. A lady guru. A sentimental attachment to be a hero in the lady's eyes. Look deeper boy. You need a guru with intellectual power to remodel the soul of others. Think now who leads black Davey around and tells him how to think.

I thought more. Not Oliver and Miller and Loomer. The professor I said.

Professor. Harry Field is that the professor you mean.

I couldn't think of any other professors.

Then you must be thinking of Harry Field. That's good Nicky because do you know what a professor does.

A professor talks.

Right there good man. What does a professor talk about.

I don't know.

He talks about talking Loomer said. A professor talks and makes everybody else afraid to talk. Do you know what this Harry Field had the nerve to do. He tried to talk Miller himself out of being God. The beginning of the end.

I shuddered.

That's your Davey Leo's guru. Think about it.

I thought.

Think.

I thought about thinking.

Think about blame. That's how the world advances blaming the right people.

I got confused thinking about blame.

That's all right Loomer said. It will come to you. Meanwhile that's what you can do for me in Cincinnati. Keep an eye on him and keep thinking. Get upset. You gotta get mad Nicky. You gotta get real mad enough to kill someone. That's what I need from you pal. I need you to get boiling popping raging mad so you can't stand it. That's what I want you to practice in Cincinnati. I want you to brood. Think all the bad things anybody done to you. Maybe when you're mad enough we can get together again how about it.

I'm mad.

Right. Now I'll tell you a secret. Would you like to hear one. Your Oliver who got killed was a jerk got what he deserved.

No.

Yes Nicky. Your Oliver was a dumb fool bringing trouble upon Miller and the Farm and all us. He shouldn't brought that baby full of trouble and killing the brown man was wrong Nicky Miller shouldn't have to put up that kind of shit. It was right to kill him Nicky.

No.

Everything changes it ain't like you think Loomer said. The world is changing in a state of flux. Do you know what flux is.

I thought it was a flower my mother talked about.

Never mind you don't need to know. Most things in the world you don't need to know. You'll get on fine following gurus with your interests at heart. Leave subtleties like flux to people who are smarter than you.

Oliver said I was smart enough I said.

Smart enough is what I'm saying. People like you don't need to be any smarter and let flux go on without bothering them. People like me with a different interest we have to adapt the flux of the world to our purposes. Gurus of the future. You see what I mean.

No.

Don't matter. The world is in a state of crisis of no interest to you because you are with people to take care of you. But around you the world is in a crisis of belief with people in a state of rage they know not why. The world is boiling and popping in a state of rage and fear thinking the devil's just waiting to grab you in its jaws.

Me.

Anybody. The world is full of thinking somebody's out to get you and take away what belongs to you popping and boiling for desperate measures to thwart the devil. What you think Nicky does it sound convincing to you.

It sounded convincing to me.

It's because of the noise and clamor of the commercial world though most people would rather blame the government because the commercial world is themselves. It's the racket of television and shopping strips with traffic and taxes and cops on the road and kids in the streets and crime and guns and drugs and programs about the guns and drugs and somebody coming along and taking your guns and drugs and highways chopping up the countryside plus the construction delays and orange barrels paid by your dollars where the fines are doubled and the insurance forms and the license forms and the commercials teaching everybody to lie and the lying columnists and the sound bites and the baseball strikes the millionaires the panhandlers and nursing homes and dying making everybody think somebody's out to get them and you'd better do something about it. Think about it.

I thought about it.

More and more people want their gurus who will stand up to the enemy gurus of the devil. They want the guru who can show a good reason for the bad feeling they got and find someone to blame. That's Miller's genius though he's not the only one. His group happens to have sole possession of the truth but actually there's lots of folks in sole possession of the truth which nobody else has. In fact if you ask me almost everybody is in sole possession of the truth and everybody else is the victim of delusion and the devil. Are you following me.

Almost everybody is in possession of the truth.

Right. And everybody else is deluded. That's the principle Nicky boy. Miller's just one of the gurus who makes his people see how different they are from the rest of the world. He confirms their intuitions. He proves their natural resentment is justified because it's not them anxious and neurotic against the world but the world that's anxious and neurotic against them. You see what I mean.

I thought about it.

He confirms what they wish to be true. If they can't understand the God everybody talks so much about that God seems to be part of the enemy Miller says I am God refuting the whole hostile world in one breath. What peace and relief that brings. The only trouble Nicky do you know what the only trouble is.

No.

The trouble is all the other gurus saying the same thing. Miller's part of a great underground movement of discontent bred by the crushing speed of civilization. He's one leak of a geyser breaking up through the volcanic soul of the earth along with hundreds of other leaks in cults and meeting groups throughout the land all venting the same steam. Some day the geysers will coalesce in one big eruption blowing the cover off the land. That's when Miller will disappear and it's God slaughtering God all over the world. Would you like that.

I don't know.

Laugh a revolution is coming he said. People killing each other's gods to save their souls until only the last ones is left. Are you ready for that Nicky.

I don't know.

228

Think about it. Meanwhile mistrust false gurus that's my word to you. If you want to kill anyone Nicky kill the professors. That way you won't do any harm.

In Bangor he drove me to the bus stop. Don't leave me Loomer I said. I don't know what to do.

Get a job he said.

I don't know what to do when I get off the bus.

Go to the Y. I'll give you some money. Go to the Y get a room. Get your job back get a friend to look after you. Go visit your baby. Get mad. Not at me though I'm your friend. Get mad at somebody else.

On the bus I cried. An old lady next to me said tell me about it dear.

You're an old hag I said. She moved to another seat.

I tried to remember what Loomer said. In Boston the bus driver showed me where to go for the next bus. I rode in the bus days and nights. We stopped at restaurants. I bought food with the money Loomer gave me.

The bus went fast on the big roads. The hills were foggy. I got sweaty and sticky.

I thought why Loomer wanted me to get mad. I tried to think of something to be mad about. I felt sad. It was a big potato in my gullet. I think I mean gullet. I felt like a bird eating a cherry too big for him. I thought about Oliver but couldn't remember him so I couldn't think about him. I remembered him telling me to shoot the black man on top of the tiger's tongue. Only then it was the elephant pecker. That was how the trouble began the black man because he wasn't really black was brown when Oliver told me to shoot him and therefore I couldn't. That was part of the trouble. Then Loomer shooting the brown man on the tiger's tongue really the elephant's pecker and it wasn't the black man or the brown man but Oliver came tumbling down.

If people called things like they look it was Loomer shot Oliver instead of the black or brown man pushing except Loomer said it wasn't so and I'm not bright enough. Only I'm thinking if Loomer did shoot Oliver that changes the whole picture only everybody says I'm not bright enough to see the whole picture. But if Loomer did shoot Oliver then I have to think for myself.

I'm not bright enough to know what to think if Loomer did shoot Oliver. I think Loomer told me to get mad and kill Harry Field but I'm not bright enough to know if that's what he told me or that's what he didn't tell me. I hate when people hint. I'm not bright enough to know what they're hinting at when they hint.

If I'm supposed to get mad and kill the professor I don't know what I'm supposed to get mad about. I thought about getting mad without getting mad at anything. That was hard to think.

I thought if Loomer killed Oliver.

I thought if should I get mad.

I thought if but David took the baby back who should I get mad at.

I thought if and Loomer gave the baby away both could I get mad at. If and sent me away to Cincinnati could I.

I wondered if you needed to be mad to kill him.

I wondered if I was mad did that mean kill him.

I'm not as dumb as people like Loomer and Oliver say I am. When I got to the bus station in Cincinnati I asked a taxi to take me to the Y. The next day I bought a gun. Dumb people don't know how to buy guns.

I found out where the professor lives. Dumb people can't find out things like that.

I put the gun in my pocket and walked to the professor's house. I remembered it. This was where Oliver got the baby.

The baby's name was George she was a girl. I thought her name was Holiness but Oliver said her name was George. When I went up the steps to the professor's house with the gun in my pocket I thought about George and cried.

I was crying when the lady opened the door. Yes she said.

I saw a little girl sitting on the rug. She didn't look like George and then she did.

What's the matter the lady said.

I took the gun out of my pocket.

The lady looked at it. Something happened to her face.

What's going on she said. Her voice was wrong.

Is Harry Field in I said.

He's on a trip. What do you want. What is this.

What kind of trip.

He's miles away. East Coast. Who are you. What are you doing with that thing.

I put the gun back in my pocket.

I took Dutton the Carpenter's card from my wallet when I used to work for him. I wrote NICK on it and gave it to her. While I was getting my wallet and finding a pencil and writing my name she kept jumping up and down and closing the door only not closing it. Ask him to call me when he gets back I said. Sorry to bother you.

I guess she didn't remember me from Miller Farm.

It would be easier if I had someone to help me. But like Loomer said this is the best way if I'm going to be independent and grow up a man.

21

David Leo

Here I am again, remember me? I'm the one the playful fellas left on the island, to figure how to get back. Fraternity stunt. I'm back now, thanks to the McCaskills. All to help out my friends the father professor and his daughter. Some people would be sick of it. They'd write a letter of resignation to said professor and daughter saying thanks, enough for me. Not me. I'm the loyal dog, like the retriever in the McCaskill bow. He sits there protecting his family by checking out every wave, one after another, each one a new problem.

When I get to shore, don't bother to kiss the soil. Too much on my mind, which is inclined less to gratitude than to a lawsuit. Trouble is, a lawsuit assumes money. Since the fellas don't have money, what could I sue for?

The immediate question on the dock (it's low tide and I climb a ladder to the deck) is what now? I look for my car, though I know they took it since they took the keys, with that funny promise by Loomer to return it to Hertz in Bangor. In any case, it's gone. I must learn the transportation facilities in Black Harbor. Civilized questions return. Food, shelter, sleep, and how do I get from one place to another? It all starts with money. Of which I have some. The precise figure is sixty-five bucks, plus a Master Card, a Texaco card and a Mobil. Also the return air ticket from Bangor. I have what I need to get home.

But in a state of confusion. It's close to five, which limits what I can accomplish in the rest of today. My pack contains clothes, with my notebook, shaving and toilet stuff. Last time in Black Harbor I stayed at the Inn. The Inn is close by, near the yellow building with the general store.

The telephone on the dock by the pumps is out of order. There's another in the general store next to the post office. Garden hoses, scythes and sickles, a lumbery smell. I forget why I need a telephone, then remember. Hello Hertz? Oddly enough the reply is quick and affirmative. The fellas, good guys after all, returned my car. Good guys after all? Do you believe that? Should I feel a chill in my spine for the innate goodness of my fellow man amid the deadly tricks? If civilization is a surface watch out for the bumps and hollows.

In any case though, I need to go to Bangor, so as to use my ticket. How do you get from Black Harbor to Bangor? Is there a bus? I didn't think so.

If you stick around, the store man says, maybe you can hitch a ride tomorrow on the truck. Another night in the Black Harbor Inn, better than the house on Stump Island anyway. Remember the uncomfortable bed, the old pine bedstead, the down home wall paper, by God it's the same room. Get dinner at the hamburger store and back to the coastal quiet of nautical sleep. Having had a little more nautical atmosphere than I need. Returning here tends to eliminate the in-between and comments on the whole venture with something like a sneer. The other time I was beginning a hunt. Now like Odysseus I'm trying to go home. I have accomplished what I intended, but without certain rewards I had no right to expect, and there's a sick feeling in the air. I need to analyze that sick feeling, since my mission was such a success. We got the child back, we eliminated the father, and now child, mother, and grandfather are safe where they belong. Only I, loyal Davey, ran into a snag, but I'm out of it now. What's sick about it?

Say it's my touchy reaction to being scared and humiliated. Ego hurt when they put me on trial and left me on the island. Shouldn't take it personally, they were beaten and only getting back what they could. I know that. It's something else. The sight of Oliver Quinn slipping or shot down the waterfall, a renewable shock, I replay it in my head. Enraptured with the horror. I caught that moment in the act, a knife slicing into the neck of time and I saw the blood of the universe. Now it stains our good fortune or separates me from it. I am being mocked. By whom? The god? Is Oliver Quinn in your way, shall I bump him off for you? The fellas, good guys both, with their mock trial. The universe, reading my mind and giving me what it thinks I deserve.

Blackmail, holding me symbolically responsible for Oliver Quinn's death. That's why I can't complain to the police or file a lawsuit. If I filed a lawsuit the death of Oliver Quinn would become known. Inquiries would follow. Millerites would testify according to their view of the universe.

I hear the bell buoy again in the night, and the bed is no less uncomfortable than before. In the morning it's the woman with long hair serving again and sun through the curtains of the breakfast room. The truck to Bangor, gee it's already gone. It left at six while you were asleep, the rest you surely needed. Inventive Davey will have to find another way to Bangor.

Are there taxis in this part of the world? Yes, if you pay. A taxi will go anywhere if you pay enough. In this case it would be double the distance because you'd have to summon the taxi from Bangor before it could take you to Bangor. An elderly fat man in a business suit intervenes. You looking for a lift, sonny?

I'm trying to get to Bangor.

Well I'm heading for Augusta capital of this state but I could drop you at Bucksport where you might pick up another ride to Bangor if you so incline.

Well thank you, it beats sitting on my ass in Black Harbor.

The man's car is the latest, its cost high, its motor silent. Its springs and shocks absorb the rocky back roads and convert them into waves. We glide cruisingly across the fields and down the dips and over the inlets and tidal runs of the Penobscot countryside. The man talks. His name is Jerome Turnbull. His face hangs down around his mouth. He requires my story, and I tell him all except what I'd rather not. Therefore I leave out the kidnapping and the death of Oliver Quinn. I leave out Miller and my trial on the island. What's left I tell him fully, patched for coherence. He doesn't see the gaps and is satisfied. So, he says, the bottom line is you're a professor?

He, he tells me, is a professional troubleshooter. You got troubles to shoot, I'll come and shoot em for you, haw. He's spent the last three days shooting troubles on the dock at Black Harbor. Told them what they need and who to hire for it.

He asks me do I like his car, and I say fine. More pleasanter than a airplane, won't you say? and I says yes, more pleasanter than an airplane. He says I can save money if I don't use my ticket. Go with him to Augusta, down by the turnpike ramp I can hitchhike all the way to Cincinnati in cars as good as his and be home in no time. Then I can turn in my ticket, get my money back, and I'm home without spending no money at all.

Not only that, there's valuable social experience to be gained from hitchhiking, the people you meet, an education not in no university or book. Himself, Jerome Turnbull, never drives without picking up a hitchhiker. He asks about their lives and they tell him and he learns something just like today, being as he never knew no black professors before. Never knew what they was like, but from now on when someone says black professor he'll remember how polite and soft-spoken you was.

So, he says, not to twist your arm but I strongly advise you to save that airline ticket and ride with me to Augusta where I'll show you where to hitchhike and guarantee you'll meet interesting people and add to your life memories you'll never forget.

I think, No way. No way will I give up Harry's comfortable airline ticket for the American adventure of hitchhiking, to save Harry's money not mine, but I'm not counting on the perverse grumbling inside me about something, how I have been treated or Harry or what. At Bucksport, which I recognize from the signs, Jerome Turnbull doesn't speak. I wait to see when he'll tell me. He cuts across to the suspension bridge on Route 1, leaving Bucksport behind. Then he says, I see you're taking my advice.

You mean that was Bucksport? I say, pretending.

Good decision. You'll get lots of good rides in Augusta.

He quiets down and the rest of the way is mostly flat across fields and through villages in the dreamy silence of automobile trips. Coming into Augusta he livens up. Explains where he'll take me, the best place for a ride. Says how much he learned from me a black professor, a lesson in race relations he'll never forget. Hopes I learned something too, like it's some specific point he has in mind. Good luck, sonny, he says.

Nine out of ten cars go by without stopping. Then ninety-nine out of a hundred, and I wonder if there are any odds at all. Also what Jerome Turnbull the troubleshooter didn't say, like what murderous kooks pick up hitchhikers even in peaceful Maine.

It's middle day, the air cool, the sun blinds the pavement. At last a car stops. I run to catch up, a two-door with three people.

A woman steps out so I can get into the back with another woman. All three are women. I'm relieved, women are less likely to be murderers. Thirties or late twenties. Jeans, lots of color. Laughing, residue of a joke before I came along. Where to, soldier? they ask me. Cincinnati, wow that's far. We're going to Rochester. You want to go to Rochester with us?

It's on the way, I say, if you can stand me that long.

We're going to stop the night at a motel, they warn me. You can hitch another ride there if you want.

Stopping's fine with me, I say.

My name is June, the driver says. This here's Veena and that's Minnie in back with you.

Glad to meet you, June, Veena, and Minnie. June the driver has short black hair. She has a small face with thin features and sharp eyes, looking smart and businesslike. Veena in the passenger seat has tumbling blonde curls, chubby cheeks, and a smiley face. Minnie in back keeping her distance from me is big. She wears glasses and has a sweatshirt with the words, DON'T MESS WITH ME, GO TO COLLEGE INSTEAD. She stares out the window and I can't tell whether she finds everything funny or disgusting.

As a trio, they're boisterous. Who am I? I keep the professor hidden as long as I can. They wish I came from the ghetto, sorry I don't. I don't use crack, either. I hope I have a girlfriend, but the baby came from somebody else. Miller calls himself God. You never heard of Miller who calls himself God? You never heard of God?

Minnie makes wry jokes for the others to laugh at. June is intent on driving. Veena laughs when she doesn't know what's going on. You're cute, Veena says. The others agree, I'm cute.

And what do you do, you women? I say.

We're waitresses.

And why are three waitresses driving from Maine to Rochester on a Saturday in the middle of spring?

Funeral, they say.

The mood is not my idea of funereal, although I know funerals produce different moods in different societies. For a while I don't know if they're going to the funeral or coming back. Then it appears they are returning home, which means the funeral was in Maine. I catch no mention of a deceased.

They learn all about me, the things I did not tell Jerome Turnbull. The kidnapping, the man down the waterfall, the trial for my life on Stump Island. Judy Field too. Wow, they say.

Veena giggles. What color is Judy? she asks.

Hush Veena, they say, but I don't mind. Same as you, I say.

And what's the nature of your relationship? Minnie asks. She's the big one with glasses. Also, I now realize, the one the others consider most intelligent and best educated. She did time at a college in upper New York State.

Ambiguous, I reply.

Are you intimate hee hee with her? Veena asks.

Ignore her, June says.

I wish I were, I say. Tell them what they want to know. Strangers I'll never see again, who cares? Maybe a stranger can see things I can't though clear as day before my nose.

Have you made that wish known to her? Minnie says.

She knows what I want.

And still says no? Veena says. She's crazy.

There's always something coming up, I say. If it's not the kidnapping of her baby it's the death of her former boyfriend.

Snack stop, a change of places, now Minnie drives, June is in the passenger seat, Veena the blonde is behind with me. She keeps pressing the heels of her hands together like an exercise.

You're cute, she says.

June asks, How come you didn't use that air ticket to go home if it's not your money you're saving?

I don't know, I really don't know. Minnie answers for me. He's fed up, she says. After all he's gone through with no reward. He's fed up taking things from what's his name, Harry?

Is that it? Veena says. You want a reward?

Dinner stop early, a family restaurant chain. All over the country the rest rooms are back in the same corner to the right. My three waitresses observe Sue who's our server for tonight. She's got too many tables is her problem, June says. She's inexperienced, Minnie says. Should we give her advice? Veena says. Let her swim, Minnie says. Survival of the fittest, if she doesn't improve she'll get fired.

Minnie is studying me across the table. Thinking. Back in the car she says, You've been meeting up these god people, maybe you should meet a goddess or two. Trojan War, kids?

Oh no, June groans.

Veena in back with me squeals. Trojan War, let's play Trojan War, she says. Whenever Veena laughs she pats me on the arm. In the car it's getting dark and she's shadowy.

What's Trojan War? I say.

It's a game, Minnie says. Did you notice our names? We're the goddesses and you're Paris.

You have to choose, Veena squeals softly out of the darkness beside me. You have to decide which one of us you like best. And then—Veena giggles again—the one you choose gives you a reward.

I don't get it.

Maybe he doesn't know the story, June says.

Of course he does, Minnie says. Don't you?

I don't get what I'm supposed to do.

Choose the one you like best. Love, fame, or money—

That's not it, that's Careers.

Love, wisdom, money, June says.

Minnie thought up this game last year when this cute guy noticed our names, June says. I forget his name.

They had to monkey around to make me fit, Veena said. My real name's Veronica.

So what am I supposed to do?

Be Paris. Just pick which one of us you like best.

I like you all equally.

No, pick the reward you want, Veena says. Pick June, she'll give you money. Minnie gives you wisdom. Pick me.

June will give me money?

Not real money. They laugh.

Symbolic money, Minnie says. They whoop.

Fuck wisdom, Minnie says. Who's going to pick wisdom in this day and age? Let's update it to fit Davey. To fit the problems of his life. How about it, Davey?

I don't know.

Well I see some questions that fit you, Minnie says. Which do you care for? Judy or her father? Love or career?

What about me? June says.

You're money. Love, career, or money.

He won't pick me, June says. If he wanted money he wouldn't be a professor.

Okay, you be career. Prestige and status. Tenure. I'll be Harry, his work, his mind. Veena's Judy.

You want me to choose one of those?

Exactly.

What happens when I do?

The one you pick gives you a reward.

Let's play it right this time, Veena says. No cop-outs, okay?

I don't understand. Which do I pick, one of you or one of those goals?

Pick the one of us you like best.

I like you equally. I like you all fine.

So pick the one with the reward you like best.

Well what are those rewards?

You'll find out after you have picked.

But how can I pick if I don't know the rewards?

Pick what you care most for, Minnie says. Love, work, or prestige. Judy, Harry, or yourself. Veena, me, or June.

I try to go along. The truth is I no longer know what I want. I'm feeling somewhat sour about everything. I stall.

Shit man, Minnie says. If it's that much of a problem, forget it. I'm sorry I suggested it.

Veena is disappointed. Damn, she says. We never get to play.

No no, I'll play. They wait, I hold my breath. I pick Judy.

Judy, Veena says. That's love. That's me. You pick me.

I knew you would, Minnie says. You're so conventional.

June laughs.

So what's my reward? I say.

You'll find out, Veena says.

Are we ready to look for a motel? Minnie says.

Yes yes a motel, Veena says.

The motel is a Day's Inn. At the desk, June says, One for the three of us, one for you, is that right? Fine, I say.

The rooms are adjacent on the second floor near the end. They open on the balcony. We go to our respective rooms together. The girls have heavy bags, they struggle up the steps. They go into their room and I into mine. I unpack pajamas and toilet kit and put the latter in the bathroom. I turn on the TV but I'm not in the mood. I'm in a bad mood I guess, although it feels like a good mood. Except the guilty feeling I expect to feel later on, though I don't feel it yet. Since nobody has said anything more about it, I wonder if the Trojan War game is over, if my making a choice was all there was to it, like Truth instead of Consequences. I tell myself I'm weary of the joke. The game was a flirtation, I decide, and it riles me like the mock trial on the island, for I've had my fill of mockeries where nothing means anything and you only pretend it does.

The phone rings. Are you in bed yet? It's Veena.

I'm watching TV.

Did you take a shower?

What? I hear giggling in the background.

I just want to know if you took a shower.

Yes I did.

Don't go to sleep yet.

All right then. A moment later I go to the door to let her in. She's wearing a gold robe, which she takes off with nothing under it. She looks pretty good.

Your prize, she says.

I suspected this.

I let her get into bed. She smells good and is soft and firm. Just pretend I am Judy, she says.

That's good of you.

Of course it is, she says. I'm good at the things I do.

She leans over me on the pillow. Would you like me to take off your pajamas?

All right. Hold me, she says. I do so. Though she was nonexistent to me as recently as this morning, when I climb on she's sweet and strong, sharing nature with the perfumed malls of America. I have a deliberate thought, this is not Judy Field. I think of Judy watching while I wash my hands of her. Veena murmurs and whispers.

242

How do you like your prize?

Later, in the silence of the settling back, I ask what would have happened if I had picked Minnie or June.

Same thing, she says. This was our way of deciding who gets to sleep with you. Thank you for picking me, she says, like thank you for calling Delta.

I consider the deep choice they had asked me to make. So any choice I make, what I get is sex? What else would you want? she says.

She gets sentimental. After tomorrow, we'll never see each other again. Don't go to sleep yet. When you leave, I'll cry. Write to me.

In the early morning I wake up with naked Veena loudly beside me. My night was stuck in the confusion of Veena for Judy, Minnie for Harry, and June for myself, with all forms of devotion translated into sex. After a while I hear grief like a train whistle down the track. I see myself as a railroad track straight between the trees and I riding along like a train. I don't know who laid that track or set me running, but there's a switch deflecting me suddenly, spinning me into the wilderness. Now there's no track and I'm stalled, I can't go anywhere. Someone should have told me, someone should have warned me. I rage in the silence of the early light.

Then it passes and when Veena wakes up, I'm ready to continue. Good morning to you, sunshine. We take turns in the bathroom and shower. When we are ready we go next door and knock, like lovers traveling with a pair of maiden aunts. We go down to breakfast together. The decorum of the morning prohibits any mention of last night. We are quiet and subdued.

They leave me by a ramp near Rochester. I have Veena's address and telephone number in my pack. I'll probably lose them. I couldn't see if she was crying when we left.

Two more rides take me home. First a couple in their twenties. They speak neither to each other nor to me during my three hours with them. Then a couple of guys, one with a pony tail, the other with a beard. They ask me to explain why I don't like the word nigger. They say they don't mean no harm, live and let live. Okay? they say. They want me to agree. Okay, I say.

They let me off at the Mall, where I catch a bus. My apartment is stuffy, having been closed more than a week. I check things out and guess it's good to be home.

I don't call the Fields. Maybe tomorrow. I think what I did on the road, my right to do it, after what I've been through without reward. Maybe I won't call them. Not until they call me. If they do. Then I can decide if I want anything more to do with them. The grief is back. This time it's for getting off the track my train was on. Like if I don't follow that track I won't know who I am. Loyal and faithful, David Leo. I realize that any choice I could have made in the game last night would have been a betrayal. The game was stacked against me from the beginning. This makes me mad once more, and gets rid of the grief again for a little while, anyway.

22

Nick Foster

After I didn't find the professor in his house I forgot. I kept forgetting.

I worked at Pompadours. One day I saw the brown man Oliver said was black across the street. He was walking along. I ran out from the kitchen with my apron on. Hey I said what are you doing here.

You jesus get way from me he said.

Who let you out you're exile I said.

Stay back or I'll call the police he said.

I thought that's wrong. He broke the rules. I called Loomer at Miller Farm. Dumb people don't know how to make long distance telephone calls. I called from the restaurant telephone and asked the operator. I said I want to call Loomer. Where is he she said. I told her Miller Farm. Where's that she said. I said New Hampshire. What town she said. I couldn't remember and then I remembered Wicker Falls. So she called Miller Farm and said Loomer. Loomer said hello.

Dumb people can't do that. I told Loomer the black man was loose. Loomer laughed.

Well what should I do I said.

I don't give a damn just don't kill him Loomer said. Don't bother me I got better things to worry about.

I thought about it. I thought if the professor was on the East Coast where the lady said then the professor escaped the black man. Dumb people don't think things like that.

I thought if then the professor would be back here home. I figured how to find out. I found his number in the telephone book and if he answered the phone he was back. The lady's voice answered. I hung up. I waited for the lady to go away and then I called again. Another lady answered. She had a different voice like an old mother or the librarian in the school library asking did I need help. She wasn't the professor so I hung up again. I thought if I kept calling. After a while the others would get tired and he would answer the phone. I kept calling and got the young lady or the librarian lady. Their voices got jumpy. As soon as I heard the voice wasn't the professor I hung up so I wasn't taking up their time. I never said anything. Then I thought they have to go to the telephone to answer it so when I heard the voice this time I said sorry and next time the voice started to say something when I said sorry so I listened and she said who is this like she was mad and I hung up fast.

One day I told Jake Burridge and he took me to Professor Field's street to sit in the car and watch if he comes out. I seen the lady with the baby George go out in the stroller and come back and five o'clock the professor drives up. That means he's back. He's got a woman I never saw like she's Mrs. Professor. They drive up and put the car in the garage and walk into the house. I went back to work and thought about it.

I got the gun but I had to work. I said tomorrow's better because I have the whole day tomorrow but today they's only a few hours left before it's not today any more.

Then tomorrow is today and they's not so much time as was which gets shorter because the day gets longer. I put the gun in my pocket and walked to the professor's street. I went up the steps again. I thought the last time I come here and gun in my pocket and the lady who answered the door and I didn't remember what I was supposed to do. I was supposed to do something here when I saw the professor but I couldn't think what it was.

The wife lady I never seen answered the door. She smiled at me like I was nice and asked what I want and I said can I see Professor Harry. Professor Field she said and she called in the house up stairs like Harry dear a man to see you. He came down. He had a sweater without sleeves and shirt sleeves puffing his arms and glasses and when he saw me he said I know you. Then he asked who and I said Nicky and he said you're the one give us the baby seat at Miller Farm and what can I do for you.

I said I need your help.

Sure he said like he was Miller and he chased the lady and we sat down in his study and I took the gun out of my pocket because it was banging against my leg and he looked and said what's that.

I told him it was a gun which surprised me he didn't know a simple gun when he saw one.

What are you doing with it. I told him I went to the store all by myself and paid for it with my own money.

All right he said like a little bit mad. I didn't want him to be mad. Sorry I said. What for he said like a little bit madder more. I know you the one who helped kidnap my granddaughter and you also kidnapped my friend David Leo and abandoned him on an island in Maine.

He escaped I said. He wasn't supposed to.

Maybe he wasn't supposed to be kidnapped either he said.

But Loomer said.

Loomer eh. He told you.

I started to say but couldn't think. I heard people in the hall and I saw the lady with the baby. That's my baby I said. The baby looked at me. Hey baby remember me I said. The lady turned and saw me and made a noise like when my sister cut her thumb with the scissors. She looked at the gun on the table.

That man she said. She ran out the door with the baby.

What's the matter boy he said. He leaned over the table like a nice old man.

That's my baby I said.

That's the baby you tried to steal.

I don't know what I'm supposed to do I said.

Do about what.

I don't know. I need somebody to tell me.

I have a suggestion. Let's start by getting rid of that gun. He put his hand out. I grabbed the gun. I need that I said.

What for he said.

I tried to remember. I'm supposed to kill somebody.

Really. Who are you supposed to kill.

I looked at him and I was scared. I don't know I said.

Did somebody tell you to kill somebody.

No I said. I tried to think. The professor looked at me smiling like trying to coax Peter Rabbit out of a hole.

Then why do you think you are supposed to kill somebody.

I don't know.

Well where did you get the idea.

It's who killed Oliver I said.

Ah he said. Your friend who got killed is that it.

Yes.

You depended on him.

Yes. I said he was my I tried to think of the word Loomer used. All I could think of was Miller and I said he was my Miller.

Your leader. Your teacher.

I remembered the word. My guru.

That's a big loss for you he said. I thought how he knew. It makes you feel rudderless doesn't it.

I didn't know what the word meant. It meant something so I said yes. Rudderless.

You need to look in new directions. Seek new leadership. Learn to think for yourself.

That's what Loomer said I said. I remembered. He killed my guru so I'm supposed to kill his guru.

What did you say.

The black man I said. I'm supposed to kill his guru.

He was leaning forward and his hands were too close to the gun. I snatched the gun away from him and he jumped up in his chair. He was breathing hard and then he smiled.

Who's his guru.

You I asked. Are you his guru.

Me. Are you saying you want to kill me. Is that what you are talking about.

My insides bumped like a dirt road.

You're wrong he said. You're not supposed to kill anyone. He said it madly and I was scared. Is that why you want my help. Well listen to me my young friend. There are two problems with what you said. One it wasn't Davey who killed your guru. Two I'm not Davey's guru. Furthermore it's wrong to kill people. It won't bring Oliver back to life and it would only ruin your own life. Turn your mind to other things.

I cried.

You need to look ahead instead of the past. Get interested in something. Maybe we can figure up something good for you to do. Would you like me to help you.

I need to kill somebody.

Why.

Because he took my baby.

What baby.

Your baby. My baby. I loved my baby and he took it.

Do you mean Judy's baby for God's sake. That's not your baby and no reason to kill anybody about.

There was a big noise. People ran into the room. They said you freeze. They were cops in shirt sleeves pointing guns at me. One of them grabbed me by the shoulder and pointed his gun in my face. Stand up you he said. Another grabbed my gun on the table and said I got his gun.

What's going on the professor said.

It's all right sir the policeman said. We got him now.

What are you doing why are you here.

Someone called us the man said you're being held up.

The lady with the baby came in. I called them Daddy when I saw the gun she said.

For heavens sake there's no need for that we were having a peaceful conversation the professor said.

Nine one one the policeman said.

He came by the other day with that gun the lady said. He kidnapped my baby.

No no it's all right the baby is safe and sound the professor said.

Where'd you get that gun the policeman said.

Bought it I said.

We're going to take you in concealed weapon.

No need to do that the professor said. This is a peaceable visit I was giving Nick advice. The weapon isn't concealed it's right out on the table in plain sight.

After a while the police were sorry and left. The lady was sorry but the professor said all right. They went away and the professor talked again. I was glad he kept me from going with the police. Call me Harry he said.

Listen to me Harry said. Let's not have any talk about killing people. David Leo did not kill your Oliver get that through your head. Who told you that is trying to confuse you. Did Loomer tell you that.

I thought who told me. Loomer told me. I thought how did Harry know. I thought how did Harry know so many things.

David pushed Oliver Loomer told me I said.

Did you see David push Oliver did you actually see.

I don't know.

Let's check out a couple of facts shall we do that Nicky.

Sure.

Where were you when Oliver died.

In the woods.

What were you doing there. Were you supposed to shoot Davey. Was that what Oliver wanted you to do.

Yes. I thought how did Harry know.

Then what he said.

Loomer came along.

Loomer came along and told you he would do it and sent you off into the woods is that what happened.

Yes. I wondered how Harry knew. He wasn't there then I thought how did Harry know.

So you didn't see David push Oliver at the top of the falls did you. You didn't because you were back in the woods right.

I guess I didn't I said. I remembered seeing him push and I remembered not remembering.

Now tell me while you were back in the woods did you hear any shots.

Yes.

How many.

One.

Who do you think shot that shot.

Loomer.

Why Loomer.

I saw.

You saw him shoot that shot you really did.

I think I did.

What direction was he shooting.

Up.

Up in the sky.

Up the waterfall.

What did you think did you think he was shooting Davey as he said he would.

I thought he was shooting the black man.

But he didn't did he.

No.

Who came falling down the falls.

Oliver.

After Loomer shot up the falls.

Yes.

Oliver came falling down when you were expecting Davey to come falling down is that right.

Yes.

Then why isn't it obvious to you that Loomer shot Oliver.

Loomer I said.

He killed your friend don't you realize that.

Loomer I said.

You saw it yourself didn't you just tell me.

Loomer I said. I thought. I knew it I said.

I knew before but now I knew it. It made me jump up and down. I stood and jumped up and down. I knew it like I knew everything. I growled like the tiger's tongue and trumpeted like the elephant's pecker.

Easy boy. You knew it he said.

I saw it I said.

What did you see.

I saw Loomer kill Oliver.

It made me mad. I felt good and mad. I hit my fist in my palm. I aimed the gun at Harry. He ducked so I aimed it at the window. I said wow.

Now do you see why you mustn't kill Davey.

Not him I said. I smashed my fist and banged the gun against my head. Careful with that he said.

He deceived you Harry said. He induced you to deny the evidence of your eyes and your good common sense.

My good common sense.

Loomer. He's tricked you Nicky.

Wow I said. Dumb people don't see how they are tricked. I saw how I was tricked and it made me good and mad. I said if Loomer killed Oliver then Loomer took the baby.

Loomer didn't take the baby he said. Oliver took her and Loomer and Miller gave her back to us.

That's what I meant I said Loomer gave the baby away. I heard a voice talk not Harry. The voice said ask him.

I asked him. Will you help me I said.

Gladly Nicky I can put you in touch with counselor types. We can give you tests to discover your aptitudes and special interests.

The voice said tell him. You help me kill Loomer I said.

Kill Loomer don't be ridiculous. Don't talk about killing you mustn't think in such terms.

I thought in such terms. The voice said if you were smart you would do it yourself. I said don't worry I'll do it myself.

No you won't Nicky you've got to rise above.

The voice said go to Miller Farm. I said I'll go to Miller Farm and kill him myself. I felt proud for doing that.

You stay here you can't go to Miller Farm. Stay right here you can come to me for help. We'll work out a program.

I went home. I worked at the Pompadour. I asked the voice what to do but it didn't say. One day I came back. Harry talked more. He said I would never amount if I killed somebody. He made me talk to a lady in an office. She had a white coat. I took a test and filled in blanks. The test was hard.

One day I went to Harry again. Harry talked about careers. He asked me if I liked to make things and the good feeling I get from making something. He said the good feeling if I make Nick Foster. I said how can I make Nick Foster. That's ridiculous I am him how can I make him. He said like I could build me out of me. It sounded like hard work. He said forming habits and getting interested. You're smarter than you think you are Harry said. He said I'm going to teach you how to think for yourself.

I liked when he said that. Oliver said I wasn't as smart as I think I am. Harry said Oliver was wrong. I liked it both. If I was not smart then I could do what Oliver said and not worry. If I was smart then I could do what I wanted and not worry. I heard the voice talking again not Harry. It talked about killing Loomer. It said don't tell Harry because Harry said I should get over it. If I don't tell Harry he won't say get over it. The voice talked and talked. I thought and it stopped talking and I stopped thinking. Then I didn't know what to do. If I thought I didn't know what to do too. If I didn't know what to do that's what I needed Harry for.

One day the voice said ask him for a ticket to Miller Farm. Harry said what do you want to go to Miller Farm for. I told him so I could kill Loomer.

He said get rid of that obsession in your mind who taught you that barbarous idea.

Thou shalt not kill everybody knows that I said.

One day I asked him for a ticket to Miller Farm again. Harry said no way. He said I'm not going to pay for an assassination no way. I said what's assassination and he told me.

Next time I asked him the voice said tell him I don't want to kill Loomer. I want to see Miller.

Why do you want to see Miller he said.

I remembered. Because Miller is God Himself I said.

He breathed and looked at the room like he wanted to lie down. He said would you like to discuss religion with me.

Okay I said.

He talked about God Himself. I don't know what he was talking about. I came back and he talked again. He said God Himself was in me. I don't know what he meant. I looked around inside but I couldn't find him.

He said most people don't think Miller is God Himself he is more like a guru. People have different God Himselfs he said. He said if I wanted to believe Miller was God Himself was up to me. He said the most important thing was.

I thought. I thought about Oliver my ex-guru. I thought about ex. I thought how nicer when Harry talked to me. I had funny thoughts about Oliver like I was smarter than Oliver. I couldn't believe it. I thought about scolding me for thinking it. I told him I didn't mean it I just thought it it just happened to think itself. I thought who was smarter Oliver or Harry. I thought would Harry ever ask me to shoot me someone across the tiger's tongue. I thought Harry telling me don't shoot him Oliver telling me shoot. I thought Loomer shooting Oliver because it was bad to shoot the black man. I thought it must be very bad to shoot the black man if so many people thought it was bad.

Harry told me the black man hitchhiked home from the island. He told me I should forgive the black man forever. He said the black man was trying to live his life like I was trying to live mine. I thought about Harry talking about me trying to lead my life and I cried. I felt sorry for me trying to live my life.

Harry said the religious way was forgive your enemies. I thought enemies and couldn't think of any. I thought who I was mad at I could forgive him. Loomer I was mad at so I told Harry I forgive Loomer. Harry said that was good of me I might turn into a saint yet. The voice said ask Harry for a ticket to Miller Farm to forgive Loomer.

The voice said I am smart. Smarter than Harry thought. Tell Harry if you don't give me a ticket I'll hitchhike. Dumb people can't do things like hitchhike.

What for he said. You don't want to go there.

The voice said Harry wasn't supposed to tell me what I wanted. I was supposed to want what I wanted without him telling me. I do too want to go there.

What for.

I want to live there.

Live there. His eyes got big like fried eggs. What an interesting idea. Why do you want to live there.

The voice said tell him because nobody fights. People are nice there. Miller takes care of you there.

He said would you make peace with Loomer.

Sure.

He wouldn't get me a ticket. It's not that I'm afraid you'd get lost he said. I'd rather take you myself if it comes to that. That way I can see you stay out of trouble.

The voice said tell him if you don't take me I'm going to hitchhike.

One morning I went out to hitchhike. I told the first man where I was going so I could kill Loomer. He made me get out on the road. The police called Harry. They told him about the gun. Harry came and took me home. I said you can't do that he said.

The voice said keep trying. If you don't take me I'll hitchhike again I said.

I can't take you he said. I have my wife only recently back and my daughter and my work to do.

That's all right I said I'll hitchhike.

On the other hand I'm retired Harry said. I have no necessary schedule if it would save you. I don't intend to take you to Miller Farm only to have you murdering people.

The voice said tell him he was my new guru and I'll do what he says. If he takes me to Miller Farm I'll do what he says. If he doesn't take me I'll hitchhike. The voice said never give up you owe it to Nicky.

One day the voice said kidnap him and make him take you. So I got my gun and I kidnapped Harry and made him take me to Wicker Falls. Dumb people can't do that. It took two days.

Harry said why I shouldn't kill Loomer. He said you are learning to be a civilized man and civilization depends on turning the cheek. We stopped at the motel. I watched television. I saw a program about a man chasing a man who killed his girlfriend. When he got the man in a garage he shot him with a machine gun. I liked that. I kept the gun under my pillow so Harry couldn't trick me and escape.

In the morning after breakfast I went out back with my gun. I shot a tree. Harry said what the hell are you doing.

I said practicing.

Practicing for what.

I said I needed to practice if I was going to kill Loomer.

He said stupid. You mustn't do that mustn't. I cried.

He said we've gone as far as we can. Now I'm going to stop this nonsense turn around and go home.

I said you can't because I'm kidnapping you.

The voice said if you give up now you'll never be Nicky again. You owe it to Loomer. We got in the car and drove on. Harry drove. I made him drive all the way.

The voice said Harry wants you to think for yourself. If you think for yourself you'll kill Loomer because Harry doesn't want you to think of that. Dumb people can't figure out things like that.

Are you mad at me I said.

What the hell do you think.

I don't know I said.

23

Harry Field

Harry took Nick Foster to Wicker Falls against everyone's advice. Barbara, Judy, Joe Rice, Connie. He went anyway because otherwise Nick would go by himself and anything could happen. He liked the unusual feeling of intervening in events.

He hoped he wouldn't run into Lena, who had called to say she had been invited to Miller Farm. How she got the invitation she didn't say. He didn't tell her he was going there too. For a moment he was irritated, thinking if she goes I can't, then decided it didn't matter.

He let Nick believe that he was kidnapping him. That began when Nick showed up one day, pointed his gun at Harry and said, Take me to Miller Farm. You have to because I am kidnapping you. Harry persuaded him to wait a day so he could tell his family. If I just go off with you now, Harry said, my wife and daughter will call the police and come after us and you'll end up in jail instead of Miller Farm.

How do I know you won't escape? Nick asked. If I let you go you'll outwit me.

Where can I go? Harry said. This is where I live. If you come back tomorrow I'll be here.

So Nick postponed the kidnapping a day. When he came back he pointed his gun at Harry and said, Now. By this time Harry was packed and ready to go, against the advice of everybody. What will you do if I refuse? Harry asked Nick.

You can't because I'm pointing the gun at you.

Would you shoot me?

Nick didn't answer. His hand looked nervous and Harry realized the gun could go off because of nervousness. If you shot me, Harry said, how would you get to Miller Farm?

I'd hitchhike, Nick said. I'm not so dumb.

In that case I guess I'd better take you, shouldn't I?

So Harry let Nick think he was kidnapping him. He thought he could rescue himself at any moment if necessary. Though the gun pointed at him from time to time, the worst danger was that it would go off accidentally, in which case it might hit anything including Nick. So he humored Nick and pretended. The length of the trip would give him time to change Nick's mind. He would rescue Nick from himself and protect him from others.

He drove in the cool morning with Nick beside him like any other automobile trip, except when he remembered the purpose. The strangeness shocked him but exhilarated him too. He had built his long eventless university career leading the life of the mind. Chasing kidnappers and dissuading potential killers was not what professors do. But if you live long enough, everything can happen.

While driving he struggled with the lightness in his head. Precursor of a stroke. He hoped it wouldn't happen on the road, and he kept conscious by force of will. They drove a long time the first day and stopped at a motel. He kept thinking of ways to trick Nick. He could drive aimlessly around the country and Nick would never realize they weren't going to Miller Farm. He had opportunities to escape at every stop. A phone call to the police would stop it. At the motel Nick slept with his pistol under his pillow. It would be easy to take the pistol then. Sometimes during the day Nick fell asleep with the pistol in his lap. Harry didn't seize these opportunities. He refrained out of respect for Nick. Since he knew he could rescue himself he wanted to treat Nick honorably. He drove and he talked, lecturing Nick. He did not think Nick would actually kill anyone but he wanted to be sure. He wanted Nick to transfer his allegiance to Miller, exchange the guru again. His colleagues would tease him about turning his disciple over to such a fraud but never mind, lives were at stake. What to tell Miller? Explain to him, Nick's a good person at heart. Miller would understand.

When they arrived at the Sleepy Wicker after two days he was still dizzy, but there was too much to think about to notice. Nicky was humble. Harry said, If you promise to give up killing, I'll take you to Miller tomorrow. I'll persuade him to let you stay. Would you like that?

Yes.

Nick had eyes like a nocturnal animal. He told Harry there was a voice in his head telling him what to do. Is that God talking to me?

No, Harry said. It's you talking to you. It's in your head.

That's what I said, Nicky said.

They took separate rooms that night because they were almost there and Nick wasn't afraid of Harry pulling tricks any more. When Harry called Miller that evening to warn him of what was coming, they said Miller was busy and call back tomorrow.

Trying to sleep Harry heard Nick's television through the walls. As long as I can hear him, he thought. He woke in the morning at eight-thirty. He banged on Nick's door, then back to his room to shave shower and dress. When he was ready he knocked on Nick's door again but no answer.

That was odd. There was no reason for him not to reply and it scared Harry, what to think. He waited and knocked again. He couldn't think of anything but to ask at the desk, but this was embarrassing and he waited some more. Finally he told the clerk. My friend doesn't answer the door; he said, ashamed of the alarm in his voice.

The woman was surprised. The kid in 19? He left.

When?

Couple hours ago. Went walking down the road.

Which way?

Village way. Maybe he got a bite at the Bonny Vista. She spoke soothingly to his anxiety.

Trying not to be alarmed, he drove to Wicker Falls. No Nick at the Bonny Vista Café. The cashier just came on, hadn't noticed anyone, she said. Harry forgot about his own breakfast. Like a zoo keeper chasing an escaped panther or poisonous snake. Don't alarm the countryside. How far could Nick go in two hours on foot? Harry was ashamed of skipping breakfast for it converted imagination into emergency, and his imagination was too lurid.

He saw a parked police car at the intersection. Uh-oh. The village was a few buildings around the intersection, and the police car sat quietly in front of the hardware store. Next to the post office and the grocery store. A small group of people stood around, pricking his nerves with sudden fear. He stopped across the street. I'll get a paper, he said. Maybe Nick is here. Maybe not. A young policeman leaning against his car chatted with three or four citizens, none of them Nick. Harry strolled over. Behind the police car a yellow tape stretched across the front of the hardware store. Yellow tape signifies caution, construction, danger. It doesn't have to mean a crime. I'm not ready, Harry said.

Already too late? Whatever was fated to happen has already happened. The newspaper rack was outside the hardware store. Pay inside. The policeman watched him. To pay for the paper he would have to go through the tape. The policeman said, You don't want to go in there.

You can pay me, a woman said.

There were four people besides the policeman. Two farmers, a laborer with a pony tail, and the woman. She was hearty swinging her arms in a big green sweatshirt.

What happened?

Man shot.

Who?

So it was a crime. Thinking furiously, that idiot, damned idiot. Calm down. The worst case in your imagination never comes true. Harry knew this and relied on it late at night when his daughter had not come home or his wife was late. Always it was something else, unrelated. Just because it happens to be raging in your mind doesn't mean a thing. Whatever happened here had nothing to do with Nick. He counted on this as a principle.

I forget his name, the policeman said. Any of you folk remember his name?

Nobody could.

An old farmer with a rueful smile. First murder hereabouts in thirty-six year, he said. He said "hereabouts" in the old New England way and "year" without an s like "sheep" or "fish."

Now we're no different from city folk, the woman said.

You don't know who got killed? Harry said.

Somebody from Miller Farm, the policeman said. Man come in from Miller Farm to identify him.

Miller Farm, worse and worse, Harry thought. Let it not be Nick, oh Nick let it not be you. But where then did Nick go, what happened to him, in the tidal advance of the news?

Nobody caught the name? Harry said.

Why, you know folks out there? the woman said.

One or two, Harry said.

You're from Ohio, the younger farmer said, reading Harry's license plate.

They looked at him, friendly and wary. The woman laughed. Well, she said, it should be familiar to you. Drive by shootings, gang killings, no different from anyplace else. Ohio.

Drive by shooting? Harry said.

The policeman shrugged.

Shot from a car? There, I knew it. Nick would not have been shooting from a car.

I'd tell you the guy's name if I could remember it, the policeman said. He's inside. You want to take a look?

No thanks, Harry said. A quick reaction, followed by thoughts. Maybe I should at that, he said.

If you like such sights, the policeman said. He went to the tape.

Harry hesitated. It wasn't a frail blond kid, was it?

Frail blond? Nah. He lifted the tape for Harry to go under. Harry declined. Never mind, he said.

I don't like dead bodies either, Luella said.

The shame of receiving sympathy for that almost changed Harry's mind. Not quite, though.

Swarthy, the policeman said. Kinda ugly. Foreign looking.

Loomer, Harry thought. Let it not be Loomer, please not. Too late, too late.

Luella was talking, grinning for the adventure of it. News, nothing like this happened in this place for thirty-six years. Tell me folks, have we got a Mafia now? I was at the desk, busy with the basket display. I heard a bang. I didn't think gun, I just thought bang. Didn't pay no attention maybe a couple minutes, maybe five. After a while I got thinking you don't ordinarily hear that kind of bang on the streets of Wicker Falls so I went to the door and there he was.

Where?

Half sidewalk half street. I seen him lying there and blood and I says, Uh-oh.

That's what I'd say too, the laborer said.

Jeannette in the post office saw him same time. We looked out our doors at the same moment.

Dead already?

Looked dead to me. I didn't care to look, I called police while Jeannette did what she could for him.

Dead when I got here, the policeman said. Coroner will fix the finer time.

Harry said, Maybe I should take a look. No I guess I won't.

Suit yourself.

I guess if you know somebody out there, you want to know who it was, Luella said. Like me. Main thing was make sure it wasn't Jacko. Soon as I knew that, I didn't look no more.

That Miller place, the older farmer said. I always said they's not good for the country to be living so close.

Any info on the killer? the laborer said.

Rose said he got away in a pickup truck, Luella said.

I thought you said nobody seen the killer, the laborer said.

Somebody seen him drive away in the guy that got shot's truck.

How could that be if nobody seen the killing and you was the first to seen the body?

Beats me, Luella said. That's what Rose said.

Truck's probably miles away by now, the policeman said.

You could set up a roadblock, that would catch him.

If they think that would work, they'll do it, the policeman said. If not they won't.

Nicky in the stolen truck, where would he go? Not back to the motel, for Harry would have seen him. Heading north? Eventually he'll bump into the Canadian border and what then? He wouldn't know what to do. They would shoot him down while he was trying to get someone to tell him what to do. Miller Farm? The voice in Harry's head, if he had believed in voices, said Nick went out to Miller Farm. Because he would want to go home. The nearest facsimile of home. Miller Farm for sanctuary, even if he lacked the concept of sanctuary.

Someone said, I just been thinking. If the killer hijacked the victim's truck, he must of left his car some place. That would be a lead.

Harry was fidgeting, thinking Miller Farm, I must hurry to Miller Farm. The laborer noticed him. You're a stranger here.

You just noticed? the younger farmer said. He's from Ohio. That's what we was talking about, all the drive-by shootings in Ohio.

Passing through, Harry said. I'm at the Sleepy Wicker.

Well you picked a good time. It don't happen every day here like in Ohio.

It doesn't happen where I come from either, Harry said.

The policeman's radio jabbered. The policeman went around the other side of the car. When he came back he looked strained, scared. Crime wave, he said. It's spreading.

What you mean, Fox?

More killing?

The policeman nodded. He looked shocked.

266

We're making history today, Luella said. Note the day, when crime broke out in Wicker Falls.

Where? the younger farmer said.

Miller Farm, the policeman said, with irritation. It's trouble out at Miller Farm.

Shit, the older farmer said. I told you, I told you.

What kind of trouble? Luella said.

I always knew that place was ready to blow up, the old farmer said. You going out there Fox?

Got to stay here, the policeman said.

You want to go? We can watch the body for you.

No thanks.

You're a good boy, Luella said.

Stay away from Miller Farm, that's my creed, the old farmer said. They got a stash of arms big enough to blow up the Pentagon. Christ I don't even drive out Rib Rock no more.

Afraid they'll shoot you, Chet?

Moral infection, the man said, the devil's out there. Stay away, my advice. He noticed Harry. No offense, he said.

He's just a visitor, Luella said. He knows people there. How come you know them? she asked.

Harry didn't want to answer but not answering would give offense. One of them got involved with my daughter, he said. It's over now.

Ah they reach out their tentacles and snare the kids, the farmer said. Brainwashing, you gotta protect your young folks.

Not my young folks, the laborer said.

It's like bringing the worst ills of Ohio into our community, the old farmer said. Drive by shootings and skinhead militias arming to blow up the government and take over.

This ain't a militia, the younger farmer said. What I heard, this is more like a religious community.

Luella looked at Harry. Are you worrying about your daughter's friend? she said.

You can look at him if you want, the policeman said.

No thanks. Harry couldn't stand it any more. Excuse me I better get going. He went back to his car.

Take care, the young farmer said. Be careful in Ohio.

Harry was thinking so loud it came out as spoken words in the car. Where am I going? Now what do I do? Look for him. Where can I find him? Miller Farm. What will I do if I find him? It's too late, he's dead by now. Don't jump to conclusions. Who else would come along and shoot a Millerite on a street where nothing like this has happened in thirty-six years? He's doomed. Goodbye Nick. Thought I could save you, sorry. Catch him, teach him, teach him what, his doom? Too late.

Going to Miller Farm was like Nick going home. Home is sleep. Whatever it is, Harry, thinking so hard he was not thinking at all, drove out Rib Rock Road toward Miller Farm. At the point where Rib Rock enters the woods and starts to climb, he heard the next fold of trouble wrapping him like a cabbage leaf, the alienating sound of a police siren in the trees. The howl of the law rising out of Rib Rock like steam, then flashing lights behind scaring him into full stop in the ditch while the sleek car tore past up the hill into the still deeper woods ahead. Sirening the foxes and squirrels, screeching the skunks and raccoons, outshrieking the hermit thrushes and white throated sparrows. A side effect of the news he had already heard, trouble at Miller Farm, like the swell from a hurricane miles away but coming closer. The sirens and armed forces of the world chasing Nick.

He waited in the ditch, opening his air-conditioned window to let the siren recede and another siren came up behind him, a new wild bird in the spring. This too got louder and burst into view through the trees with flashing lights heading to whatever it was. Again he waited for the sound to fade and disappear and the forest silence to return, hoping to hear some bird voice, running water, falling twigs, leaf rustle, to reestablish himself before leaving the ditch and crawling back onto the road.

Ten minutes of whatever it takes to get out of the woods at the top where Rib Rock flattens out between fields and he could see ahead one of those flashing police cars stopped at the side of the road like an enameled calico turtle. Parked by the Miller mailbox where the drive goes in. He stopped behind it.

The police car was empty. It blocked the entrance to the Miller drive with its lights flashing. He figured it was intentionally blocking the way and the policemen themselves were down in the compound.

He sat a while in his car, while the lights in the police car buzzed his eyes. He turned off his engine and listened. What he heard was veins and arteries. He got out of his car, taking his keys. Walked up to the police car and looked in. A newspaper on the seat. The car would have been easy to steal. He looked at the gate and the electrified fence and still thinking in spoken words said, What should I do?

Walk in, he replied. The gate behind the police car was shut but not locked. He opened it, trespassing, and walked down the drive toward the woods. The distance looked greater when he was on foot. As he walked he listened for news. Mostly he heard his thoughts saying Jesus are you scared? Making every thought loud to prove he was alive, so the birds in the field could hear. Imagining rather than seeing meadowlark, bobolink, redwinged blackbird. The villainous cowbird that lays its eggs in other birds' nests. Telling the birds in his out-speaking thought, we're just going down to Miller Farm to see what's going on. If we see any trouble we'll retreat. I am looking for Nicky Foster. My young mostly innocent but murderous friend, to make sure he's all right and had nothing to do with the crime wave that has alarmed the people of Wicker Falls. The good people of Wicker Falls.

Explaining further: You'd do this too if you recognized the power you had over such an innocent yet deformed young person. Responsibility for the power of years teaching the young how to think for themselves. Opportunity not only to make a moron think and a madman sane but to save lives, an opportunity that doesn't come to just any professor in a lifetime.

Yet if the madman has chosen through stubbornness to doom not only his victim and himself but this whole community of believers whose gullibility I may scorn but whose goodness I would never question, it's not my fault. It's not my fault, Harry said to the birds as he descended toward the clearing.

He heard a car straining up the hill from the compound. A large black luxury car reeking elegance, Cadillac or Lincoln. He stepped onto the grass to let it pass. The driver looked at him, an old woman. The car stopped, she opened the window, called, Harry, get in. Hurry.

Lena. She looked a hundred years old.

The gate's blocked, he said.

She looked ahead. What's that car doing there? she said.

She looked as if she were fighting off a stroke, if a person can fight off a stroke.

That's the police. They're blocking the entrance.

Tell them to move. She blew her horn.

There's no one there.

How can I get out?

You can't.

Oh help me, she said. How did you get here?

That's my car out there.

Can we go in it?

Yes, if you want to. What's going on?

Never mind. She got out of her car. Come on, she said.
Quick.

Are you just going to leave your car? he said.

I'll leave a note. I'll pick it up later.

Why are you so eager to leave? he said.

Get out of here first.

He followed her to the gate. He didn't want to go without
finding out about Nick. I'm looking for somebody, he said.

Not now, she said.

He opened the gate for her and she went to his car. Are you
staying anywhere? she asked.

The Sleepy Wicker Motel.

Take me there.

He held the door while she got in his car.

Are you going to tell me what happened? he said.

The world just ended, she said. She looked white and with-
ered. Just get going, won't you please?

24

Lena Fowler Armstrong

It was Harry Field and he drove me in his car down Rib Rock Road through Wicker Falls to the Sleepy Wicker. What happened? he said. He was impatient, I shocked. Give me time, I said.

You didn't tell me Miller had only one eye, I said.

I didn't notice, he said.

(That's how I knew he was God, when I saw his one eye. It was big when I approached, full of the brutal universe contradicting the sweetness of his smile. But when I looked from the big eye to the other, I saw the big one was dead, made of glass, the live eye was the other. That's how I knew Miller was God.) You never noticed his glass eye, I said.

He said Miller had his back to the light. What happened back there? he asked. Why did you say the world just ended?

Give me time, I said. I told him why I went to see Miller. (I went because Harry was all scoff and scorn. The force of his negative thoughts crossing my field reversed them to positive. I went to Miller propelled by Harry's solar wind.) I was mad at you, Harry, I was mad.

So I wrote to Miller. Miller Farm, Wicker Falls, New Hampshire. Obsequiously polite, asking for the right to visit. I told him I wanted to meet God, and he invited me to come. So I went. (I took the Lincoln and drove. I reached Wicker Falls in the evening and stayed at the Sleepy Wicker Motel. I called from the motel and announced myself and they told me they'd send a man in the morning to direct me.)

Lena, Harry said. The world just ended. There's a police car blocking the entry. A policeman in Wicker Falls said somebody was killed, and somebody else was killed in Wicker Falls. Will you please tell me what happened?

I'm telling you, I said.

Can you jump to the end, and then go back to the beginning?

The end? I said. The end is the end.

What do you mean?

The end is they killed him.

Killed who?

I couldn't say it, but I did. God. They killed God.

Miller? They killed Miller?

That's what I meant, yes. The car continued to bump down Rib Rock Road.

The space represents the story's impact. The story is a tragedy.

Who killed him?

That's what I'm trying to tell you. I loved him and they killed him, I said through my tears.

That shut him up. It shut us both up while the car rumbled into Wicker Falls and then zip down the highway toward the motel.

I loved him, Harry, I said.

He looked gloomy and didn't speak.

I said, I presume you'll insist on getting me a room of my own at the Sleepy Wicker?

That would be best, he said.

With no point in getting mad anymore, though you wonder why he keeps pursuing me if he doesn't want me when he has me. Why else did he come all the way to Wicker Falls?

After a long time he said again, Tell me what happened.

Here's what I told him. The man sent from Miller to direct me, this stereotype, farmer with felt hat, long mustache, red chest where the buttons open in front, I followed his pickup truck, driven like a tractor crawling up the country road into the woods and across the field and down to the compound, which fit Harry's description well enough. A woman on the porch of the Victorian house said wait inside. Waited on the sofa by the big staircase while people went in and out, up stairs and down, wondering if I would recognize Miller from his description, a face like Emerson, hair like Liszt. Tableware clacking, which made me think of lunch, so I went out. I saw the building Harry had called the altered barn and through its open doors two long tables with people coming in to eat. I asked a boy in an apron if Mr. Miller was here. I should have recognized him without being told. As I approached (across the length of the room) I saw that an accident had befallen the Emersonianism of his face and realized it was the enlargement of his eye. It was a single eye and I almost stopped. He looked at me with that enormous universal eye blasted (I thought) by the same electricity that created life. He stared at me and I faltered. The woman on his left beckoned me and Miller bowed his head with a smile.

When I looked next I realized the awful eye was false. Dead. The live eye was the other, shrewd, partially concealed under the eyebrow. That was the eye that saw me, and when I switched from the false glass to it I recognized divinity. Next to the false display, concealed by it, the real thing.

I told Harry my belief. (God looks through every living eye.

If you look directly into someone's eye you'll see and be seen by God. You see him fleetingly, God dispersed. Miller's false eye led me to God concentrated. It deceived me until the falsity made me look at the live eye next to it. From then on the glass was merely an advertisement to warn that I was in the presence of God's Eye, not where I thought but shrewd and observant in the shade. When I found this live eye with God looking through, I saw God concentrated.)

He said, Do you want to interview me for the papers or do you want to sit at my feet?

I told him I wanted to give myself to God.

How do you propose to do that? he said.

That depends on what God wants from me.

Then you want to see me in private.

Yes.

Have lunch first. Sit at the end of the table. When you have finished ask the boy to show you to the guest room and wait there. It will be a long wait so you'd better have something to read unless you'd rather pray. I'll come to you.

I waited all afternoon. Eventually I heard a bell and saw people returning to the altered barn. A woman invited me to the dining room. Do you think he's forgotten? I asked. Patience, she said. She had a long braid down her back like a guitar player. I returned to the dining room. I saw Miller across the room. From this distance I could not see the disfiguration of his eyes, and he looked like any farmer, animated and jovial.

He left before I was finished. I hurried after him, heading toward the woods. I haven't forgotten, he said. Wait for me.

I returned to the guest room, and the light faded. The guest room had a bed and a small table with a clock, a single wooden rocking chair, a faded glass-framed picture showing a child looking at her reflection in a pool. The window was open with a

screen outside. I heard spring birds in the woods. Music somewhere, a radio, a cottage door shut. Footsteps, but mostly the
house was still. I read by the bedside table while I waited.

He came after ten. I heard the quick step, then a knock on the
door, like a doctor entering the consultation room. He wore a
dark blue robe like a cheap magician. I saw the false advertising
eye before I found the godlike real one.

You stayed?

You told me to wait.

He looked me over. How old are you? he said.

Seventy.

You don't need to stay if you don't want to.

I wanted to see you, I said.

You've done that.

I wanted more.

You want me to see you?

Why yes, I said.

If you stay the night you'll need your luggage. I'll send Jeff
for it. What do you need?

Just the bag in the trunk.

Give me your car keys and he'll bring it. Go to bed. I'll be
back.

Are you going to visit me in my dreams?

God don't fool around with dreams, he said.

Jeff brought my bag and I got ready for bed. I showered and
perfumed and made up my face. I sat in bed by the lamp and
pretended to read.

Waiting for my lover. The worldly cynical half of my soul
laughed. This was not a question of being deceived. I did
wonder which came first, the gratification of lust or the pleasure of suckering me. I estimated Miller to be sixty. Does he like

seventy-year old women? Or all women? Will he have to over-come repugnance to make love to me?

He came back in the blue robe and sat in the chair beside the bed where I was propped up. What do you want to say to me?

I hear you call yourself God.

Do you believe me?

I do and I don't, I said. Were you born with a glass eye?

He smiled and did not reply. Do you want me to overwhelm you? he said. Watch. He leaned over me, supporting himself with his hands, one on either side, his face looking down at me close.

Look me in the eye. Not the glass one.

I giggled. Are you hypnotizing me?

Do you want to be hypnotized?

I want to know what I am doing.

Then look in my eye.

He removed the blankets that were covering me. You were waiting for me, he said. He opened his robe and there he was, ready for me as I was for him. Look at me, he said.

He descended. I felt him and I thought, filled with God. I had forgotten how good it could be. This guy was a charlatan, a fake, I knew that because he knew it, charlatan, fake, mere man. It makes no difference, though, and that's the point. Even a charlatan can be God, which I suspected when Harry first told me about him and knew for certain when I saw the false eye leading to the real eye, and confirmed in my body when I felt him in me.

That's what Harry can't understand. For him it's one or the other. If he's God he can't be fake. If he's fake he can't be God. But of course he's fake. He's God in spite of that and when he surged, I fell in love with Him all over again.

He lay beside me afterwards and spent the night. My wives don't mind, he said. Of course he has wives, the old rooster, taking his pleasure, why shouldn't he?

I said, You like me in my seventy-year disguise?

Seventy is beautiful, he said. God is in you too.

Just not to the same degree, I said in my sarcastic mode. He didn't mind. He knows what I think.

Eventually he slept. I looked at him on his back with his open mouth, his breath clacketing like the gear works of an old farm machine, and I said, God is sleeping too. I knew what I was doing. Pretending, as good as real, I've been pretending all my life. I have pretended all my beliefs, my devotions, spirits, mediums and horoscopes. My Gods. Everything I ever believed was pretend, nothing else is possible. My marriage, which I pretended for forty years. Love, often. My home and family with my children. I planned to tell Miller when he awoke. Harry too, because I suspect he pretends his things as deliberately as I pretend mine. His pretense is logic, rational argument based on a prior pretense, whose premises he never questions. Let us suppose, if this, then that. I admired the audacity of the man who pretended to be God, believing in his pretense like any other person, so I went along with it, a good story. Lying awake while God slept, I pretended to debate the question of moving here to live, which would be a strong gesture but would mean leaving Anchor Island. I decided to ask his advice in the morning and was already thinking up ways to become a member of Miller Farm without giving up Anchor Island.

He got up early. Work to do, he said. I went back to sleep. I woke later full of love with the tenderness of Godly flesh remembering itself inside me.

Then I saw the police car flashing its lights in the sunny grove. People stood around and a policeman talked to them. In the barn tables were set for breakfast but there was confusion. A young woman directed me to a seat near Miller's. No one else was there. Go ahead, start, she said. I'll serve you.

I asked what's wrong. Somebody got in trouble with the law, she said.

They came then into the dining room, animated, exchanging opinions at their assigned places. The women around Miller's seat took their places, but Miller was not there. The woman next to me told me. She was in her forties with fair hair and a strong boned face. Someone's killed, she said. Miller went to Wicker Falls to identify him.

Who's killed? another asked.

That's what Miller went to find out.

What's the police car doing here?

That's a different police car. One car came for Miller. This came later. Katie, what's with the police car?

Katie at the other end of the table. They thought the killer was here. Somebody thought he escaped in a Miller pickup. But all the pickups are here. Now the cop don't know what to do.

Has anybody offered the policeman a bite to eat?

Ask him in.

The policeman came in the far door. He was young and shy.

Sit down, officer. What you like? Ham and eggs?

Just a single poached egg on toast would be nice if you have such a thing.

A man came in with a rifle. He had white fuzz around his chin and his eyes were hot. He leaned the rifle against the wall and sat down. There was a row of rifles next to it. Others brought more rifles to stack next to those already there.

It was quieter in the dining room after the policeman came in. I saw his golden head down the row, leaning forward as he forked his poached egg and toast into his mouth. The people around me were worrying who was killed, eliminating those who were here, leaving others.

Miller's back, someone said. A word flashed down the table and across the room like electricity: Loomer. Loomer? Loomer. I saw shock but I didn't see anyone break down in grief.

Miller came in the door with another policeman. Set the room up for a meeting, he said.

Hey Miller, was it Loomer? The word Loomer bounced through the room like a tennis ball.

The boys and girls with aprons picked up the tables, which were boards on saw horses, stacked them on the side, took the chairs and converted the dining room into a meeting room. Table in front with a microphone. The golden poached egg policeman left. The other policeman, a football player with a bulldog jaw, watched from the side. He noticed the stacked rifles. What are these? he said.

What do they look like?

Whose are they? the policeman said.

Our God given right. You don't like it, ask God.

The policeman placed himself near the wall where the rifles leaned. He folded his arms.

We hunt with them. We protect ourselves. They guard us from the government.

Make sure you know how to handle them, the policeman said.

We can handle them, don't you worry.

People filled the room, all kinds, work clothes, country dresses, jeans, sweat shirts. I sat near the back. As the people returned Miller scrutinized them, grave and wrathful. His false eye grew like the cyclops. Facing that wrath I thought deliberately of last night's penis, the whiskers that scratched my neck, the loving sensitivity which was my secret.

All were seated except Miller in front and the puzzled bulldog policeman among the rifles. A long silence. I thought oddly of Harry whose scorn was responsible for my being here. Myself in combat with Harry, refuting him with my presence. My superiority in being able to see not only what he saw, namely, the fraudulence of Miller, but also what he could not see, the divinity of Miller. I saw the little arguments by which Harry cut Miller down, scoffing at his small backwater camp, quibbling questions such as where was God before Miller and where will God be after he dies. The limits of Harry's number-based faith that could not conceive of the multiplicity of God and Miller everywhere. How that language of numbers blindered him with simple-minded propositions, like that if there was one God there could be no others. Or if Miller was single and God was single then every other manifestation of God was a refutation, whereas I knew from my eyes that God and Miller were not only one but everywhere. It made no difference how many Gods there were because the idea of number has no meaning.

At last Miller spoke, his voice loud through the speaker. I went with the police this morning, he said, to identify Jake Loomer, who was shot to death in Wicker Falls in front of the hardware store.

I expected an exhalation, a gasp or moan, but the room was quiet. Jake Loomer, he repeated. One shot from a pistol, close range. No one saw the killer.

He looked around the room as if the killer were among us, or some one would know who he was.

The police would like to know if Loomer drove his own truck to Wicker Falls this morning, Miller said.

Loomer's truck is right here where it belongs.

That's why the police would like to know if he drove it. Someone was seen in one of our pickups after Loomer was shot.

I heard people looking at each other, realizing things.

He went to get eggs, a man in the back said.

Loomer? With his truck? Did anybody go with him?

Not as I know.

It was silent while Miller's glass eye searched the crowd.

What are you suggesting, Miller?

It grieves me, Miller said. The history of God is a history of followers who have fought each other for proximity. A history of warfare. We came here to escape the rivalry of churches. We came to unite the follower and the source. To make God and disciple one. I have seen the rivalry even among my own believers. Jealousy and envy. I didn't realize it had gone so far and I'm at fault. Now we have a tragedy and I must do. There will be a meeting of my elders directly following. Sit down please.

Sit down, Miller repeated.

He was looking at the back of the room. Take a seat, he said. We're having a meeting.

I saw a young man with yellow hair. He walked up past the bulldog policeman and the rifles.

You've come back to us? Miller said. What do you want?

The young man, scarcely more than a boy, was working his mouth. He looked like trying to speak but unable. Finally it came out. Are you Miller? he said.

You know who I am, Nick.

Are you God?

If you say so.

The boy began to moan. His voice reminded me of a wary cat warning off another and it turned suddenly into a screech with words. I didn't hear the first words and then I did hear. Why did you do this to me? he cried.

I don't know exactly what I saw. The young man showed something in his palm to Miller. Miller leaned forward to see. From the side someone shouted, Drop that, and the bulldog policeman drew his gun. I heard a bang or pop like a cap pistol. Miller ducked behind the table, I thought he was looking for something he had dropped. The bulldog policeman ran to the door behind the table. I don't know what became of the boy, he disappeared. There was a roar of outraged voices. There were men scrambling over the chairs knocking over women to get their rifles against the wall. Several raised their guns, with two or three shots that went off like bombs in the room full of smoke, and I saw they had shot the bulldog policeman in the back as he ran out the door. The men with their rifles ran past the fallen policeman, I don't know where they were going. I heard shots receding. I didn't know what they were chasing or running from.

People crowded around the table where Miller had ducked, and someone screamed, then a lot of screaming and shouts of No. Other policemen ran in and out with radio voices and static.

I was in the crowd around the table. My lover—I thought of him as my lover—lay on the ground where the people stooped over. He had blood on his face and his mouth was open the way he had slept in my bed last night. I recognized something lying beside him and picked it up. A woman put her head with her long black hair on his chest and another held him by the hand. His mouth was moving slowly, he was trying to speak, but there was no sound, and he had no eyes.

Next, though I don't remember a transition, we were standing back and Miller was stretched out flat on a table and someone had closed his eye, and I handed the other eye to someone who tried without success to put it back in, and his face was ashy and someone folded his hands. They slipped down by his sides, and whoever folded them tried to fold them again but they kept slipping down.

Who are you? a woman said to me.

A visitor, I said. I came to see Miller.

Well there he is. Take a look.

What's going to happen?

They'll kill that boy.

I remember him, one said. He was simple and sweet but not no more he ain't.

How can we live without Miller?

We won't have to. The police will come and massacre us.

A man came in where the others had left. What's happening? they asked him. They're chasing the boy and the police are chasing them, he said.

The woman said to me, You better leave.

I forced myself to think that until yesterday this man was nothing to me. Now he was the world and it had come to an end. I got ready to die. I went back to the room, got my bag, packed and went to my car. I sat in it. I couldn't move.

I heard fireworks in the woods and guessed it was gunfire. I sat in my car a long time not knowing what to do. Waiting for something like an astronomer looking through a hole in the universe. I heard the sirens and saw another police car coming down the hill into the compound. Two policemen jumped out with drawn guns and two more came running down the hill behind them. They ran by me and toward the woods and then there was another eruption of fireworks that I knew to be gunfire. I saw the smoke coming out of the woods. I heard shouts and a woman screaming. The scream unhooked me from where I hung, and I started the car. I drove up the hill leaving the compound behind. I didn't know what had happened, nor what I had seen, nor what was yet to come, except that I had been granted a view of the world. If I had arrived a day earlier or later, I would have missed it. That narrow time window proved that it was designed for me. World, seething volcanically just for me. The devil had escaped from Miller's body and spread in sulphur and gunpowder into the earth's atmosphere. I thought I had mistaken the meaning of his eye and the lure and sweetness of my love was devil-born. Later I recovered my vision and understood the three persons of his divinity, Miller the God, Miller the Devil, Miller the fraud, my three lovers in one, while numerical Harry knew nothing.

I told Harry most of this in some sort of order while he drove me to the Sleepy Wicker Motel. I thought he would try to go to bed with me there but he didn't. He kept shaking his head and clucking as if it were his fault. His fault? The trouble with Harry is the enormity of his desire to think he's important. I brought the murderer, he said. I brought him in my car. If I hadn't brought him it wouldn't have happened. I thought I could prevent it.

His morbid guilt irritated me. Well you couldn't, I said, so you'd better stop moaning about it.

PART FIVE

25

Jake Loomer

What is this place? I must have slipped and fallen, it's too damn cold. I'm talking, can you hear? I tell you half the people at Miller Farm are simple stupid folk who just want God a little closer than church. They're disaffected and easy to recruit. Tell them, if God came to earth in Christ why can't he come to earth in Miller? If Miller treats them well like love, they'll join, some will. It's the other half, or maybe a third or so. Some, anyway. I've forgotten why I came, do you recognize where we are?

Okay. As I was saying, these people are sore, angry, mad. They want to hate something and don't know what. Some hate government, some the TV, some hate teachers and well dressed people in the parking malls. That's hate growing all over the world, popping up where the old restraints are cut away, like the molten earth when you cut the crust open. This looks like a mountain, higher and colder every step. Are you getting tired? Me too. I told them it's me against you or them, especially them. Most people are afraid to hate God. But if you tell them God's not out there but here, living as Miller, that makes the rebellion colorful. Miller the new God against the God of the world. Let me explain. They believe or don't believe in Miller, they don't have to if they don't want to. What they do believe in is the enemy, out there in the world. Hate is war, fight, guns. For them Miller is gathering place to revolution, the fight coming. Different kinds, we take them all.

This damn shivering cold. I ask you, Will we take over the world? The only way to take over the world is to organize all us little groups into a bigger group with a leader. Listen to me. In the long run Miller's an impediment. He's stuck on saving people out of the world, hide away happy by ourself. Bullshit. He lacks the long view to take back the world. He stands in the way when we join others so at some point he'll be a martyr. Listen to me I'm talking to you. We need to decide what cause to martyr him to. Not sure I'll stay around that long, because delayed gratification is not my strongest. Where was I?

I'll tell him if he asks, I get my gratification from the remote of a gun. Like when I saw what Oliver wanted to do and did it to him instead. Better than my cop days when I always needed a legality excuse. Which took some of the pleasure away when it got me trouble. The pure gratification is how the squeeze and focus produce bang by remote control. Remote is the finger and hand squeezing gradually enough you don't know the exact moment when it will bang, and when it does the further remote is the jolt of the target which was as good as you until now caught, dropped, made dead. That's the top in my experience.

Never mind. As for us I said the true outcome of all things is anarchy. Entropy you said, not me, what I said was anarchy. I said the advance of destructive technology which gives any small group the power to hold the rest of the world hostage by blowing up people in stores or subways or city squares producing a condition of universal terror until every small community is an armed fortress. Tell Miller this. He talked about this sovereign community independent of the world, tell him it's the shrinking of defended communities to tiny groups where every man for himself is every man a God.

If I could remember how I got here. It's hard clinging to this cliff, it scrapes my face. Do you remember Oliver? Oliver no mistake. When I met him and told him about the murdering God and he talked about Raskolnikov I thought what an ass. Invented the Raskolnikov Society to draw him on, see what he would do. He came through past all expectations, bringing a child to Miller Farm without forethought of consequences, dumber than even I could have guessed. Physical disgust. Oliver who thought he knew me, his fat face, eyes like uncooked eggs. Bringing the attention of the police and world. The FBI don't know we're a sovereign community, Oliver forgot to tell them. The disgust of being stupid. His cohort Nicky is considered stupid, but at least he doesn't think he's smart. Oliver's dumb because he thinks he's smart which revolts me.

I talk all the time. Keep talking while the river runs downhill, draining out. Where was I? Oliver, not only is he dumb, he's a homicidal maniac. This I saw when he arrived with that baby, thinking Raskolnikov with no sense of Raskolnikov maybe because he only read him in *Cliff's Notes*. So when the guardian angels come roaring after the baby and he's wondering why I'm disgusted, he gets this dazzling genius idea of murder by water-fall, using his sidekick for executioner, which is when I decided enough is enough and gave him tit for his tat.

The river draining out of my side like Christ bouncing down the rocks in the waterfall. Which killed two birds with one rifle shot. Down comes Oliver in a smart way. Smarter than getting rid of Davey Leo, using his own waterfall as comeuppance, a word I learned in college when tit goes for tat. I told him getting rid of Davey would bring the whole university and police force of Cincinnati looking to see where he went, precipitating

Armageddon before we've had a chance to name our cause. But getting rid of Oliver was no sweat because nobody was around with enough shit to ask what became of him. Only his pal Nicky. If he got a parent or a sis or bro I don't know and gals are most likely glad to be rid of him sooner the better like Judy the mother. He came to live among us, which is already disappearing from the world, so you could say he's already disappeared before he disappeared down the waterfall, already dead so nobody'll notice when he's really dead.

Do you remember where we are? If I keep talking I'll live. As long as I talk I'm alive. The other bird was the glorification when I held the rifle against my shoulder and sighted the cross hairs in the mist free at last to squeeze that trigger and watch him fall without a twang of conscience to maim the joy. When he got to that elephant pecker and I said Go! down he came, just like he said he would, his own idea, boomboom and splash. Because the only real thing in this world I discovered long ago when I wondered why I wasn't getting gratification from being a cop is the feeling when you find in your hands the removal of the world from the life sights of some other human being, which I could write a book about. It's what I expected when I was a kid from sticking my pecker inside some gal, but it wasn't the same. I never had much go with gals and women, always disappointed, them and me, never quite compatible with my methodical ways, I preferring the quick bang and long consequences which a gun gives.

This looks like a cliff I'm clinging like ice scratching my cheek like a pillow of rock. I'm getting thin and still nobody hears me to help even if it looks like a mortal wound which I have been looking forward to all my life. As I was saying, it's like how this joy of killing I mentioned a moment ago came out of looking forward to being killed. Like what right has God to kill

me? And what will happen when I die? Like I discovered long
ago the world isn't just me dreaming about God, it's filled up
with people crowding me, dreaming too, and none giving me
credence, me just another stranger down the street. So I figure
introduce myself. What better than knock them out of their
dreams. If God or somebody knocks me out of my dreams and
nothing follows and I am all by myself in the black without even
myself to keep me company and if that's my eventual state and
condition, nada null and void my life, what's worth living except
make myself known to some other people going to be dead like
me soon anyhow? So I figure they're all thinking about going
into the black like me, or maybe not as smart as me (this more
likely) it never occurs to them they're going into the black all by
themselves with no self for company or even thinking dumb
like heaven next to Daddy old God, which nobody with brains
believes, I say what's the best way to make myself known to
people about to die but be the one to make them die. That's the
pleasure which I never knew enough to connect to being off
dead by myself myself until here where I'm beginning to get
cold.

I told him it comes down to two things in this world. One is
the thing itself. The other is the rationale. Everything depends
on the rationale, which helps you decide who to kill, Oliver not
Davey and no stranger in the street. The rationale joins you to
Miller as God and the Miller Farm, and fixes your arguments
to get the right people on your side like my recruiting arguments for Miller Farm at AA meetings around the country.
Rationale gives your folks motives which make them feel better.
Rationale helps you scare people like how the world is getting
hateful and we need to gather together like a bunch of sticks.
Rationale talks of the future when all the various Miller Societ-
ies in the world get together and make Armageddon on earth.

But rationale is nothing compared to what rationale is for, which is what I feel with the adrenalin popping like drug and my heart thumping in the sky looking at Oliver waddle in my sights on the elephant's pecker and see I can do it free and nothing touch me.

The question arises, what if Davey steps across like he was supposed to if Oliver's plan had its way? I don't know. Sometimes you don't know what you want until you do it. Maybe I was thinking of it but I doubt. It would have been Oliver's plan for Oliver with all the reasons that made him disgusting. I didn't know the real joy then, I only had a notion, which was why I took the rifle out of Nicky's hands in the first place. The point is when Oliver not Davey appeared, stepping carefully onto the elephant's pecker (which he was dumb enough to think was only a tiger's tongue, the last straw, not to know a tiger's tongue from an elephant's pecker), that was all it took to know my true self and mission and clarify in one second what Oliver Quinn was and squeeze the joy out of him into that trigger and up the misty waterfall. Down he came.

Like is this a mountain peak or my bed like a dream? Am I talking or only thinking? It can't be a dream but a blot in my mind, momentary amnesia, like Miller's amnesia can't remember what it was like to be God so here am I, can't remember who it was I can't remember I was. You asked about Nicky. I remember him, crazy about that baby like he was its mother. After the Oliver funeral Miller told me get rid of him. Kid's dangerous, if he stays around sooner or later he catch on who killed his buddy then hell to pay. Nick's simple, Miller said, Nick thinks slow but after a while no stopping him. Reality principle Miller said. Get rid of him, he told me, do it your way, just get him out of here.

Meanwhile Nicky himself wanted me to catch Davey to punish him for giving his baby away or killing Oliver, he not sure which. Even though his own eyes saw me shoot Oliver, it was easy to make him think Davey did it for a while. Then he didn't know what to do, because it takes a while for the kill notion to collect in a mind slow like his, while I'm thinking how to satisfy Miller until I think the two birds with one stone principle. Utilize, I say, that's economy. Utilize David to get rid of Nick. Not on Miller Farm though. Out somewhere it wouldn't be found for which Stump Island was just fine. So I masterminded that expedition for Nick's benefit to catch Davey, take him to Stump Island, and get rid of Nick in the process while he thinks I'm helping him. Thinking who would check out Stump Island and find them here if I weighted them both with rocks?

What I'm telling you is, I changed my mind. Which I have a right to do, like maybe my mind changed too when I saw Oliver step into the cross hairs only then it didn't. With a rationale. The rationale was the mistake in calculation, like in Miller Farm, if Davey disappeared he'd be missed. With witnesses, the geezer at Jake and Jim's, the harbor master, all them who knew where Miller Farm used to be. Me thinking if I can't get rid of Davey then I can't get rid of Nicky either. Like Oliver should have known, we're not as sovereign as we say when it comes to particulars.

I told you, when I got to the island the joy went out of it. Not to kill this black man, who had nothing much killable in him, while killing Nicky would be just brutal if it didn't have a plan or something clever about it. Like I said, did I tell you this? Truth is I hate killers. Hate them worse than anything in the world, damn pricks going around taking God's life away from people. That's why I killed Oliver, because the guy was a damn killer, his true colors showing as soon as he confused that elephant's pecker with a tiger's tongue. Now if I had to kill anyone on the island, the joy would rather kill Nick, not because Miller said to but because what it wants most to kill is stupidity, like Oliver was stupid, and though Nick is not as stupid as Oliver, he's stupid enough to want to kill somebody and that's stupid enough to be killed. This Davey on the other hand was not even stupid enough to kill. He was just dumb, which is different. Stupid wants an excuse to kill and does something else it thinks is as good as killing, whereas dumb doesn't know what it wants and doesn't know about the joy of killing. Dumb is ordinary. Dumb reads Raskolnikov and thinks he's somebody else, not you. Dumb thinks the Christian end is the truth about Raskolnikov, not the killing beginning, and thinks Raskolnikov got what was coming to him, which he did, but only because he turned dumb without having the joy to carry it out.

I think back to Miller's command, to get rid of doesn't necessarily mean kill if I could get rid of them in my own way. Leave them both on Stump Island to eat each other up. Double exile, that would be fun. No better than weighting them with rocks though because of the witnesses, plus the fact that two exiles together gives them more brain than they would otherwise have over a period of time and sooner or later they find a way off, which is trouble to avoid. So I changed my mind again to get my kick out of letting the black man go and leaving Nick stranded alone on the island. Putting the black man in my debt, I'm on your side buddy, the world is yours, life saver. Only then I'd have the black man's conscience to worry about, if he makes a fuss about leaving the guy behind even if he does want to kill you. So that plan's no good either. It ended up I left the black man on the island in fake exile only I forgot to tell the man with the boat, and found myself on shore with Nick still with me like nothing had happened and I still hadn't got rid of him. So in the end I took him to Bangor in the car and then just told him scram, here's money, go home and don't come back, which I could have done in the first place without the bother of Stump Island and just as good results.

So I take my joy where it's left me to take. The world used to be full of joys if you knew how. I caught Davey for Nick, then let him go, leaving him and Nick in a state of maximum confusion. Sending Nick off to the bus all by himself wondering what to do, so maybe he'll look up the professor, that would be vicarious, if you can plant that joyful an idea in his idiotic soul to make interesting consequences. I should have been a religious terrorist, too bad I didn't realize that before. Get my gratification by the principle of maximum surprise, sowing shock and surprise by remote making everybody live in a state of cringe. Emulate God and the irrationality of all fate. What's the matter with me?

It looks like pavement, that's what it is. What am I doing here? I remember. I took Davey's car to Bangor. Nick went home. What I told Miller, I got rid of him, let him wonder how. Miller's dumb, not stupid. He doesn't understand the joys of killing and not killing, though a man in his position really ought to is what I think. What the hell. There's a day coming. I know it, I feel it. It's concrete and damned cold. If it's the big day, I don't yet know. It's coming and I was waiting for it. I was ready. I intended to speak to a few guys next week. Sound them out, get a little start. Call it the Raskolnikov Society, good name. Wouldn't tell Miller, no need for him to know. Gave it up for some reason. Why did I do that?

Milk. I remember. When was that, yesterday? Today? This morning? That's what I thought. I came in town early this morning to get milk. Milk. Loomer went to the village to get milk. Because this woman with the kids, stepping out of her cottage when I was on my way to tune up my truck, she asked can I get milk which she ran out of and I said sure. Showing what a nice guy when things are ordinary and no great stress, why not go to town to get milk for this woman whose name I forget because she got kids and needs milk having run out? It comes back, I remember now. So that's where I am, which I would know if I could open my eyes and lift my head and look around. Is it already too late? I must be losing blood is why I'm having such trouble keeping things straight. If you ask I'll tell you if I can open my mouth. Milk. I get in the truck and drive to town, just in time for the store to open, and when I come out there's the kid just walking along front of the post office looking at the sky. The kid himself Nicky it takes me a moment to remember I sent him away so how'd he get back, another moment to why he got back, another for him to recognize me like he seen a ghost. Never saw anybody so scared in my life, not even when I was a cop busting in the door to arrest the guy. And him backing off like I was the ghost, though he himself looked like a ghost to me, a ghost looking like he had seen a ghost. Then he asks me my name like he's not sure, he says, Loomer? like he doesn't know and needs to be reminded.

Loomer sure, Nicky I say, what you doing, you come back to live with us? Already I have a bad idea about why he's here though I don't yet know the precise nature of the badness. He says, Wait.

Wait what? Wait what for?

Stay there, he says, don't move.

Why should I move, like he sees me about to arrest him, what did he ever know about me as a cop, did he even know I was a cop?

What's the matter with you Nicky?

Don't you outwit me, he says.

Disciples

Outwit you, what would I outwit you about? He's fiddling in his pocket. A dirty handkerchief comes out and drops on the ground. He tries another pocket, gets a little white spiral notebook, puts it back, says to me again, Wait, hey Loomer, wait.

I'm waiting, it doesn't occur to me what I'm waiting for.

Back into the first pocket which looks bulgy to me, now the bulge comes out, a pistol, where'd he get that, what does he want with that, a pistol for Christ sake.

Wait, he says. I wait. While he looks at it and fiddles with it, like he's not quite sure how to work it.

What's that you got?

Wait. I ain't no idiot.

Then he gets it to click properly and he puts his hand up like he's going to hand it to me. I step forward to take it and something inside me goes bang and maybe the pistol too, mainly it's what happened internal to me like my insides suddenly decided to explode. Knocking me off my footing, a surprise to find me on the sidewalk like somebody knocked me down with a baseball axe.

I see his feet standing next me. His floppy brown shoes with the long laces like he could trip over. Some reason I can't turn my head enough to look up at him.

You dead? he asks.

Yeah I'm dead, I say.

Okay, he says and walk away.

Leaving me here. Too damn bad, like to make me mad if I could think about it, but there's a big telephone pole lying across my middle. Getting cold. Once in the zoo I saw an elephant in a cage slamming his pecker into the ground, bang bang bang. That was a sight to see, the pecker bigger than his trunk, three times as thick. You never see a sight like that on ordinary visits to the zoo. I always admire the elephant, keeping that thing to himself, knowing so much he never tells and always moving calm and slow. Not like the tiger licking his chops.

If I cared, but the spots are moving in, I don't see so well, and I'm tired. Maybe I don't really care what the hell. Maybe I never did, if you think about it.

26

Nick Foster

Harry said we'll go to Miller Farm in the morning and talk to Miller. The voice said if we do I won't kill Loomer. It said if Harry doesn't let me kill Loomer I have to do it myself. I thought how to do it myself when I am with Harry. I thought how to not be with Harry. I didn't know how to not be with Harry.

I had my own room in the motel and I was not with Harry there. The sun woke up and I was still not with Harry. The voice said how to not be with Harry and I went out not with Harry. I walked out of the motel and up the road and I thought about not being with Harry all the way to Miller Farm. The morning was early and the grass cried. It said dumb people who can't go out without Harry are not as smart as me walking on the road by myself. I even knew the way to Miller Farm by myself.

In Wicker Falls the Bonny Vista Café made me hungry and I had breakfast. I saw people pay the cashier. I didn't know who would pay for me but I found money in my pocket and I gave the cashier. She figured out the change and gave it back to me. Now I had more money than I started with. I thought how smarter I am getting.

Across the street I saw Loomer coming out of the store. I

wasn't supposed to see him there I was supposed to see him in Miller Farm. I thought go to Miller Farm and wait for him or go now. The voice said there he is am I ready. I didn't know what to do like he come to make it easy for me only it was hard and I wondered if he was Loomer and I ask. Loomer I said. He was getting into his truck then come out. Well Nicky what you doing here.

I thought if he ducked behind the truck he would outwit me. It said be careful don't outwit me. I come back.

So I see. He come up with his hand and I thought he could outwit me shaking my hand so I didn't. The voice said why I come to kill Loomer and there he was what was I going to do.

Wait I said.

He said what do you want now Nick are you coming back to live with us. The voice said my gun where is it. I looked for my gun. I couldn't find it. It said watch he'll get away.

Stay there don't move I said.

He backed up like he was going to get behind the truck and I came along like not to let him because somebody said he was trying to outwit me be careful. I couldn't find the gun.

He said what's the matter with you Nicky. He smiled friendly which was funny because I never saw him smile before and it made him look different like he wasn't Loomer after all. The voice said him smiling to outwit me and be extra careful again.

Wait I said don't you outwit me.

Outwit you Nicky. What would I outwit you about.

I ain't no idiot I said.

He came toward me. I found the gun. He stopped. It said he was going to outwit me so I took the gun and shot him. Quicker than I thought.

I had the gun in my hand and the trigger in my hand was no no. The trigger was like my fly not to open except when. I had

302

to say now before I could pull the trigger it had to take the no no off. When it took the no no off it was easy. The gun went bang before the trigger was all the way. It went bang like it was waiting for me to pull the trigger and all I had to do was. Bang came out of the gun and all around too. It came out of the air and my head and Loomer's belly where the gun was. Bang pushed my hand back into my chest step back my balance. Bang felt good and the push on my hand and all the things happening from my finger on the trigger. Bang felt good because Loomer dropped like somebody holding him let go. Now I can get my baby back I said.

He lay on the ground and kept talking. I didn't expect him to keep talking I thought when you shot someone he died. He lay on the ground and said mumble mumble get a doctor.

Sorry I said. It said make sure he's dead.

Are you dead I said.

Yeah I'm dead.

Okay I said. Don't call me an idiot.

Blame God you're an idiot God made you what you are Christ get help.

What kind of help I said.

He stopped talking. Something was wrong with him he wasn't Loomer he turned into something else.

He was lying his head under the truck. The voice said take the truck is free. I got into the truck. I drove around his head. Dumb people don't have the sense to drive away in Loomer's truck.

I thought if I go back to Harry but the voice said Harry took me to Miller Farm that's where I was going. I drove the truck to Miller Farm. I didn't see anybody. I sat on the bench by the horseshoes and waited. I thought how to get my baby back now Loomer dead. I tried to figure how. I figured and figured and couldn't make it come out. I thought the voice will tell me what to do. I thought who and I thought Harry and I waited for Harry.

I heard a siren like the city. I remembered Loomer on the sidewalk and it said I killed Loomer probably. I went into the woods and I hid in the trees and I watched. I saw the car with lights and a policeman and I thought who will be my guru now. The policeman went into the house and Miller came out and got into the policeman's car and they drove up the hill. Another car came down the hill and the policeman got out. People came out of their houses. They talked. They went into the altered barn and ate breakfast. I already had my breakfast at Bonny Vista.

I thought I don't know what to do. I thought if I go into the altered barn and say hello. Nice people and Maria will take care of me. It said no no. I thought why no no. It said if I killed Loomer. I remembered shooting Loomer. I remembered Loomer on the ground his different look. I thought if that meant I killed him. I wanted my guru. I thought I'm not smart enough to know. It said would they chase me. I thought I wish I were smarter. I thought how I was smart enough to be not with Harry. Smart enough to kill Loomer and not let him outwit me. Not smart enough to know what to do.

I thought about not being smart enough. I thought about Oliver helping me and Loomer helping me and Harry helping me. I thought who will help me now. I thought how rotten not to be smarter. I thought if I was smarter then I wouldn't be here. I thought whose fault was that.

I thought whose fault. Everybody talking whose fault it was not theirs. Oliver Quinn got killed whose fault was that. Not David Leo. Loomer. David Leo escaped from the island whose fault was that. Not Loomer. David Leo. Nicky Foster killed

Loomer whose fault was that. Not Harry. Not Nicky. Nicky is dumb whose fault is that. The voice said if not nobody somebody.

It said if Nicky wasn't dumb I'd know what to do. I thought why isn't Nicky like Harry. I thought Loomer said don't blame me blame God God made you ask him. I thought that. I thought it again. I never thought it before.

I thought if God made me dumb why. If God made me dumb and Loomer smart why. Oliver smart why. Harry smart why. David Leo the black brown man why. If why I'd know what to do.

I thought like I'd never thought before. I thought if Loomer killed Oliver Nicky killed Loomer. If Nicky killed Loomer they'll kill Nicky. I thought who will kill them who killed Nicky. I thought if I don't do it no one will. No one will care. I thought about nobody caring for Nicky. It made me cry.

I sat in the woods a long time. I was thinking about God made me dumb. I remembered the lady said God loves you. I thought how she knew. Loomer said God made me dumb. I thought how God made some people dumb and me dumber than anybody. I thought if that was fair. I thought if God could change it if you asked him.

The police car came back. Miller went into the altered barn. Everybody ran around. People said meeting. I thought if meeting I should go. I was scared. I thought if people think I killed Loomer. God will save me. I remembered people said God would save me.

I went to the meeting. I walked in the back. Miller talked about Loomer. I don't know what he said. I saw the policeman and the guns. I thought about the guns shooting me.

I went up to Miller. Somebody said if he's God he's my guru. Miller told me to sit down.

It said if Miller's God he owes me something. It said he doesn't know I have to tell him. Dumb people don't know things like that. Dumb people don't know when they know something that somebody else doesn't know. It said even God doesn't know he owes me something and I am not as dumb as he thinks. I went up front to tell him.

He told me to sit down. It said not yet first I have to tell him. But I have to be fair so I said are you Miller.

He said I knew who he was like I was dumb to ask which was dumb of him since I knew who he was and it wasn't why I asked.

I said are you God. He said he was the lord God almighty maker of heaven and earth and all the critters material and spiritual living therein and there was no God but he and if I didn't take it up with him I couldn't take it up with nobody. His voice clanged like my aunt's silver set and gonged like the sun and crackled like the earth falling down.

I said if you are God why did you make me like you did. I said why do I always need somebody else to think for me and tell me what to do. I said why do I need a guru to lead me why can't I see for myself like a guru and why did you make people laugh at me and kill my gurus and make me kill them back and why did you make me so now they'll chase me into the woods for the things you made me do and make me die under a leaf and rot away.

He said come closer I can't hear you. It said he was outwitting me like Loomer. I wouldn't let him so I pushed the gun into his middle and squeezed the trigger. It went bang in my hand inside him like a pillow and I pulled back and felt good like Loomer and the TV. He made a face and fell down. Someone grabbed me and somebody pulled me away. Someone shouted and I heard another bang and another bang and I ran out the door.

I saw them chasing me so I ran to the woods and the path up the waterfall. I watched me run. I run up the waterfall path hard and I heard some bang banging behind me but mostly not and it was quiet in the woods except the heavy breathing.

The heavy breathing climbed up the path beside the waterfall. The path was steep. It never climbed so fast before.

I didn't hear anybody chasing me. I got to the top and said what am I going to do. I wished I had a guru. I thought Meditation Point where people sit. I thought if I stayed would they come after me.

I sat down at the top. The water poured over the edge like a pitcher. I couldn't see the tiger's tongue. I couldn't see the elephant pecker. All I could see was the edge where the water poured. I remembered Oliver and wondered how I could kill David Leo if I couldn't see the tiger's tongue or the elephant's pecker. I thought if Miller didn't know what I was talking about. If Miller didn't make me an idiot. If nobody knew what I was talking about. If nobody made me an idiot. I thought if I was not an idiot what was I doing here. Harry said I wasn't an idiot I was a moron. I said what's the difference. Harry said I couldn't ask that question if I was an idiot was the difference. I said was it normal for a moron to be what I was doing here. I said would they stop chasing me if they knew I was a moron. I said would they stop chasing me if they knew I was not a moron. If I was not as dumb as they say I am.

I saw the men at the bottom. They were standing at the foot of the falls looking up. They were next to the spray with long guns in their hands. They were looking up at me. I thought if I can't see the tiger tongue or elephant pecker I am safe. Then I thought but they can see the tiger tongue and elephant pecker and I am not safe. A dumb person wouldn't think like that.

The Meditation Point was on the other side. I had to cross over the water like David Leo. Like Oliver Quinn. I thought if I don't cross they will climb up and catch me on this side. If I do cross I will be David Leo Oliver Quinn. It was because I let Loomer kill Oliver instead of me kill David Leo. I owed this to God because I let Loomer do it instead of me.

I thought if they kill me I will die. I thought what that would be like. I thought most people don't like to die. I thought why. I thought if I am going to die I wouldn't know what to do with my life if I didn't. I thought a smarter person like Loomer would not have come up this path. A really smart person would have taken the empty police car that was sitting in the clearing with its lights going around. Loomer would have taken that car and roared out with his sirens going. I thought a smart person like Harry would not cross over the waterfall. A really smart person like Harry would go to the back of the pond here. Such a person would be out of sight of the people below. He would cross the stream at the back of the pond instead of the front. Then he would go through the woods to Meditation Point and the people down below wouldn't know. That would make him smarter than them. I thought when he got to Meditation Point a smart person would keep on going. He would go back into the woods and into the mountains. He would cross the mountains and come out someplace else and nobody would know where he had gone. That's what a smart person would do. I thought why can't I do that. I thought the reason I can't do that is that Nicky Foster is a moron. That's why people love him. If he wasn't a moron he wouldn't know what to do and people wouldn't love him any more.

This made me happy. I stood up and started across the water-fall. I looked down and saw the men raising their guns and pointing them at me.

27

Miller

When Miller woke in His bed with the old woman, He knew His time had come. No source told Him, the knowledge seeped through the Amnesia. The old woman slept and He looked on her with pity and blessed her with happiness.

He prepared for the day neither pursuing nor dreading what was to come, which He knew would arrive in time. He took His coffee and roll in His office and read the day's documents to be signed. The first indication was the police car that silently entered the compound and the policeman who told Him of a man killed on the sidewalk in Wicker Falls. They believed the victim lived at Miller Farm and they wanted Miller to identify him.

As He rode in the police car to Wicker Falls He knew this was the final day. He knew who had been killed needing only the sight of his face to draw the veil of Amnesia from that knowledge. He went with the policeman into the hardware store where the body lay. It was on a table by stacks of screens full length on its back, face like a Roman dictator, the body of Jake Loomer. When Miller saw him He grieved. He was my heir, He said.

They tagged the body of Jake Loomer and brought Miller back to the Farm. They used the sirens now because a suspect

had been spotted driving Loomer's pickup. When Miller returned He called a meeting. His disciples assembled and Miller
told them the news. A moan of sorrow went up. Let there be
peace, Miller said, deploring the tendency of the godly to divide
into factions. He was about to say more when the man whom
history will remember as the Deprived appeared in the back of
the room. When Miller saw him He knew through the Amnesia
what was about to happen.

Are you God? the Deprived said.

If you believe it.

Did you make me what I am today?

If you believe it.

Why did you do that?

Miller answered him. While the man held a pistol to Miller's
body Miller explained the world. He read the law that separates
wheat from chaff. Some die that others may live. The flower
yields to the plant. Your father died to make room for you. He
spoke of the evolution of life from one-celled creatures and sea
urchins and trilobites to lungfish and lizards and ocelots, with
species going extinct that others may grow, for millions of years
before mankind rose on the backs of the extinct. He spoke of
the men and women who have lived since men and women first
appeared, ancestors before language and after language, before
and within history all in the flash of an eye, all before you came
in your own life that like all others stands upon the dead. The
dead that you too shall join. He spoke of the would-be lives,
millions swarming even now in the body of every future father
and mother, protected in the deep inside where they wait in the
warm juice of life. In the moment of surge and connection
these millions of potential lives rise like salmon into the stream
where all but one will fall, the lucky one who can outreach the
million dead competitors against odds greater than a lottery,

though this winner may never know or acknowledge that winning luck. And Miller told the Deprived how even these luckiest survivors live only for the briefest of spans. And among them, the temporary survivors, creatures in the sea slime or individuals in a nest or people in a crowd, there will always be some whose manufacture is flawed. A detail gone wrong. A minor error in transmission, with consequences sometimes unnoticeable, sometimes inconvenient, even disabling. A deformed leaf, the feebleness of a runt, mental deficiency in a child. So Miller explained the Deprived's condition but the man did not have the understanding to follow. Intent upon his grievance and the machine in his hand, his finger activated God's chemistry in an explosion forceful enough to drive a pellet through the body of His incarnation. This pellet, innocuous as a pebble at rest but rendered monstrous and terrible by the energy of speed, tore God's organism, severing enough vessels and lines of communication to block their functions. Obedient to God's own laws of chemistry, physics, and biology, God's body could only die.

Now as Miller lay mortally wounded among His disciples He faced the questions of His existence. In pain, afflicted by His inability to will a remedy against His own laws, He asked, is this what my creatures go through? His eyes open, He could see only people's feet, muddy farm boots, sneakers, sandals, open shoes with painted toenails. What have I done? He said.

God is dying, He told Himself, shocked. But God cannot die or be shocked. The Amnesia must end. He looked forward to that, the release from sixty years in this body back into knowledge and power. Lying on the floor He tried to regain the divine memory forfeited when He adopted this shape, searching outside His mind for the shining of eternal knowledge.

Remember, remember, He urged Himself, trying to overcome the Amnesia by thinking back to its origins. He remembered His youth, asking the question that once seemed so mysterious: Who is God? Who was God when as a boy in a state of innocent amnesia he thought he was only a boy? Why, he thought, God is the Father, capitalized, not his life father but the Father of us all, ruling and judging. He loved God in place of his unknown biological father just as he loved the good foster fathers and mothers, three different families, who raised him. He loved because he believed God loved him, and he grew up in that spirit of love extended to life which God gave him emulating his foster mother Clare and his other foster parents, and he thought himself obliged to please this love-judging God just as he pleased his loving and judging substitute parents. As a child he imagined talking to God, reciting the formal phrases that God expected and adding in his own impromptu language what he wanted God to hear. He grew up so enamored of God that he thought God said things to him that He said to nobody else, that God shared secrets with him and loved him more than he loved others.

He observed with amazement how fortunate he was, just as the agency people said, to have such good foster parents even though each foster visit came to an end, terminated in one case by death, in another by a family breakup, in the third by causes he never knew. Yet even as he grieved for these transient parents good fortune followed. How gently and indulgently the kindly families in their different ways gave him what he needed. How fortunate not to be poor. To be healthy. People called him good looking and women loved him. Everyone praised him for qualities he did not have to work to develop, and he cultivated their praise. He praised himself. He heard God in his ear telling him what a good boy he was, how special. Someday you'll be famous, God said. The world will look up to you. How different it could have been if you had been one of those people around you who are not you. If you had been the wheelchair cripple across the street or a black boy or a dog. Whose mind are you? God seemed to ask, which could only mean that he was unique. No one else saw the world out of his eyes. No one else was he. Only he was he. How extraordinary that was, like a miracle.

He went to high school and college and seminary. He went to seminary because he loved God in exchange for God's loving him. His love for God was indistinguishable from his love for life. He was ordained and went first to assist another man and then to a congregation of his own in a suburb of Philadelphia where he was welcomed as our handsome young minister. He acquired a minister's wife and his congregation was pleased.

Yet as he preached his sermons and practiced his love for God, something happened to him, beginning perhaps as a strain between the minister and his young wife. He was drawn to other women. The attraction of certain women in his office was so compelling that it could only be the voice of God telling him clearly not to refrain but take lustily what was offered. Which he did, with the scandal that ensued. Nor would the scandal die as the voice of God encouraged him to replenish it. He mistrusted this voice of God that now seemed so full of contradiction. The more he spoke to his congregations about the word of God the more he wondered if he knew what that word was. The fatherly God of his childhood withdrew. The God speaking in his sermons now sounded like an automaton invented by himself.

He lost touch with the God he used to know. This did not kill the idea of God in his heart but it made him wonder where God was. He envisioned God now as deep in the universe among the stars and dispersed in life through geological ages from the sea. He read philosophers and scientists and listening for the voice of God he could no longer distinguish between what he heard and what he wanted to hear. The voice grew more remote until it seemed like no human voice at all but the stars speaking.

Ousted from his church, he took his best followers to support him in the Philadelphia apartment while he tried to find God to tell him what to do. He no longer knew where the voices in his head came from. Some urged him to forget a God that perhaps did not exist and utilize his charm to advantage as by becoming an automobile salesman in a well stocked modern dealership. Others told him to confront the abyss. They said the voices he heard were noise generated by his head. The universe made itself and he was its accident as perishable as a paramecium on a slide.

The truth or what he took to be the truth came to him while he sat on a park bench a few days after he had been attacked by a mugger on the waterfront. He was slashed in the eye but struck back with such rage that he killed his attacker, leaving him in the street. He expected to hear from God about what he had done, but no word came, nor was he apprehended by police. On the bench with a bandage where his eye had been, he brooded about the silence. This was the moment known in the Miller annals as the Revelation, although the total revelation was more gradual than a moment. The first step was a vision of the absence of God, the emptiness of the universe. The paramecium revelation. Which would have filled him once with despair but now with relief except for the followers who thought he had a private line to God. Now they were stuck with him for something in which he no longer believed. It occurred to him that an ordinary person in such a situation would think of suicide, but not he because he enjoyed everything too much. This first light did not look like light, it looked false, like visible darkness, an opportunistic idea rather than a godly revelation.

He did not yet realize that he had been the victim all his life of Divine Amnesia.

No God above or within, the universe an abyss, this was freedom, for if no one is watching he can do what he likes, even the most radical and amoral things. Look up to see who's in charge. If no one's there how high can he rise? If he wants to rise, what constitutes up? What formerly constituted up was God on a throne. If there's no God what's to keep him from claiming the throne himself? That's how he began, a game, a gesture, an act. Suppose I were God, with appropriate explanations easy to invent for why I take this embodiment in this time and place. He brought his followers into the game, or mystery, tactfully nurturing their love to try it out, see what it was like. Suppose I were God, what would we do, how would we live, how would we explain ourselves? He lost a few of them that way. They said he had gone mad or they took it too seriously confusing sport with fraud, but enough remained and were persuaded just as he was persuaded.

He practiced the part of incarnate God as a gesture to the void. A life-giving act of maximum audacity. As he did so he became habituated. The thick wall of the Amnesia began to leak. Hypothesis became knowledge. Metaphor turned literal. Pretense was reality. So too with His followers who became prophets and disciples. There was never a deception between Him and them. They shared His perception of the abyss and the Original Hypothesis, a deliberate construction of What If? What if?, the basis of the Miller Church. Let Miller be God as given and we His disciples. As supposition turned into belief, fortified with enthusiasm, their numbers grew, they became a community with property, a place to live, an institution.

Once near the beginning Ed Hansel asked, Aren't you afraid you'll be struck by lightning? Thinking it worse to impersonate

God than deny Him. To which Miller, who was learning his new theology fast, replied that it's the idea of God that counts since God is One despite the variety of his appearances to men.

Soon Miller discovered that this trained belief could do good. Assisted by his original followers, he became a rescuer of people in despair, his community a haven. He saved them in the same way in which he had found himself, by making them name his divinity, state it in words repeatedly until the absurdity disappeared. Strange became familiar, false became true. It was a technique like twelve steps and the rituals of psychiatry. Postulating Miller as God and discovering thereby how to create belief made it easy for the sufferer to make a new world indifferent to whatever had oppressed him, failure, death, and the chains of what ordinary people called reality.

All this Miller remembered as He lay on the floor with human life draining away. He tried to speak, thinking, This is the arc moment, and my words should be heard. But his body was weak, the words were not audible enough to be taken down.

He tried to penetrate the Amnesia and was afraid. What if the Amnesia failed to yield? What if the memory loss were permanent? Would the Godhead be lost too? Can God die? Can He die and the universe remain the same?

No one knows what happened to Miller in the end. So who is this speaking for Him, telling the last moments of the dying mind? Or does the story simply write itself as it always does, pretending as usual to know what it can't, imagining in this case how the feet of the people and their voices faded as Miller went blind and deaf? Supposing that instead of expanding the universe closed around Him like a box. That He gasped for memory but instead of dispersing, the black Amnesia moved in closer deleting still more memory as if it meant to leave none at all. That drowning He prayed to Himself for the light to be restored. Yet perhaps (for now everything in the record is enclosed in perhaps as certainty grows dim) as the light refused to come His spirit ceased to struggle. He lay where He lay in the dark and wanted to rest. Memory reduced to fragments, (perhaps) He was yet able to remember the boy with the gun who wanted an explanation for the unfairness of life, and (perhaps) He was still able to murmur in the darkness, Forgive him his ignorance. Let's hope so. (Perhaps) He awoke enough to add, Forgive me too. To whom would He be speaking if he did? He wondered (perhaps) if the godless vacuum in which He had found His divinity were not godless after all, if there were something he had overlooked. And (perhaps) he noticed something skittering around in the box that contained Him, scurrying away like a mouse or other little animal, something that skated over his blood and out of reach like a pronoun, a letter, a capital I, a name like God, disappearing like a marble down a chute, and after it a name like Miller, dropping down the drain, and his long forgotten first name which the women at the orphanage gave him because his father and mother were unknown, the name Christian (Christian Miller) which he abandoned later as inappropriate for a reason now forgotten as the name itself was forgotten, this also scampering away with patter feet leaving him without any name at all. So that ultimately he found himself (perhaps) in a position where he had forgotten everything except that he had a message to tell, or story, or gospel, though he had forgotten what it was, and the tragedy was that he had no teller, no disciple who knew the words, so that if he was dying his message and godhood as well as the universe would die with him and never be known. Except for what we can guess or imagine by looking at him dead on the floor.

28

Lena Fowler Armstrong

The oddest detail in this story is the waterfall murder. I noticed it when Harry told me David Leo's story. As a murder plan it's so strange it must have meant something to the murderer. The three murderers. When I returned to Miller Farm I visited the waterfall trying to make it speak.

I came to Miller Farm to live. I gave the Millerites an endowment asking only that they let me stay with them. I moved in July and have been here two months. I keep Anchor Island for visits, but Miller Farm is my home.

I am learning how to live, for it's different from my life before. They gave me a bedroom on the second floor next to Miller's, which is now a shrine. They treat me like their new leader, though I didn't ask for that. I'd prefer to live inconspicuously but because I paid for the land and living expenses in perpetuity they regard me as priestess or even a new Miller.

Maria Garn calls me Saint Lena. I am the saint who rescued the Farm. I told her saints are not named to their face and if she calls me saint how dare I show my face? I couldn't stop her. It hurts her feelings when I scold her so I let her do it.

I walked the grounds with Maria and Ed Hansel. We stopped at each cottage, and I spoke to everyone, the children too. They showed me the garage and the padlocked shed where the guns are kept. I don't like guns, why do you keep them? I asked. Oh my goodness, Hansel said, after what happened last spring? I kept my silence. Let me not be rule maker here. Saint Lena. I have the best room in the big house. I sit at the main table where Miller sat. I open and close the prayer meetings. I look over the accounts. Tradesmen and reporters deal with me, I am the Miller spokesman by default. A group from outside once asked me to make a statement condemning the police for the Miller Massacre. I refused. I don't like the word Massacre, considering that only three of the seven deaths were actually caused by the police. Though I agree the police response to the Foster panic was excessive, I refused to say they started it or that it was a government conspiracy. I explained this to the people in the Farm and they agreed with me.

Our walk took us to the pond where Quinn was cremated first and the six victims collectively later. The grass was still scorched, which brought the rites to life for me. I'm an old lady and walking was tiring, even with my cane, but they were kind. Ed Hansel is no younger than I and Maria is heavy, and we moved slowly together. It was healthy and I felt good.

But when I asked to see the waterfall and Meditation Point, they said it was too hard. Show me anyway, I said. We went into the woods to the base of the falls. I saw the spray over the rocks and the water stream leaping off the cliff into the chute. I saw where the water jumped like a hose off the projecting rocks. Tiger tongue or elephant pecker, I couldn't apply those colorful terms, but I knew this sight would become a tourist attraction some day unless the people of Miller resist. I imagined how it would look, billboards and souvenir shops and walkways with rope railings and outlook posts for pictures.

They wouldn't let me go up, but for two months the waterfall called and I thought until I go I won't belong. Finally yesterday I went. I went alone, telling no one. In the mid afternoon, sunny and quiet with September insects buzzing while the older folks took naps. I thought this will test whether I was right to come. I was not afraid of the climb. I'm an old lady but if I go patiently there's no reason I can't. I took two canes.

It was steep but not impossible with my canes bracing me at the hard spots. I rested often. At times the path rose almost vertically and I clutched the projecting roots with my hands. Then I came out. I saw the pool and the stepping stones across the narrow current like a tube of glass and I stood close to where David Leo must have been when Quinn fell. I looked down at the mist over the rocks where he landed. I took the path around the pool and thence along the top of the bluff to Meditation Point. A bench and wooden shelter, a noble vista of the mountains south. I imagined Miller contemplating his world. I sat and contemplated myself. Thinking Saint Lena, am I transfigured by my gift? I fought vanity. Lena, I said, always so foolish, your errors and good intentions, why should you be no longer so? I changed my way of life, I replied, does that mean nothing? The argument made me sleepy. I sat in the peace of the destination and wondered if I died here, how peaceful a death that would be. This bench, this forest sanctuary.

After a while my curiosity about the killings revived, and I went back to the waterfall. I reviewed the story as told me. I thought about the people whom I would never meet, legendary, the quixotic Oliver Quinn, the deprived Nick, that malign mover of events, Jake Loomer. I wondered most about Loomer, whom the good people of Miller Farm blamed most for the tragedy as if he had planned it, even his own death, like a devil. Yet Miller had loved him and intended him for his heir, to be their next leader. I wanted to tell them he was no devil but a man among you like any other, but though I had the authority of Saint Lena such words ran up against their stubborn feelings and had no weight.

I stood by the pool watching the clear waters converge and roll over the edge. I tried by heavy concentration to waken the spirits of Oliver Quinn and Nick Foster who had died here as well as that of Jake Loomer, hoping they could show me by some spiritual osmosis what they meant by death in the waterfall. I heard no recognizable voice but my own. Maybe because none of them made it across to this side. So I went around the pool back to the other side and stood again where David Leo watched Quinn. Now it was in front of me, the innocent waterfall that never changes, the same as when they died and in the centuries before they died, before the white man or any man in this place, and still the same in the busy short times since. The peculiarity, the idiosyncrasy, the whimsicality of the murders. Ask the spirits why any killer would require so much ritual, in which he and accomplice and victim must all play their parts with timing exact and respect for the rules (such as not to detour behind the pool) if a murder is to succeed.

If it works, the waterfall will do the job well. It conceals the crime in a mist, so that no one will suspect it was not an accident full of natural beauty. What is a waterfall? Geologically it's a temporary moment in the erosion of the mountain, the process by which the mountain is leveled step by step until reduced to nothing in the plain. The waterfall is one of those steps. It expresses a discontinuity in time as in the earth, where softer rock is cut away more quickly than adjacent hard rock leaving the latter to stick out like a pecker or tongue for the water to spill over. Water on its way to the sea leaps off the broken edge it's trying to erase and gouges out the trough below in a spray that will rainbow the sunlight when there is sun and someone to see. People think it beautiful and will come miles to watch. What's beautiful about it? The swelling in me like music, where does that come from, I ask?

I strained my intuition and extended my sensors to pick up some residue of Quinn's remembering soul. I listened for the ghost thought, some words other than my own. I inquired, Is it the image of power in the waterfall, the power of subjecting your victim to it? No answer. Is it the lure of the silence which sucks up human voices and rifle shots? No answer while I noticed that what I called silence was really noise in a rush, the same now as on the day New Hampshire was declared a state, newer only than geology itself. I stretched my sensors to ask the Quinn or Loomer or Foster soul if the use of the waterfall was intended worshipfully to cleanse the deed of foulness.

Thinking how much murder by waterfall depends on chance, I asked if the waterfall itself created the motive for murder. Making it just Leo's luck to be in Quinn's way when the waterfall entered his head. Quinn's in turn when he told it to Loomer. If there had been no waterfall then no murders and no tragedy. Think Quinn thinking (for example) if Leo crosses the falls I'll do it, if he doesn't I won't. So that if he really does cross you can drop him with the rifle and blame it not on yourself or the rifle but on Leo for crossing after you had given him (in your mind) the option of not doing so. Was this what you meant? I said. But the disembodied memories still have nothing to say.

Standing over the waterfall I tried to enter a trance. Open your secrets to me. I invoked myself as Saint Lena, saying to the waterfall, speak, Saint Lena bids you tell what attraction you inspired that brought death to this place? I sank my spirit in the cool soaring mist, soaked my imagination wet, rode on the falls to ask, does the waterfall make me want to kill? Is it telling me this is how I would like to die, or am I only asking myself if that's what it's saying? How can I distinguish my questions from the answers they imply, how can I tell if those answers come from a source other than the questions? I think this question: am I thinking of riding on the water to the crash below or am I only postulating it as what Quinn's spirit or you or someone else is thinking?

Is it my idea which I am asking you to confirm or is it yours spirited into my head by the trance, namely, that the waterfall is a lesson I want to teach you about life, my victim? That it displays what I know about life that you don't.

Is it my idea or yours, spirited by the trance, which says the distance between us is the thing about life that you don't know? Are you telling me or am I telling you what you don't know that I know (or is it the other way round?) is pictured by the streaming of the falls, whether it comes off the tiger tongue or the elephant pecker, the fall of life free and catastrophic onto rocks? The discontinuity between our souls bleeding down the discontinuity in time? Which only I know. Or only you know, determined as you are to make me know it too. Am I picking this up from Oliver Quinn and Jake Loomer and Nick Foster or am I only asking if I am picking it up from them? That what I know you don't know will always require me to send you up the waterfall so I can teach you with my rifle what it is?

I looked into the pool at the leafy bottom where little claws and legs wriggled for cover. At that moment I heard a voice out of the falls, my reply addressed to me, startling and sharp, harsh and real. Saint Lena watch out. I looked up and saw them, not Loomer and Quinn but two men from the path below, running to me. I don't know their names. One of them with tattoos on his biceps grabs my arm. I thought you were going to fall, he says.

How did you get here? the other asks.

Climbed, I say.

You scared us. We saw you up here. We'll help you down.

I descended with them. Still ignorant whether the thoughts by the waterfall were my own or those of the spirits. Never mind. The two men helped me over the steepest parts lifting me by both arms. It's good they came for I would probably have fallen.

29

David Leo

The bulletin board says Professor Field will teach a seminar called "Writing About Science," Thursdays at 4. Graduate students, permission of instructor.

Who's that? one student said.

He's retired, the other said.

Is he famous?

Depends what you mean famous, the other said.

What the students don't know. Nor I, for nobody told me Harry planned to teach this fall. Proving how out of touch I've been, which made me sad. Remembering how I used to go to the house almost every day. How often I went to dinner. Harry's advice and his requests for my advice. Their friends were my friends, like Joe and Connie Rice. With babysitting for Judy thinking marriage. Thinking of the Field family as my own.

That was then. When I hitchhiked home after being mugged on Stump Island, I was mean and angry and full of spite. Standing on the inhumane pavement like a rat in a foreign country for the pleasure of two guys of no importance who hijacked me, ran me through their rituals, and left me a refugee. It was impossible not to blame Harry and Judy too. It was all connected, Harry and his daughter and the baby and Miller Farm and the quack god and the thugs and the island and the hitch-hiking highway and raw country. Not using Harry's airline ticket for spite, probably, because I was fed up with being their boy. Spiting Judy likewise with the obliging gals on the highway before the hypocritical guilt and real sorrow set in. Here was a new way to feel bad, remorse for not being the loyal Dobbin I was meant to be. Mean and ashamed. Dirty and scared too, since I had not protected myself when Veena came to my room naked like a painting, as if paintings were prophylactic.

Nevertheless, by the time I called Judy I was full of love again. We sat in the living room like a formal call in the afternoon. I described my latest heroics like Othello. Poor David, what you have been through, while I tried to steer her back to her sexy gratitude in the motel. The story continued, and my hitchhike journey brought me into dangerous narrative territory. Three waitresses from Rochester, I said, while the unsayable buzzed louder in my ears. The narrative took over like nausea. A fatal switch in my integrity circuits omitting nothing for David Leo's honest soul. I told about Veena with a vengeful relish in my voice that I could not for my life suppress.

I don't know if I can take this, she said.

That was the end, though not all at once. She put me on probation. She moved into an apartment. I visited her, even took her out sometimes while Connie Rice babysat. Connie and everybody thought we were lovers and my best friends wondered why I didn't move in. I didn't tell them. I was cleared medically. After a while Judy forgave me for Veena but though we didn't know it right away, it was too late, too much of a strain.

I lost touch with Harry too. I heard the news about Miller Farm before I knew he had gone back there. It was on television, a gun battle between law enforcement personnel and inhabitants. Miller Farm is the stronghold of a cult leader named Miller, hotbed with a stash of arms. The trouble began when police raided the place to seize the arms. And shot the leader Miller in full view of his followers.

The news appeared in the morning and afternoon papers on the first inside page. The television presentation featured one shot of the mountains, one of a road going up through the woods, which might have been Rib Rock Road, and one of a covered body unloaded at a country hospital. There was a discussion in *Time* magazine and an editorial here and there. The editorials talked about the breakdown of society.

The news that Loomer and Miller were dead stirred a strange feeling I didn't want, like regret. Like my wanting to say to them, I told you so. Nick too, later, when I learned about him. Not them though, it was Harry I wanted to say it to.

When I learned that Harry had been there at the time, I thought he had gone mad. When he got back I sought him out in hopes that talking to him would restore his sanity for me. I asked why he went.

I had to take Nick, Harry said. If I hadn't taken him he would have hitchhiked.

I said why couldn't you just send him on the bus?

Nick wanted to kill Loomer, he told me.

So you took him to Miller Farm where he could do it?

I took him to prevent it.

Why did you think you could do that?

Because I had influence over him.

I thought in Greek and Latin. Hubris. Arrogance.

I was teaching him to think for himself, Harry said. He told me the police had asked the same questions, as if that made my questions superfluous. They cleared him of suspicion.

Suspicion of what?
Aiding and abetting. Conspiracy.

I felt like a fool. The aura of foolishness was a stink in my memory, though it was hard to say exactly which thing I had done was particularly foolish. Or to escape the feeling that the real fool was Harry. I was sick of something, not sure what, sick of his mentorship, of being a protégé, of being a second son or whatever it was the whole Field family seemed to think I was. I avoided him in the lunchroom, surprising myself, not wanting to eat with Harry? We drifted apart.

I was sick of probation with Judy. It went on and on, and it became a chore. Her mind was elsewhere, it never focused on me. In July Charlene came back to me. Or I went back to Charlene. I missed her. Or she missed me. Missing Judy Field turned into missing Charlene. I thought Charlene wouldn't treat me like that. I called her one night to ask if she would treat me like that and she said no.

So Charlene came back and lives with me again. I told Judy I was back with my old girlfriend. It was sad. When I remember that conversation sometimes it seems almost unbearable with sadness. It caught her by surprise, it made her apologize, and I could hear the courage grinding in her voice. That's all right Davey, I understand, she said, as if she didn't.

With regret ever since. Regret and relief, I can't tell them apart. Lying beside Charlene at night after she has gone to sleep, I think of Judy restored to loveliness and glamor. I remember how much I did for her all for love and the memory of my heroism makes me mourn. I remember the dark New Hampshire roads at night and the mental intimacy we had as we made plans and tried to judge how terrible reality could be. I tell myself it's better with Charlene, that my time with Judy was a crazy interlude, but then I get lost trying to figure out if I could have done something differently. If I had spoken more forcefully at the Sleepy Wicker motel. If I had refused Veena on the road. If I had not mentioned Veena to Judy. If I had refused to accept probation. If I had put Charlene off a while yet. All these possibilities and others appear as my thought rolls on forgetting itself and everything on the way to sleep.

Charlene wants to get married. I don't but I guess I will to calm the seas. She wants me to invite the Fields to the wedding, and I guess I'll do that too.

30

Judy Field

In a moment of pique, Davey said, You've been kidnapped by your baby. I admit it. Preoccupied, I ignore the problems of others. My parents forgive me, they think it natural. I listen and try to sympathize, but my mind is busy and won't engage.

My mother is kidnapped by her mother, my ninety-six year old grandmother, recently widowed. Everyone expected her to die first, not Gus, the old pixie man. So my mother went to San Diego to help her adjust to widowhood. The old woman was afflicted with loss, her life was nothing but loss, she wanted only to die. She listened to stories of the living generations without interest, sustained by the habits of old roles, what a mother and a grandmother and now a great-grandmother should care about. She asked about the children and the children's children, repeated the questions and got the same answers, ate the soup Florence Byrd served her, took her nap, got back into her wheelchair and fell asleep with a book. Sleep gave her no rest, and when she wasn't asleep she thought about pain and the things that were no more, and each day she asked Florence or her daughter or whoever was there (the good senior people who brought her entertainment, dishes to eat, books to read), Why can't I die? What point is served by my staying alive? Who benefits?

Finally my mother came home, with this question which she has not yet answered: should she bring the old woman to live with us, with all the reasons not to, in which it is so hard to distinguish what is selfish from what is kind and what is practical from what is cruel?

That's what my mother worries about these days, which I forget while I take care of my baby. My father's worry is different. It began with a letter he got one day late in the summer.

Dear Professor, You may have fooled the police with your cockeye story taking the Miller Murderer to Miller Farm but you don't fool us. Justice waits.

Why do you get such a letter as this? my mother asked.

It's some ignorant echo, Harry explained, of the question the police had for him back in Wicker Falls. The question was, Why did you bring Foster to Wicker Falls? Since you knew his purpose, why didn't you notify us, why didn't you warn Loomer and Miller? The police questioned him, and the district attorneys, and he went back to speak to the grand jury. They had to decide whether he was an accessory, but they accepted his explanations because of his professorial authority. They treated him deferentially because of his position in the class structure (though it never felt like Ruling Class to him). They let him off and that was the end of it or should have been. Evidently somebody reading the abbreviated accounts in the paper, someone who didn't care what class he belonged to, was not satisfied.

Soon after that came in the mail a pamphlet from North Dakota with a full description called "Cover-Up of the Miller Massacre." *This little-noticed event will get the attention it deserves as patriots around the land are made aware of the resemblances to Waco and Weaver. Once again the government has moved to terrorize independent religious groups while they destroy our rights to bear arms. Proof of the conspiracy to pull the wool over your eyes was the release without a single charge of the so-called professor who transported the hired gun to the Farm. Ask the authorities about that character. Ask, keep asking. This case stinks and must not be forgotten.*

"The so-called professor." Is that you Harry, my father, because you drove the murderer to Miller Farm? What an outrage, Connie Rice said, speaking for all of us on Harry's behalf, for Barbara, Joe, David, me.

Other letters followed, they came every couple of weeks. They came from North Dakota and Idaho and Texas. Someone sent an editorial from a respectable New Hampshire paper. *A rumor has been spreading*, the editorialist wrote, *that the Miller Massacre last June was part of a government conspiracy to suppress dissent. We have been asked to call for an investigation of suspects who were released without charge. We think the request is uncalled for. Such innuendo does not serve the community.*

Someone told us that references to the Miller Massacre were popping up on the Internet. When names of outrages were listed the name of Miller was often added to the list (Waco, Weaver, Oklahoma City, Miller). Someone anonymous wrote an attack on Saint Lena, the moneybags lady who bribed the survivors of Miller Farm into silence. *When you realize that she was the longtime mistress of the CIA professor who trained the murderers you don't need other evidence.*

When the ruling class abandons justice people take justice into their hands. Bare that in mind, professor.

Barbara called the police about it, and a policeman came to the house, just like the one months ago when the baby was kidnapped. His name was Theodore Lord with a white mustache like McKinley. What can we do? he said. If you get more calls maybe we can trace. Notify us more threats. Suspicious package, don't open, call us.

Who are they? he said rhetorically. Crackpots. Even a tiny number of people can make a lot of noise and this is probably a tiny number of people. They have their underground communications and their grievances. A rumor starts, someone thinks it useful, and they pass it on. You'll have to live with it I guess. Hope they get tired, but I don't foresee that soon.

Mother was shocked. She's a good Christian woman who goes to church without Harry and keeps her differences to herself. She believes God is always present in her life, whispering to her and listening to her thoughts and she has always been secretly a little afraid that her husband's skepticism could provoke divine retaliation. The notion of Miller's claiming to be God outraged her and she couldn't help believing his death was God's punishment. Now it's hard not to think Harry is being punished too. She never actually said this. I read it in the marks around her eyes.

Meanwhile, Harry minimized the threat. What could happen? he said. Probably nothing, though anything's possible. More letters. A slight chance a real fanatic would take stronger action. Like what? Hitchhike from North Dakota to throw a rock in the window? Car bomb? All it needs is one crazy person with energy. You can't prevent it if it wants to happen.

It doesn't seem to bother Harry. What's the use of worrying if I can't do anything? he said. His voice was cheerful as if he enjoyed it. It sure would bother me. Glad meanwhile that my apartment with my baby is not in his target range, I hope.

No, I can't be intense about anything but my baby. I work in the office, writing and filing, and I go home to her. I have no other life. And now I have lost David Leo. He thought he was in love and he used to visit and I tried to pay attention for I owe him much. But even when I saw he was getting bored I could not exert myself. So I let him go. Now he'll marry Charlene, and I won't interfere because I have no right.

No one criticizes me for my obsession. Everyone says it's natural, the instinctual thing. The baby needs me at this most important time, especially since there is no father. It's like everyone is conspiring to clear the way for my monumental selfishness like an ocean liner swamping all the boats. I appreciate the indulgence. I wouldn't give myself the same indulgence if I were someone else. Maybe when Hazy is older I'll turn into a normal person again. Then I'll regret not having helped my mother in her difficult decision, nor having stood by my father in his nightmare. I know I'll regret letting Davey go. If I know that, why can't I make myself do something to prevent it?

31

Harry Field

Harry never did find out how he had reconciled himself to death on the kidnap day. The memory of that excitement was gone. He couldn't even remember why the death of consciousness was bad. He was distressed to forget something so important, but he couldn't bring it back.

It took him a while (although not really as long as you might think) to get over the shock of his connection to the Miller Massacre. The worst was that first evening at the Sleepy Wicker when he and Lena gasped together trying to civilize the horror. That was the moment in his life when he felt most inept and stupid, in which his contribution to this tragedy lit a flare that made everything he had ever done look stupid.

There there, Lena said.

I brought the murderer, Harry said, expressing remorse like the hero of a romance. I brought him to the site. If it weren't for me it wouldn't have happened. I made it possible.

There there, Lena said.

She had her eye on the future. She asked him, Will this start a new religion?

I doubt it, he said.

A martyr. A charismatic leader shot down. His people outcasts.

There's no message, Harry said. Only personality.

He saved people.

A few.

She told him her plan to endow Miller Farm. He congratulated her and said it was a worthy thing to do.

After the police cleared him of suspicion, he felt better. He went home and got over his gloom. Old habits of cheer restored him. He ate lunch with colleagues. He thought up another book. He played with his granddaughter. By the end of the summer he felt almost normal. Life was exciting again.

He imagined conversations with Lena, who seemed to have become a voice inside his head saying strange outrageous things.

So that's why you went to see Miller, this imaginary Lena said. You wound up with Miller, everything ends with Miller. You went to see Miller like any pilgrim. Me too, you knew I'd be there, you went to see me like a lover. Furthermore, the vigilantes are right to suspect you of Nick. You were attracted by the risk. You wanted to see if it could happen. So said the atrocious imaginary Lena in his head. She told him that he and Miller were just the same. You make the same claims, she said.

Lena, Lena, he reminded her. Your Miller claimed he was God. Words, meaningless words.

As he cheered up over the weeks, he found himself once again thinking about the mysteries of death. He couldn't remember why death was terrible. He found an imaginary Miller in his head and asked him. Ambition, the imaginary Miller said. Once you give up ambition you won't mind death.

Now he felt euphoric, exhilarated, some crazy old age thing. The threatening letters stimulated him. As if nothing could happen in the remainder of his life that wasn't good. That

thought was shocking. What a dangerous and foolhardy atti-
tude, he told the imaginary Harry in his head. Illness, suffering,
loss, terrible things are about to happen. He thought of his
wife's poor old mother, her fate. You must face the reality, you
never did face the reality. The Harry in his head ignored his
warnings. Thinking what a wild ride this journey to death.
Aren't you curious? Don't you want to know how it will happen?
The cause of death? The process, the time? The contingent circumstances? What people will say? The impact?

Good Harry was horrified by this premature rush to the end.
Blasphemy, he said. What an odd word to pick. You'll be punished, the imaginary old mother said, as soon as the first illness
hits and the dreary painful way down from that. But he forgot
because he had something else to do. What was it? Don't ask
me, how should I know? And there it was again, that physical
knot of excitement, impossible to tell whether it was the excitement of living or the excitement of dying, only that it was
physical, that it was a knot, that it accelerated his pulse and his
breathing.

Since Harry Field obviously has only a partial understanding
of himself, the last word goes to David Leo. This happened
yesterday. As he approached the door of Harry's classroom he
heard Harry's voice. The sentences gathering speed, the excitement gaining. He couldn't make out the words. But he
remembered from when he was a student how you believe it's
the thought capturing your attention, the connections, the
logic, as if the presentational magic were the highest exercise of
mind, into which you have been led by this powerful professorial energy.

He remembered that feeling. He passed the door and glanced
into the class. He saw the graduate students, twelve around the

table, mature adults, many already teachers, all proven and tested bright, with careers and names destined to appear over articles and on books, sitting around the table leaning forward or sprawling, some shaggy with beards, women with scarves, others in T-shirts and others prim and neat, and all of them, all twelve transfixed with their attention upon Harry (himself intense and passionate leaning forward over the table, with his bloodshot eyes like a hound) attending to the intricate journey of his mind with a shared look of devotion and belief.